THE FINAL SHOT

THE FINAL SHOT
RICHARD BARTH

ST. MARTIN'S PRESS
NEW YORK

Design by Glen Edelstein

Library of Congress Cataloging-in-Publication Data

Barth, Richard, 1943–
    The final shot / Richard Barth.
        p.   cm.
    "A Thomas Dunne book."
    ISBN 0-312-07748-3
    I. Title.
PS3552.A755F56   1992
    813'.54—dc20   92-3018
                                                                        CIP

First Edition: June 1992

10 9 8 7 6 5 4 3 2 1

Dedicated to:
My two favorite
Golden Girls,
Felice and Thekla

ONE

Call me crazy. I'm Greek, and for the longest time I thought "whiskey down" was something you heard in a bar and not in a diner. The closest I'd ever gotten to slinging hash was twenty years ago for Uncle Sam, who was paying a lot more than my Uncle Spiros up in the Bronx. But then my uncle was just starting out with his hole-in-the-wall coffee shop that he named, fittingly enough, Spiros', and all he could afford was fifty a week and a lot of stale doughnuts. Uncle Sam was paying twice that, three square meals a day, and a chance to see the world. I saw the world, the world according to Haig and Kissinger; lots of bamboo villages, rice paddies, and winding caves that held tiny men who for some reason wanted to kill me. I suppose I would have been better up in the Bronx cracking eggs, but who knew that one day Spiros' would become the Acropolis Diner with separate parking for over forty cars.

Somehow I avoided the little men and made it back home to the States. I'd grown up in Staten Island, where my parents had moved in the late forties from a little village outside

Athens. One thing you could say for Staten Island back in the forties and fifties, it was real America. . . . Open spaces, hardworking people, not much neon, and not much crime. People respected their leaders, and the most important person around was the man in blue. First thing that happens out of Kennedy Airport, back from Vietnam, is I get ripped off by this Pakistani cab driver. I figure, two years fighting little men for this? I was so pissed off that within the week I decided to become a cop. The rest, as they say, is history, eighteen years of it, until the incident.

I suppose all cops have incidents. That's a polite way of saying a fuck-up. Walking the streets there are a hundred ways of finding one, and when you do, if you're lucky, you walk away from it intact. If you're unlucky, the other guy walks away and then they start your benefits, or maybe, if you're real unlucky, with your funeral arrangements. I was lucky, I walked. The problem was the other guy didn't have the gun I thought he was reaching for, and instead of taking my time with it, I hurried the shot. What worked in the tunnels of Vietnam was definitely not SOP for a New York ghetto.

Now if this had been the first person I'd killed in the line of duty it might not have come down so hard on me, even with him being the son of the local Shinto priest or whatever down there on the fringes of Chinatown. But it wasn't; it was my third in eighteen years, although on the two others I hadn't been alone and my partners had stood up for me. Hell, how was I to know the kid was editor of the school paper? No gun, but they did find the crack he was dealing on him, not that it did me any good.

The community exploded and things got pretty hot. My two previous fatal shooting incidents came to light, even though the latest was eight years ago, and the local newspapers ran with them. I found out quickly enough that facts can be like whores working a barroom, they'll go with anyone if the price is right. In this case, the price was my head, and the papers and the community finally got what they wanted. I got a

2

"temporary suspension" with no promises while the brass down at One Police Plaza decided what to do with me. Most of them were cops who came up through the ranks and were sympathetic. But sympathy wasn't good enough. After a while Everett Barnet, the chief of police, let the word trickle down that his hands were tied. I guess, politics being politics, the mayor needed the Chinese vote or something. So I was hung out to dry.

Suspension is a nasty state of limbo without any fixed end point. It can go on for years, and the whole time there's no salary and no benefits. It was my decision, but I hung on. The alternative for me was to quit, forgo the pension which I was only two years away from earning, and forget about ever getting back on the force again. For eighteen years it had been my life, and the last thing I wanted to do was turn my back on it. I was a cop, that's how I saw myself, and the only thing I could do was ride it out while the "official departmental investigation" was going on, and it had been going on for well over a year. A year's a long time to wait for a community to shift its attention, but I guess the Chinese have long memories. My friends on the force kept telling me to hang in there, something would break soon. I kept wondering if they weren't talking about my heart.

My wife, Helen, who's the cashier at the Acropolis, tells me not to worry. Our kid, Hector, is in high school and talking college to me, and I'm not supposed to worry? But then Helen has always been an optimist. That's what drew me to her in the first place. We met the year Nixon resigned, 1974. In the depths of the Watergate anguish, when every morning's newspaper had some further incredible disclosure about our corrupt government, she would tell me not to worry, things were going to get better. We waited, and even though we got Ford and his "full and absolute" Nixon pardon, things did seem to get better. That same year the string bikini made its first appearance, and streaking naked in public places became an art form. People lightened up, and we all went on with our lives.

3

I remember this because even then Helen was taking the half-full glass approach to life rather than the half-empty one.

So when she suggested I go up and see Uncle Spiros after it became clear that the suspension was not going to be an overnight affair, I decided to eat my pride and go see the man. He had become a crotchety old man with a number of grand-children. He gives me coffee and a doughnut, a fresh one, and tells me business is bad. "Unless you want to work the dishes in the back," he says. I figured if I took the job I'd wind up breaking every one of his goddamn plates I was so angry.

So, that's how I came to be at St. Bartlett's College wearing gray pants, a blue tie, and this cute little maroon coat that has a badge on it, in my case, number 8079. Except the metal is too shiny, gold plate over zinc or something, and the emblem on the shoulder says St. Bartlett's Security Service instead of NYPD. There's no gun, but the job does come with a walkie-talkie direct to security central, and to Verne Newton, my guardian angel.

We go back a long way, the two of us; and from the first, it was always this strange kind of relationship. Verne, the 220-pound, black ex-linebacker sergeant, looking after rookie patrolman Costas Agonomou, 160 pounds dripping wet, white, and naively overconfident. It didn't take long to find out that the streets of New York were as deadly as the smoky fields of Vietnam. And Verne guided me through for the first couple of years until he made lieutenant and was kicked downtown behind a desk. I suppose a shrink would have looked at it and said "father/son relationship," but actually Verne, at fifty-four, was only ten years older than I was. I can honestly say, though, that he saved my ass a few times when I got into trouble on the streets; so when he went downtown I missed him. Then, for the last five years I'd see him occasion-ally at the PBA meetings and once every six months when he and his wife invited us over for dinner. I noticed the last few times that we'd somehow gone through three bottles of wine, but I didn't think much of it. Then I heard from one of the lieutenants that he was being asked to retire. He was having troubles at home, drinking, and bringing it into work. I meant to call him a few times, but somehow I never got around to it.

Then the next thing I hear he's swung this job at St. Bartlett's College as head of security, a kind of golden parachute for cops. We always knew on the force that the private sector loves ex-cops, the same way car dealers love ex-sports figures, on their payroll. St. Bartlett's was buying into the big leagues hiring Verne, an honest-to-goodness frontline fighter against crime; but at a place like St. Bartlett's, Verne was a little like a shark in a goldfish bowl.

Not that he didn't do his job okay. There's just a limit to how much enthusiasm you can bring to a job that is 90 percent lost-and-found, petty theft, and door control when you've cut your teeth on the pavements and alleys of New York. Verne did it, patched up things at home, cut down a little on his drinking, and when he heard about my troubles, asked me if I needed a job while I waited for reinstatement. God love him. By that time I had figured it was either going to be drive a cab or wash Spiros' dishes.

That was ten months ago. Now I am his Johnny-on-the-spot for dealing with the daily tinkering of running a twenty-man department. He sits above it all, making decisions regarding deployment of his resources and dealing with the administration, while I actually get the work of checking on whether bodies are where they're supposed to be, punching people in and out on the clock, and occasionally answering phones when Verne is on a break. Basically, the job's a snooze. I would say the most exciting time is the moment my payroll check is dropped off on Friday afternoon. But then, at this point in my life, the only excitement I am looking forward to is a phone call from Barnet telling me to come back.

More than half the time I'm just out patrolling the corridors of academe, and, believe me, there are plenty of them. Six buildings, over sixty stories total including basements, taking up two city blocks in Brooklyn, with enough nooks and crannies to hide a battalion of armed guerillas. Fortunately, the kids who go to St. Bartlett's are for the most part out for an education, not for blood, so our daily routine is relaxed. When I walk, I check doors, I talk to the students and teachers, and now and then I just stand by the front door. I guess you could say I'm also supposed to be a presence, which is flattering for someone five-foot-eight. But by and large the job is quiet and gives me a lot of time to wander. Imagine a place with over fifteen major departments, each with its own classrooms, laboratories, studios, dark rooms and computer rooms, not to mention gyms and weight rooms, restaurants and lounges, game rooms and auditoriums. . . . A regular city of busy industry where the only product is a commodity called education. Who knew, maybe a little might even rub off on me? Like everyone else, I want to learn something new every day.

A month ago what I learned was that Verne was about to lose his job. Hap Wilson told me. Hap's the basketball coach, and around four in the afternoon I make it a point to drop in to watch how the practice is going. St. Bartlett's is in division one, which includes some pretty strong teams, only one reason Hap had troubles getting his guys to coordinate. Four years without a winning season, with last year's nine and sixteen not looking all too good on anyone's books. Fortunately, this year's record was a lot better; not really Hap's doing, word had it, but because of Jason Sanders, a freshman guard with the hottest of hands. I didn't envy Hap. Unlike the other associate professors at the college, Hap's future depended on how successful his students were. If a bunch of kids failed on a history exam up in Markowitz's Ancient Civilization 102, it mattered little to anyone, least of all to Markowitz, who had seen dozens fail before. But just let one of Hap's forwards miss a backdoor, or a pick-and-roll, and the team go on to lose by two points, then Hap would rant and rave, and in private worry about how much longer he had.

Anyway, Hap's black, and at the college there's this black thing, sort of an underground news service that works well for those initiated. I got my bulletins both from Hap and Verne, but for some reason I hadn't been tuned in too closely lately. I was down on the floor, watching this give-and-go lay-up drill, when Hap sidled over. He knows Verne and I go back a way, or else I don't think he would have opened up the way he did.

"Costas," he began. "Do me a favor. Go back and tell your thick-skulled boss that he'd better get his act together."

I didn't say anything as I watched one of the taller players seem to float toward the basket from ten yards out. He hung like a glider on a summer thermal until the last moment, when he released the ball into the net with a whisper.

"That Sanders?" I asked.

Hap smiled lightly. "Mr. Sanders to you. Yeah, but the subject was Verne, not basketball. Word is he's pretty close to being offered an early retirement."

"Whose word is that?" I asked. At St. Bartlett's there were so many words flying around that you had to establish at the beginning which direction you were getting it from: the source, the rebound, or the dead file.

"Jeanette."

Jeanette was a very good source.

"I was having lunch in the cafeteria with her and she tells me Malloy is hearing some negative things about Mr. Newton. . . . From a few people."

Dr. Malloy is the president of the college, and Jeanette is his secretary. The best thing you can say about him is that he was a safe choice for the Chancellor. If he'd gone into business instead of education, he'd be branch manager of a bank somewhere out in Suffolk County.

"Drinking?" I asked. It wasn't such a long shot on my part. Verne had had problems with that before, but I was under the impression he'd got it under control. Hap looked at me evenly. He had the kind of face that didn't show much emotion, which in his job was good if you were six points down with a minute to go.

"Yeah, that too, but mostly people think he's coasting. I suppose they're related. This fall he didn't respond all too creatively to the vandalism over in the library, and he got on some people's shit list. You know how goddamn parochial they are over there."

"I suppose it's hard for him to get indignant over some Magic Marker scribbles in a bathroom after spending the seventies in New York."

"This isn't the South Bronx, Costas. I'm telling you, he's skating on thin ice. He hears it from me, it doesn't make an impression. He hears it from a few places, then maybe it will sink in." He motioned for one of his assistant coaches to come over. "Do him a favor, huh. He's too young to be watching the soaps at home." The young coach came over and Hap asked him to run through a few ten-second drills. Then he gave me a nod and headed off toward the end of the court.

I checked my watch and figured it was time to do the rounds in Flagler Hall. I'd catch Verne in the morning and share Hap's wisdom. As I left the gym, I took one last look behind me and was just in time to see a Jason Sanders twenty-five-foot jumper swish through. The kid definitely had hot hands.

TWO

Flagler was one of the smaller buildings. It held all the art
studios. While St. Bartlett's College concentrated in the business technologies and liberal arts areas, they had a creditable
arts program. Besides the gym, it was my favorite place to
browse. Ask anyone on the street what they picture when you
say "art studio," and they'll probably describe a large well-lit
room with many easels surrounding a raised model's platform,
paint drippings on the floor, old still-life setups resting on
shelves and windowsills, the smell of oil and turpentine everywhere. Flagler had rooms like that, but it also held a print
workshop with heavy presses, a graphics and silkscreening
laboratory, and a metal shop with arc welders and heavy
grinders. It was a place throbbing with energy, unlike some of
the other buildings on campus that held only classrooms, or
administration offices. Flagler was usually a beehive of activity
where smells, noises, and odd visual effects were produced
from students in the process of making their own personal
statements. Three weeks before I had spotted a canvas, three
feet square, suspended from the ceiling near the vending ma-

9

chines. From it there hung in a neat gridlike pattern, maybe two hundred unrolled condoms, each dipped into a different color paint. No doubt it was a statement, but of what I'm not sure. In this place it lasted just two hours before President Malloy got wind of it and ordered it removed. A Catholic college with condoms hanging from the ceiling! Like I said, a place full of energy.

But late in the day most of the classes are finished, and only the more compulsive students are still at it. Teachers in the art areas are more lenient about kids clocking in and out, and it is a rare studio that, at four-forty-five, has the same number of bodies it had say at three o'clock. All, that is, except Professor Ponzini's Drawing Class 114 that met in the large studio on the second floor. Vincent Ponzini was one of these middle-aged guys with a reputation for filling up all his classes. He'd been represented by one of the better galleries in Soho for the last ten years, but the way I heard it was that he was just a damn good teacher. Riding the elevators you'd always overhear how much of an asshole teacher so-and-so was, but never had I heard Ponzini mentioned like that. The students worked hard for him.

FA114 was a class with a live model, so of course the door was closed. Ponzini was a professional, but if he hadn't set the standard, the models would have insisted. It's hard enough to hold a pose without moving under hot lights for twenty minutes while twenty pairs of eyes dissect you inch by inch; it is impossible to do that with every Tom, Dick, and Harriet passing by in the hall leering in. So the doors were kept closed, which, to the non-art students, added to the mystery of what happened within. But I knew. One of the things I had to check on was the ventilation system inside the room, and besides, I was told, the female models welcomed the idea that the security department was near at hand.

But forget glamour. The models came in every flavor, shape, and age. The instructors all had their own preferences depending on what they were trying to do with the class, so the characters that passed through the art department office to have their model worksheets stamped were as varied as the people emerging from the 104 Broadway bus. A few were old hands at it, bringing in their foam rubber posing pads to make things easier on their feet—or backs, depending on what position they took. Like Marta, the sixty-two-year-old grandmother who always dressed in black and had a face powdered so white she almost looked like one of those Kabuki dancers. I had heard she was a short poser, unable to go the distance on the twenty-minute jobs. But the few times I walked in she was absolutely dramatic on her five-minute sketch poses, which is why they kept asking her back. Once I rode down in the elevator with her after a session, and we chatted about the weather or something. Just a polite conversation with an older lady I could have had waiting in the checkout at Grand Union. Who would have guessed that ten minutes earlier she was bare-assed in front of a bunch of kids with enough hormones flowing through their bodies to bring Elvis back to life. She didn't care about that. What she cared about was the temperature in the room and not catching a cold.

But today Ponzini didn't have a sixty-two-year-old grandmother, he had a young woman with a body that flowed over the posing bench like a silk curtain. It was a difficult pose, with her head drooping on one side and her lower body sliding away over the edge, but as I watched she held it without moving. Only her rib cage raised and lowered with her slow breathing. She had long legs that glided effortlessly into her torso, a stomach that you could play billiards on, and shoulders that were meant for hanging slinky black silk dresses on. The rest was covered by her long, golden hair as it played down her arched front with only her two little fireplug nipples sticking out on their own, disembodied. Being a married man, I'm not supposed to be moved by such academic sights, but let me tell you, she was a treat. Being that there were so many things to look at, it took me a few moments to realize that I had seen the model before. She was one

11

of the first-year fine arts students. That kind of threw me because as unusual as it is to have a world-class body modeling in any of the fine arts courses, it was more unusual for that body to also be a member of the larger student body. It takes a person with a strong self-identity to take off their clothes in a room full of friends, but from the looks of it, this young lady didn't have the slightest problem with it.

Ponzini leaned closer to the model. I had to give the guy credit, he was good looking in an Italian, outer-borough kind of way—sort of like an aging Travolta on a bad day. But then I'm Greek, have light, curly hair, and carry on a long tradition of being jealous of our neighbors to the west. Our culture had been up and going for over a thousand years before the Italians got their act together, and we've been playing catch-up ever since.

Ponzini cast a nod in my direction, which is about as far as he went with the hired help, and I took a walk over to the ventilation system. None of the students looked over at me as I tapped on the blower switch and checked the gauge. They were too busy concentrating on Ponzini as he barely brushed the end of a pencil up the model's leg.

"The left knee," he said, "is on a level with the right shoulder. Do not drop the knee. The knee drops, the back breaks." Ponzini looked at one of the students. "Mr. Strickland, you in particular have a way of making the torso like a pretzel. Even Ms. Cunningham's body here, as lithe as it is, could not do what you are asking of it. Maybe a Chinese acrobat's . . ." He lifted his pencil once again and placed it an inch away from the model's right nipple. "And from the top of the breast we flow diagonally across the chest to the point of the chin." He moved his pencil parallel but not quite touching the draped hair. "Then a vertical line to the left ear. If you remember anything from this course, remember this. The lines must be correct. Without the proper foundation, the edifice will crumble."

I took one more look at the edifice before turning back to

the door. In my mind there was no way that structure was about to crumble, with or without a foundation. Some of the students were now frantically erasing and resetting the points Ponzini had been discussing. I glanced over at Strickland's drawing and could see nothing wrong with the way the guy had placed the leg, but then, what do I know? To me the Mona Lisa looks like she's frowning. An alarm clock went off somewhere near the model's stand, and a general grumbling went up from the young people. Ms. Cunningham unwound herself from her position, reached down from the bench, and found her robe. In a few seconds, she was covered and brushing her hair to the back of her. As she passed Ponzini going toward the changing room, she sent him a hot little smile, which made it all the way back to where I was standing. After eighteen years as a cop you get kind of sensitive to body language, and what I saw spoke eloquently. Ponzini was either fucking her or giving her free art lessons, and he didn't look like the charitable sort. I had always heard about the perks of professorship, and here it was staring me in the face. Give the guy credit, all those nights I'd seen him working out in the school's Nautilus room were not being wasted. I supposed keeping up with the coeds could kill you if you weren't in shape. I turned the door knob slowly and exited as the students were packing their drawings into their portfolios. The clock in the corridor over the row of lockers said five o'clock, which meant my shift lasted for another hour. That gave me just enough time to run through the other five floors of Flagler, and then take a swing through Nathan Hall before reporting back. Nathan would be easy, just a bunch of administrative offices. Nothing ever happened there.

THREE

Nathan Three was the floor for the fine arts faculty offices, and it was usually a quiet, deserted place. Fine arts teachers didn't spend much time in their offices; in fact, they didn't spend much time in the school, which I'd heard was a source of friction with the other faculty members. The studio teachers didn't prepare lectures, assign homework papers that needed to be graded, write proposals for new curriculum, or even do work on their doctoral dissertations. They just came, taught their courses, and went away. Their offices, which were granted to them by force of the union contract, were used as storage for some of the better work by their students, or for supplies. The rooms were generally a mess inside, as unlike the technology department faculty offices as a Columbus Avenue flea market was from Tiffany's.

There was usually no one on the floor after 5:00 P.M., so I was a little surprised when I stepped off the elevator and heard loud voices coming from the end of the hall. The two men were arguing in Howell Tandy's office, the only office on the floor that didn't look like a pigsty. Tandy was the head of

14

the art department, a man given to wearing three-piece suits while most of his faculty were in jeans. But then Tandy came from the academic side of the art world, the art critics and historians; and he would no sooner touch a wet brush as he would know what to do with a *sumi* stick. I knew, because I kept picking them up from the floor of Professor Konisha's Japanese-drawing class.

. I had heard that Tandy had been the compromise selection by the warring factions of the art department when they came to choose their department chair a year earlier. At St. Bartlett's they group the small faction of historians and critics in with the artists, so when the expressionists were fighting with the figurativists, and the postmodernists weren't speaking to the minimalists, everyone turned to the aloof historians to represent them in the councils of higher learning. Then they found out that even historians have points of view and political agendas, but by then it was too late. Tandy was in for three years. With his nine hours of release time from teaching he had plenty of opportunity to meddle, and meddle is what he did with a special gift. From the sounds coming from his office, he was in fine form.

The other voice in the room came from Gregor Ostyapin, the big Russian sculptor. He had reportedly escaped from his homeland in 1976 with little more than the clothes on his back and a bag full of sculptor's chisels and chasing tools. By some quirk of luck, he arrived at St. Bartlett's—this is from Verne—just when the art department was looking for someone to set up a marble-carving studio, someone outside the department who they could get as an adjunct. Ostyapin jumped at the opportunity even though, for twice the work, he was going to be paid half of what the full-time faculty was paid. Since then Ostyapin had walked the corridors of Flagler, a bearlike figure with what seemed like a permanent coating of white marble dust over his beard and clothes. After a few years they bumped him up to a full-time instructor which entitled him to health benefits as well as a livable salary. Maybe the administration figured he'd sue them for white lung disease if they didn't show some concern. All of this, of course, was common knowledge outside of the department because at a place like St. Bartlett's there were few secrets.

Now this normally placid artist was shouting at his department head with as much restraint as Al Sharpton at a convention of honkie bond salesmen. It was hard for me not to catch what they were saying.

"Is not fair," Ostyapin repeated, "that you not recommend me for tenure. What is this that Ponzini comes first? I set up all carving studio, I go find good marble, I order tools. I do everything and what does Ponzini do? Ponzini paints and fucks the students."

"Ponzini's classes are always closed," Tandy shouted back. "Ponzini is on the union health committee, Ponzini's student evaluations average over nine-point-two." Tandy took a breath. "Look, I try to do the best I can for you, Gregor. I block your program into two days, which is against the contract, but I can't recommend you both. I'd like to but you know there's only one tenure line for the art department now that Simmons retired. Ponzini was my choice. Maybe the dean will see it differently."

"The dean sees it the way chairperson sees it, you know that. The dean has rubber teeth like you." I heard a fist slamming down on the table and wondered whether the situation called for some intervention. What the hell, I thought, it couldn't hurt. The way I figured it, St. Bartlett's was paying me for precious little real work as it was. I walked to the doorway and showed my face.

"Everything okay, gentlemen?" I asked in my normal airy way.

The two men turned around and looked at me in silence. Ostyapin's hand was still closed into a fist, but now it was at his side. His face was red behind the white frosted beard, and his eyes held more anger than I cared to deal with. Tandy, on

16

the other hand, looked as unruffled as an air-conditioning repairman in December.

"Yes, quite all right," he said. "No problem."

You hope, I thought to myself. What if Ostyapin decided to practice some chipping away on your facial bones. But instead I nodded politely and turned back into the corridor. Hell, let them work it out. Tenure fights have been going on as long as there were students to fight over. I moved down the corridor and started checking to make sure all the other doors were locked. By the time I hit the staircase to go up to the fourth floor things had quieted down in Tandy's office.

FOUR

Tuesday is my night out with the boys, a night to get away from Helen and Hector and try to make some sense out of being a forty-four-year-old Greek man with a VCR, a microwave oven, an expresso maker, a subscription to *New York Magazine,* and a peptic ulcer. I can explain away the ulcer after all those years on the force, not to mention the anxiety of waiting daily to get called back on, but *New York Magazine?* So Tuesday night I salvage a little of my former self and go and do some heavy male bonding. It's really all a joke since the other guys are as wrapped and tied as I am. But I've always played a decent game of poker, and it was nice finally finding a steady game.

Winston Taylor got me started in the game about a month

after I arrived at St. Bartlett's. They needed a sixth and had run out of candidates. Winston is down in maintenance and custodial and is one of the guys you always see around the school fixing things. The guy's a genius with a screwdriver, but to be truthful, he has no idea what to do in a high-low game holding a nine. I've told him a dozen times it's no crime to fold, but he always gets sucked in. Then he'll look up with his "I can't believe I did that again" grin and pass the chips over to whoever had the seven or eight hand. I like him, and so does everyone else at the school. Here's a guy out of Bedford-Stuyvesant with a sweet temperament, a guy who finished high school on time, finished two years of trade school, is the youngest deacon his church ever had, and has a hard time saying a bad word about anyone. Give him another five years and he'll be head of the entire maintenance and custodial department, which at a place like St. Bartlett's is no small job.

The other guys around the table are a mixed lot. Very democratic. Some are there because they just love to play the game, and some are there because it takes place in Winston's apartment across the street and is convenient. There's Pete Howser from the purchasing department, a man who wouldn't even bet a pair of kings in a five-card draw game; Dory Stabler, an outspoken teacher from the English department, who also happens to be president of the union; Eric Westman from personnel, who's got the lowdown on everyone; and Chester Rooney, ex–farm team ball player, and current freshman dean of students. It's a bunch of guys that have no more reason to be sitting at the same table than do Yasir Arafat, Johnny Cash, and Harry Schwartz, my local dry cleaner. But somehow we pull it off, and at the end of the session everyone leaves a little taller than when they arrived. What the hell, the stakes are a quarter to a half-dollar, and psychotherapy costs a lot more.

Tonight, Howser was starting in again on the AIDS issue, the latest cause célèbre on campus. Rooney was rolling his eyes and hoping that whoever was the dealer had the good sense to hurry up the shuffle.

18

"Christ, if President Malloy ain't right," Pete Howser was saying. "Hey, I got a kid in high school, and I wouldn't want her being taught by some creep with AIDS. Guy could cough right in her face."

"As far as medical science has shown," Stabler interrupted, "coughing is not one of the vectors of the disease." He turned to Rooney. "Deal the cards."

"Call me a bigot," Howser continued, "but in my book a teacher with a communicable disease shouldn't be in a class-room. I'm glad the president is taking the hard-line position on it."

"You're a bigot," Rooney said, and started dealing. The cards slid across the table evenly, but people hadn't started picking them up yet.

"Well, they're holding a meeting on the subject tomorrow afternoon," Winston said. "I got a note to ready the audito-rium. Dr. Malloy is going to meet with faculty members, trust-ees, and concerned parents about AIDS in the classroom. When I asked how come they needed such a big space, I was told they're going to talk about the Father Simmons thing."

Westman groaned. "Didn't they have enough blood?" He interrupted. "Christ, the guy only retired because they hounded him out. He could have finished teaching out the year, maybe even gone for another year. He's been with us since sixty-eight."

"And how many kids would he have contaminated?" This last comment came again from Howser.

"Contaminated?" Stabler snorted. "You got it all wrong. Teachers don't contaminate students, it's the other way around. The other day I caught myself asking the checkout girl at Sloans if I could be using a check. Fortunately, she didn't see anything wrong in my choice of syntax." He collected all his cards in front of him and started arranging them in his hand. "Anyway, it's like those McCarthy witch-hunts. They ruined good people back then, and they'll do it again now."

He looked down at the exposed cards on the table. "Pair of jacks bets."

"Wait, pot's light," Howser interrupted. "Who didn't ante?" Leave it to a purchasing agent to discover a light pot. Six voices said that they had, which in my book is a mathematical impossibility. I hadn't seen Stabler throw in his chip, but I wasn't willing to make an issue of it. It happens maybe twice a night with him, but I figure his lousy play more than makes up for chiseling the extra fifty cents. I chucked in a chip and looked down at my hand. The jacks were mine, so I opened with a another chip.

But I was still thinking of what had happened to Father Simmons. I remembered because it took place back in September, only a few months after I had come to work for Verne. Simmons had been denied his classes because so few students had signed up for them. Why? Because before registration the word was making the rounds that he had AIDS. A priest with AIDS, at St. Bartlett's. . . . Now that was interesting. To bypass the problem, the administration offered him early retirement, which he grudgingly took. The other option, for Dr. Malloy to talk to the students about their shameless reaction, apparently never crossed the president's mind. Father Simmons was, by reputation, a good teacher and he must have been deeply hurt when he couldn't continue teaching. I watched as the bet went around the table and chips landed in the center. Now they're already fighting for his tenure line. How the world turns, I thought, and bumped the bet up to fifty when I got my next card. Two jacks up with another in the hole. My lucky evening. Now if only I could keep a straight face.

But Westman wasn't buying. He folded his hand and sat back to watch. The others stayed in, and we had a lot of fun through the next rounds. When I raked in the pot there was some slight grumbling, but with two jacks showing what did they expect? When the banter died down, Howser started dealing the second deck. I guess everyone in the room was thankful that he had something to do other than mouth off on

20

his favorite subject. Even at a place like St. Bartlett's, gay-bashing was not a common activity. Just to make sure, West-man short-circuited further conversation by changing the subject.

"You guys want to hear a joke? This is one of those good news, bad news stories. Word's going around the personnel office that our request for a new copier has been approved. The bad news is that President Malloy has asked us to approach the alumni council for it. You know what that means?"

Winston laughed. "Lord, don't I though. Some sharpie with a forty-million-dollar company gets to unload a fifteen-year-old broken-down copier and take a big tax deduction. We get to wrestle with the son of a bitch trying to get parts and supplies for it. I can't tell you how many broken-down machines are around this place, machines that should have been put to death long ago. But if it's a gift from some big-shot alumni, who're we to shove it back in his face?"

"Precisely my sentiments," Westman said. "I told Dr. Malloy that his solution was not acceptable." He smiled at the other men and picked up his hand. "He is reconsidering."

"He's always 'reconsidering,'" Stabler said with a snort. "Then it just dies. That's what I like about the union contract negotiations. It's the one time he can't just 'reconsider.'" He took a breath. "Now, what's this garbage you've dealt me, Howser. Just because I took the moral high ground on Simmons?"

The game continued. Money changed hands until around 9:45 P.M. Stabler was the first to go, claiming he still had a lecture to prepare for the next day's class on Shelley's *Prometheus Unbound*. He left claiming he'd only lost seven dollars. A good night for him.

The rest of us kept at it for another hour until the pretzels were all gone, as was the suitcase of Budweiser. A real man-to-man macho evening. Before we left, Chester Rooney, the freshman dean, mentioned the issue of date rape and asked me if the security department had any complaints. I hadn't heard of anything specific, but then date rape was the dirty little secret of every coed school. If the administration ever found out about it, my guess is it usually came through the counseling service, not through security. Howser's position, of course, was expected. He said something like, "How does anyone ever know whether the girls asked for it or not?" Typical. As a cop I saw a lot of rape cases pass through the precinct houses, and after the first one I didn't ever have to ask a question like that. After the rest of us were finished jumping on him for that one, we decided to call it a night. I went home twelve dollars richer and maybe two pounds heavier. This male bonding thing takes its toll.

FIVE

I missed being a cop. From the beginning of the job with St. Bartlett's, I had always assumed it would be a temporary thing. I still did, although it was getting harder holding onto the thin edge of hope the department had given me. So I plodded through my days, feeling as out of place as a sports-caster covering a bingo final. After more than a year, I still felt nervous leaving the house without my gun, and a lot more vulnerable without the vest. But why the longing to get back? If asked, I would have to admit that by any reasonable yard-stick it was eighteen years of chaos. There were times I would come home with stories of fellow cops blown away; stories of families living like animals in the rubble of some abandoned building, pulling knives on each other for the last pipe of crack; stories of soul-numbing violence for absolutely no reason. And I would ask myself what the hell was the attraction? I'd done my duty to my country, two years of it in Southeast Asia. So why was I still out there on the edge of insanity? I never got tired of asking myself that question, and to be truthful, I never had the answer. Except that maybe what kept me in were those few occasions, brief moments when the job opened onto a world of almost religious dimensions. It happened when you saved lives, when your being there resulted in some unknown soul's salvation; not in heaven, but here on earth. It happened with Hector.

Two years on the job. One night Verne and I are cruising down some street in Manhattan near the old West Side Highway, and Verne spots this woman running out of an alley. There was something funny about the way she was holding herself, kind of loping like a wounded animal. Verne does a U-turn and goes back. She saw us and ducked back down where she came from. Only it's dark, and by the time we're out of the car with the flashlight, she's disappeared.

There were maybe a dozen doors and the open end of the alley. We figure, why go and make a federal case out of it? No blood, no shots, no bodies. We try all the doors, check the back-up street, but she's gone. It's maybe fifteen degrees outside, and a wicked wind is blowing in off the Hudson. On the return to the car we passed back through the alley and by some garbage cans. Inside one of them I thought I heard this kind of sniveling sound, like a cat laughing, only cats don't have a sense of humor. Verne was down the alley already, but I turned back and lifted off the lid. A week-old baby in a dirty blanket was inside with the tin cans and old newspapers. A week of buying formula and changing diapers and the bitch had given up.

In those days it was easier than it is now. We got him, Helen and I, after going through the right channels and agencies. But then in those days, the bureaucracies of the city had at least half an eye to logic. I had found the child and had given him

23

back his life. . . . We were entitled. Hector's been our son ever since, a little Hispanic baby who has a last name of Agonomou and will never have a yearning, as I do, to go and see the real Acropolis one time.

So when I say I miss being a cop, it's not such an innocent statement. Our lives have been shaped by that job, both good and bad, and I suppose now that I am on hold; Helen is both relieved and sad at the same time. But not me. I want to go back.

SIX

There was something funny going on at school the next morning when I arrived. I knew it immediately when I passed three girls openly crying in the halls. One, maybe you could expect, a flunked exam or kiss off from a boyfriend, but three? When I swung into the security office at nine the place was littered with men in blue, some of whom I recognized, including Captain Dass Dougherty. Verne Newton looked beleaguered. He motioned me over as Dougherty inspected me from the tips of my fake leather Favas to the little gold badge on my maroon jacket.

"Well, well," he smiled. "What is this, Newton, a little storefront PBA? Any other old cops on your staff?"

I felt like strangling the son of a bitch, but I don't think that would have helped my case. Besides, it wasn't Dougherty's fault. His Irish father had married an Indian lady from New Delhi back during the war and Dass was the unfortunate result. There were chromosomes there that never dreamed they'd be swimming around in the same gene pool together. He had the temperament of an Irish-Catholic bricklayer and the tolerance of a Hindu dog catcher. I could think of a better combination to represent the fine people of the city of New York as the number one crime stopper from the 67th Precinct. I'd worked over in the 67th for a couple of years before being transferred down to Chinatown. Dougherty and I were never on great terms, but we did manage to coexist or at least keep out of each other's way.

"Good to see you again, Dass," I said. "We have a problem here?"

"You do," he said pointedly. "But not us. I'm trying to tell that to Verne here, but he seems to disagree."

I looked over at Verne, who was rubbing his jaw with the back of his hand. At any other time I would've said he'd be heading for his special drawer, but not today, not with all those witnesses in the room. But his eyes still had the need in them.

"What happened?"

Verne sat down heavily. "We got a murder on our hands."

"So you say," Dougherty interjected. "As far as I see it, it's no more than an unfortunate accident. We'll check it out, but I'm always right on these things."

"That's why you're a captain," Verne said sarcastically.

"And you're the nursemaid."

Verne raised up out of his seat and started around his desk, but I got in between them just in time.

"Goddamn it," I said. "Hold on. You're not going to solve anything that way. Who's dead?"

"One of your art teachers," Dass said. He looked at his little notebook. "The maintenance staff found him this morning at six-thirty down in the weight room. Guy by the name of Ponzini, Vincent Ponzini." He closed the book. "From the looks of it he didn't feel a thing."

Verne went back to his seat behind the desk and lit a cigarette. He's been trying to stop for as long as I've known him and has it down to four a day, one after each meal, including his coffee break. Since it wasn't anywhere near ten-thirty yet, this was not a good sign.

"He was lifting weights," Dass Dougherty continued, "on the press bench, and I guess he got too much on the bar. He was trying to lift one seventy-five up onto the rests. Maybe he thought he had it seated or maybe it just slipped out of his outstretched arms. Anyway the full weight came down on the bridge of his nose, broke his face and pushed some shards of cartilage into his brain. Happened sometime after midnight. The weights were found a few feet away with a little blood and skin tissue smeared right where they came down on him. Seems pretty clear cut to me. I always thought lifting weights was a dangerous way to get exercise."

"And the school knows?" I asked unnecessarily. I remembered those three girls in the hall.

"Word has gotten out," Verne said. "There's going to be a meeting in Dr. Malloy's office in a half hour. We have to come up with some statement quickly. Students will want to know what happened . . . also the parents."

"After coming back from the gym I told your president to release his initial report that it was an accident," Dougherty said. "He is in agreement."

"Of course he is in agreement," Verne said. "How would you like to be the president of a college with a murderer running around loose. Especially now when the Middle States accrediting thing is coming up again this year. Of course he wants it to be an accident."

"You don't think it was, Verne?" I asked. I was still a little shocked. After all, I might have been one of the last people to see Ponzini before he died. Me and about thirty-five students.

"I don't know. But I do know I wouldn't shoot from the hip and say anything until I had all the facts."

"Sure, it's better for you if it was murder, isn't it Newton?" Dougherty said. "Otherwise your ass is on the line. No one

26

was supposed to be in that room after midnight using weights, were they? Think of the negligence suits you're up against from his family. Your boys are supposed to have kicked him out, and if they had he wouldn't be dead now. Great security department you got here." Dougherty turned and walked to the door. "Now, if it's murder you're not quite as responsible, right? Obviously you got a vested interest, Mr. Newton. So, I think for the moment, or at least until I interview everyone involved, we shouldn't let our prejudices cloud our thinking." He looked into Verne's eyes, reddish from traces of swollen veins. "Or anything else, for that matter." He motioned to his men then turned and left the security office.

Verne looked up at me and shook his head. "Prick. He always was a prick," he said.

"Who was on last night, Verne?" I asked. "What's his report?"

Verne's hand hesitated, then went for the top drawer of his desk. There were just the two of us in the room, and he knew I wouldn't say anything. He found his little bottle and the neat stack of Dixie cups and poured himself what looked to me like two ounces. Three swallows later he crumpled the cup and tossed it into the waste basket. He closed the drawer and looked back up. There was a tired expression on his face, but the liquor didn't seem to have any other effect.

"Gonzales had the graveyard shift covering Cameron and Flagler."

"Christ," I said. "Just your luck."

Verne smiled lightly and shrugged. "You can't stop being a nice guy just when your friends need you." I don't know whether he said this pointedly or not, but he got his message across. Gonzales was not a suspended cop, like me—he was an ex-con, put in the slammer by Verne ten years earlier on a robbery charge. But there was something about him that had kept Verne interested. For all his street-smart talk, Gonzales was little more than a frightened kid with an IQ that was struggling to make it up to body temperature. Verne followed him through his contacts up in Greenhaven, wrote him letters, encouraged him to take courses so he could get an equivalency degree, and when he finally came out on a good conduct parole, offered him a job.

Gonzales had been doing three graveyards and three evening shifts a week since before I got here. The best thing you could say for him was that he was reliable. He always showed up on time. Then after arriving, what he did was walk the corridors looking for people to say hello to. If I were grading him, he'd get an A for friendliness, and maybe a D for observation. He once spent five minutes chatting with a guy who had no business being in the building and who had just stolen a thirty-five-millimeter camera from the photography lab. A real man-child, but like Dougherty had said, Verne had a vested interest.

"Obviously he didn't look in the weight room after Ponzini was dead," I said. "Did he look in before? Did he see him working out?"

Verne gave me a look of infinite pain. You spend a life doing good deeds and one day it has to backfire. From Verne's expression, this one didn't backfire, it imploded.

"No," he said. "He never went down there."

"What? What the hell was he doing?"

"This is a big place, Costas. Sixty floors to cover and only six men at night."

"Hey, it's me, Verne, not President Malloy. The man's got two buildings to cover, he's supposed to do it." I took a breath. "He didn't go down there, why?"

Verne's hand inched toward the drawer again, hesitated, then retreated to the arm of his chair. "Because I told him not to," he said simply.

I had to sit down on that one.

"You want to be more specific?" I asked.

Verne rubbed his eyes and leaned back. He waited a long time before he spoke again. When he did, he wasn't looking at me but out his window down at the campus. "You know,

28

Costas, sometimes the people who make all the decisions don't know shit. Malloy looks out there and sees a bunch of buildings and students, that's his college. But his college is set down right in the middle of one of the worst neighborhoods in Brooklyn, with some of the poorest people, and what does he do for them?" He turned back. "He lets them hold a flea market on the block where they won't be able to go inside and use the facilities. Maybe three or four times a year he lets them in the school to use a classroom for a meeting or something. Then he gives them one evening a week when they can use the library, but not to take out books. Big fucking deal. This is what he calls his community relations initiative."

"Don't tell me," I said, stunned. "You're letting them in after hours?"

Verne shrugged. "What's the harm. We got the facilities, they got the need." He stood up and walked to the window. "About a year ago a bunch of guys came and asked me if they could use the weight room. That's all. I knew them all from around the neighborhood. You know, I walk to work. I said okay, Tuesday and Thursday nights, ten to one A.M. They guaranteed they'd be out of here by one."

"Why didn't you ask permission from Dr. Malloy?"

"Because I know what he would have said. Insurance problems and all that crap." He sighed. "It was just a little gesture on my part, that's all. And for a year it worked well. But I had to make sure that none of the guards would put it in their report by mistake, so I always put Gonzales in that slot. He and I had an agreement. He would let them in and then just not bother to go down to check on them. It was the same bunch of guys every time."

"I'd say you have a problem, Verne. A big problem." I shook my head. "You got to be crazy. You're supposed to be the fucking head of security, not the head of unlawful entry."

"I know," Verne said. "But they're all good kids. For over a year it worked well. But hell, Dougherty's going to find out, so I might as well tell Malloy now." He looked at his watch

29

and stood back up. His eyes traveled down to his desk drawer and lingered there for a long moment.

"Go ahead," I said. "You'll need it."

Verne shook his head. "No," he said, "not this time. I don't want to make any mistakes."

"I'd say you're a little late with that." As he headed toward the door I asked him one last thing. "Did you at least find out from the guys you let into the weight room if they saw anything."

Verne looked back at me and frowned. "Nothing. I checked. When they left at one A.M. last night the place was empty."

"Makes no sense," I thought out loud. "Ponzini must have been killed after they left. So why would he come to work out in the middle of the night? And how did he get in?"

"That's what I'd like to know," Verne said. "Too bad Dougherty's not as curious."

SEVEN

For the next hour I felt like I was the receptionist at a year-end clearance sale. The phone must have rung on an average of three times a minute, which is about two times a minute more than normal. Fortunately another guard by the name of Clarence came by at the end of his shift, and I had him pick up a few of the calls. Normally, when someone wants to know anything at the college from the daily schedule of events to the time of day, it's security that gets the call. We even field calls about tuition and holiday schedules, so you can imagine what it was like when there was a stiff on campus. We said the same thing to everyone, which was essentially that we didn't know a thing, call back later. By the time Verne walked back in I felt like a cash register that's been punched once too often. If it was possible, Verne looked a lot worse than I felt. He tumbled into his chair and didn't hesitate. The bottle was out before I even had a chance to nod Clarence out of the office.

"So, I'm on probation," Verne said, and upended the little cup. "Dr. Malloy said he wanted a few weeks to review our security department in light of what he termed 'gross laxity in judgment.' " He looked up at me with eyes so ridden with guilt that I thought he had leveled a punch at the president. But I was slipping. It had gone the other way.

"Gonzales is history," he added. "Malloy told me any guard that could overlook a dead body on his shift had to go. I tried explaining my part in it, but he was out after immediate blood. Manuel's was the easiest. My turn will come when he finds a replacement." He splashed another drink from the bottle into the cup, finished that, and threw a beautiful, one-handed set shot with the crumpled paper into the wastebasket. Then he bent over his Rolodex and came up with a number. I knew where he was calling even before he punched the first digit on the phone. A block off the campus there is a restaurant run by two Puerto Rican brothers that specializes in eggs, steam table food, and hot meat sandwiches. They also serve cheap beer, which makes it the local hangout for many factory workers who want to take the edge off before going home. There was no doubt in either Verne's or my mind that Manual Gonzales was there right now, having a breakfast washed down by a cold Budweiser. Verne spoke into the phone for a moment, waited until they located Gonzales, then asked him to come back up to the office. Slowly he replaced the phone.

"At least Manuel gets to clear out right away. With me, I got to linger like a rotten vegetable for maybe two, three weeks." He took a deep breath. "President Malloy's already issued a statement that Ponzini's death was an accident. Isn't that great?"

"I think it stinks, both ways. And I'm sorry about Gonzales. You haven't fucked up too many times since I've known you, but this sure makes up for it." I was angry, both at Verne, for being so goddamn thoughtless, and at Malloy. I found myself nervously rubbing the smooth, black anodized case of a little penknife I keep in my pocket, a habit that goes way back to Vietnam with me.

"You just going to lay down for it?"

"What else did you have in mind?"

I could tell that the liquor was finally getting to him. He looked at me, his eyes like those of a sun-baked snake's searching for some cool shade.

"Well, one thing you might consider is finding out who the hell killed Ponzini. I think if you pulled that off, it'd give you some leverage with Dr. Malloy." I didn't tell him that if I helped it wouldn't hurt my chances of getting back my old job.

"Man, you're crazy," Verne said. "How do you think we're going to figure this one out when Dougherty's already kissed it good-bye? Would make him look like a fool." He stopped, thinking of what he'd just said and a new look came into his eyes. I caught it and pressed on.

"You still got some friends over there could help us if we needed something, right? I know a guy in the lab section. Verne, we could pull this off. Dougherty doesn't know anything about St. Bartlett's. No one's going to talk to him. We're right on top of it." I stopped for a breath, aware for the first time that my heart was beating like I'd just run the police school fifteen-hundred-yard training run. "You just going to lay down and take it like they want? Verne, you can't walk away from it."

"There's other stuff. Dr. Malloy said there's been other complaints."

"Yeah, Hap told me. But you know what I figure, I figure it all comes from the same problem, and this is just what you

32

need to get you off your ass. You're director of security at a place with over two thousand kids, Verne, not some glorified school crossing guard. You've been playing this job for as long as I've been here like some early retirement plan. Time for you to step up and be the man once again." I hesitated. "Me too."

Verne closed the desk drawer and leaned back. He didn't say anything for a moment, then a little smile crossed his face. "Shit, you really think we could do it?" he asked.

"We could give it a try," I said. "I got sixteen hours a day when I'm not on duty here. From what I can tell, Ponzini was no hermit."

"I didn't know the guy. Sitting behind this desk, I didn't get to know many of them." He rocked back up and leaned forward. "Costas, we got two weeks. Hell, I might as well go out swinging as feet first." He bent over and wrote something on a piece of paper on his desk. Then he tore it off and handed it to me. "Ray Matthews was one of the guys I let into the weight room. Here's the address. Might as well check with him when you can."

"And Gonzales didn't see *anything?*"

Verne shook his head. "I grilled him this morning and he didn't see anything unusual. But you can ask him, he'll be right in."

We waited for the next few minutes in silence, Verne making himself look busy, nervously shuffling papers around his desk, me trying to remember the last time I saw Ponzini in front of his class. Then we heard some footsteps down the corridor and Manuel turned the corner into the office. He looked at Verne right away and somehow picked up a signal because his head started to quiver.

"Sit down," Verne said softly. Gonzales sank slowly into a chair. Some of the guards changed their uniforms before going home, but he was still wearing his maroon coat, gray trousers, and gold-plated badge. From what I'd heard, he wore them even on his day off. He was incredibly proud of his job, and of his responsibility and authority, all of which were made visible by the threads of office. He leaned forward in his chair, closer to the man who had yanked him away from a life of liquor store holdups and court appearances. His eyes searched Verne's face.

"You wanted to speak to me?" he said slowly.

Verne cleared his throat and tried to sound calm, but I knew this was hurting him almost as much as it would Gonzales.

"Manuel," he began, "the president has asked that I relieve the person who was on duty last night and whose obligation to immediately report the incident was neglected." Gonzales's head wagged up and down now like a schoolboy listening to the theory of relativity. I realized he had no idea of what Verne had said. He still waited expectantly. "Yes?"

It took a few seconds, but finally Verne understood. He held out his hand. "Manuel, I need your badge. You can't come back to work here."

Gonzales looked down at Verne's outstretched hand and slid back into the seat. "Not come back?" he said. "Why?"

"President Malloy's orders. I'm sorry. It's all my goddamn fault, and I tried to take the blame, but something had to be done right away. It's like you were in the wrong place at the wrong time. I'll probably be following you in a few weeks." He closed his hand and pulled it back. "I'll try to find you something else. I still have some contacts."

Gonzales looked around at me like he'd just been sucker punched, and to tell the truth, he had. Some moisture began to form in his eyes as he slowly turned back to Verne.

"But I love this job, man, the students, the other guys."

"I'm sorry," Verne repeated. "I really tried my best."

"What about my wife? What will I tell her? We just got a new set of bedroom furniture. . . ."

"If you need any help with money," Verne said, "I'll chip in on the monthly payments until you get something else."

Gonzales shook his head. "There won't be anything else. No one wants to hire an ex-con." He said this so flatly that I realized he wouldn't even try. I also realized that Verne

34

couldn't keep chipping in for the bedroom set, and the monthly rent, and the food, and that sometime in the future it would all get to be too much. Especially when Verne lost his job. And there were all those liquor stores out there with full cash registers. I didn't know what to do, cry or take a poke at Verne. Either one would have helped with what I was feeling. Gonzales slowly unpinned his badge and placed it on the table.

"But it wasn't my fault," he said. "I didn't see anything."

"I know," Verne said. "You already told me that. Unfortunately, that's not the issue——"

"Not exactly," I interrupted. "It's one of the issues. In fact, I wanted to ask you some questions about last night. Verne and I are trying to get to the bottom of things."

Gonzales nodded numbly, and Verne relaxed into the back of his chair. The hard part was over. I asked for some details of his last night's shift, and Gonzales answered almost as though he were now the suspect. I tried to make it as easy as possible on him, but after twenty minutes I gave up. Verne had been right. Gonzales had been the Puerto Rican version of "hear no evil, see no evil." When he pulled himself out of the office he looked like a man that had just lost his family in a plane crash. How long would it take him to get back to the streets, I wondered? Not long enough.

EIGHT

The weight room at St. Bartlett's was the only one I'd seen, so I can't judge how it compared to others. Lifting heavy chunks of cast iron is just not my idea of fun, no matter what it's supposed to do for your pecs and deltoids. I'm not even jealous of guys like Schwartzenegger who seem to have the lovelies swooning at their rippling physiques. My motto has always been "no pain, no sprain," and I leave it at that.

The room was maybe twenty-five feet square and had a red mat covering half of it. On the uncovered part were two press benches, one sit-up bench, and an assortment of weights and bars that could sink a small trawler. A city policewoman eyed me as I poked my head in. I recognized her from my earlier life around the 67th. She nodded me inside.

"Agonomou," she said, "how's it going? What are you doing here?"

I shrugged, which I guess was all I needed to do to jog her memory.

"Oh yeah, I forgot." There was an awkward silence for a moment as I stepped in.

"This where it happened?" I asked innocently.

She pointed to the closest bench and a set of weights two feet away. The bar had already been dusted for prints but you could still see the splotch of blood in its center. Other than a dusting of powder here and there, the floor was clean.

"Hell of a way to go," she said.

I could think of worse, but I didn't say anything. The body had been removed, the photographs taken, and now she was just waiting to get the word from Dougherty so she could leave the scene of the "accident." Nothing seemed different from the hundreds of times I'd looked in on my rounds. There were mirrors on the walls to enjoy the fruits of everyone's hard work, five other bars full of weights, a rowing machine in one corner, and a mammoth Nautilus machine in the other. It was a real torture chamber as far as I was concerned. There was a door in the back wall, which I knew led to a storage closet. I walked over and opened it and saw another four mats stacked to one side. There was cleaning equipment in a separate locker and a few extra supplies around like boxes of chalk for gripping the metal bars. Nothing special. I turned back to the weight room and crossed over to the bar. Looking at Ponzini you wouldn't guess he'd even attempt 175 pounds. I bent down and gave one end a lift. I got it off the floor but it took two hands.

"Heavy," I said, trying to be polite.

"I think that's the point."

I grinned. "Were you here with the body?"

She nodded and gave a frown.

"See anything unusual?"

"Yeah, he wasn't breathing."

A comedian. I had half a mind to tell her to try the Improv club but instead I said, "Exercise sometimes has that effect. Dougherty has no doubt it was an accident?"

"No blood anywhere else. The doctor said his body hadn't been moved. If someone hit him, it had to be done while he was on the bench. With all these mirrors around he should have seen it coming. No bruises on his hands from warding off a blow. . . . You figure that adds up to foul play?"

Apparently she wasn't considering how difficult it would be to ward off a blow if you were holding 175 pounds over your head.

"Were his clothes sweaty?"

"What?"

"Sweaty. Every picture I've seen of some guy working out he's always got a ring of sweat around his neck and down his back."

The woman cop thought about that for a moment and narrowed her eyes. "I don't think so," she said. "But he could have just begun. Also, he'd been dead for over five hours by the time we arrived."

"Yeah, maybe," I tossed out. "I suppose Dougherty's right. They find a locker key on him?"

"If they did, I didn't see it. He was dressed just in shorts and a T-shirt. His clothes were next door in one of the lockers in the men's changing room."

"Unlocked?"

She shrugged. "Ask Dougherty. I wasn't in there."

I took one last look. Somehow, it didn't add up. Everything was too pat, too clean. I've been to accident scenes a lot, and the overwhelming impression is always that something was out of place, a crane toppled on its side, a car upside-down, a twisted bicycle. Here there was none of that, not even a drop of blood on the polished hardwood floor. Just a smudge of it on the bar. I started walking. "Thanks," I said, as I headed toward the door. "I'll keep the kids out."

A bunch of students were now peering into the room and pointing. I made my way out the door and closed it behind me.

"Show's over," I said. "Back to classes."

"Hey, Costas," I heard one of them say. "What's the story?"

I looked over and saw Strickland, the kid from Ponzini's drawing class who made human bodies into pretzels. The fact that he knew my name didn't surprise me. After all, that's what name tags are for. I walked the two steps over and put a light hand on his upper arm, light but not lacking in a certain authority.

"Where you headed?" I asked.

He looked down at my hand, then up into my face. "Print-making," he said.

"Over in Flagler?"

He nodded.

"Good, let's walk. I'm headed that way myself. I got a few questions for you."

"About Ponzini?" he asked.

"You're not such a bad student after all," I said.

NINE

St. Bartlett's is not known for having very bright kids. Few of the students could put together a set of SATs above 750, and even fewer showed anything unique in high school in the way of personal style. But the guy I was walking with was an exception. In fact, if they gave style points on the SATs, he would have gotten all 800s.

He was tall and dressed entirely in black right down to a pair of heavy thick-soled brogans. His collar-length, straight hair had been dyed an intense raven color. But where he had shown true creativity was in his subtle choice of face powder, a light dusting of white, which gave him a slightly eerie presence. He was The Joker as a young art student. The only thing lacking was the lipstick. He reminded me of Marta, the sixty-two-year-old model with the Kabuki face. The two of them would have made quite a striking mother-son act.

Strickland's first name was Charles, and he was a nineteen-year-old first-year fine arts major from Bay Shore, Long Island, the birthplace of Scrabble. Notwithstanding, he had been avoiding the written word ever since grade school. This I got in the first hundred yards of our walk. He had come to St. Bartlett's because all through high school he had been told by his teachers he had an "aesthetic flair," and they recommended he pursue a career in art. He suspected that his teachers told him that because he was, on the one hand, atrocious in English and, on the other, the only kid in class who sharpened his pencils. It didn't take him long to find out that the other young aspiring artists at St. Bartlett's could do a lot more than grid paintings with sharp, thin lines. They could actually draw. Maybe that's when he decided to turn his artistry inward and use himself as a canvas. He told me all this when I asked what he was doing at St. Bartlett's. Then, the preliminaries over, I asked him what he thought of Ponzini's class.

"He was rough on me," he concluded. "Some teachers just need to have a whipping boy around. To amuse the class, I guess. Amuse themselves. I suppose I learned some stuff in there." He shrugged. "The man certainly knew how to draw."

"Most of the kids liked him," I said. "I guess you didn't fall into that category?"

We kept walking in silence for a moment. I had dropped his arm and we were keeping a steady pace down the linoleum halls. Suddenly he gave out a short laugh.

"It's hard to love a man that's constantly on your case and insists on you calling him Professor Ponzini. Besides, he hated the way I looked. He once told me that it was just an excuse for not being able to cut it as an artist. He suggested I consider accounting for my life's work."

"That must have hurt," I said.

"He had a knack," the young man replied tightly.

"With others too?" We were just getting to Flagler, and there were still a few things I wanted to ask.

"Not many. Most of the other majors produced good work. But he taught an elective drawing class, which he kept referring to as his wretch-a-sketch section. I'll bet he made mincemeat out of them. They're all business and technology majors."

"Know any names in that class?"

"Only one, Jason Sanders."

"The basketball player?"

"You got it." He opened a fire door and we swung into the basement of Flagler. The elevators were twenty yards away at the end of the corridor. "But the art students I knew saw Ponzini as kind of a hero," he continued. "They're all so sensitive about the difficulty of making money as artists they compensate by loading up on pride. Ponzini played into that; he was always making fun of the business faculty and their pretentiousness; their endowed chairs from the cardboard-manufacturing associations or their tool-and-die worker's union scholarships. A class wouldn't go by when he didn't make a joke at their expense." He nodded at some students that were getting out of the elevator, and then the two of us stepped in. "Besides, he seemed to be a very successful artist. At least from the way he talked and from the stuff he had. Did you know he drove a Porsche?"

I let that sink in for a moment. "Did your model, Ms. Cunningham, also think he was a hero?"

Strickland gave me a quick, sly look.

"Ask her," is all he said. "Then ask Jason Sanders."

"Cunningham also modeled in the elective class?" I had an idea what he was getting at, but I wanted to hear it from him.

"Hardly, not with Sanders in the class."

I was about to ask another question when the door opened on the second floor and a bunch of students crowded on. Nods and hellos all around, and a series of breathless "have you heards" about Ponzini. Everyone got off on four and headed for the printmaking shop. Strickland held back for a moment and tapped my shoulder.

"So if it was an accident, how come all the questions?"

I tried to smile, but I think it came out crooked. "Loose ends," I mumbled.

"Very loose," Strickland added and hurried down the hall to catch up with his friends.

TEN

There are two ways to get to talk with a particular student. I could put a note in a mail folder in the lobby of Cameron and wait a week until I got a response, or I could find out the student's schedule and catch him outside a class. The best way to do that was to find a friend. I checked my watch and saw that it was getting near to lunchtime. Chances were I'd find who I wanted in the cafeteria.

As far as I was concerned, St. Bartlett's student cafeteria was the Sodom and Gomorrah of the private college educational system. More sins were buried in the stews, chilis, and vegetable thatches than in the workers' pension fund. The salad bar with its wilted lettuce, tofu, and mung bean sprouts was there to show how health conscious the school's commercial food service was, right alongside the racks of Twinkies, Oreos, chips with nacho ranch dressing, and soft-drink dispenser. Besides, a trip through the lines here could cost a week's allowance.

I took a few steps inside and scanned the room. The cafeteria was not a popular place for faculty because the noise level was so high. Music blared from dozens of ceiling speakers at a pitch that has actually set Cheerios dancing in their bowls. But the students seemed to love it, and the large room was never empty. It was their place to strut, and the sound only helped bring out the jive in everyone. If the library was the mind of the college, this was its soul. Looking at the faces of the scores of students, I could see it was a soul full of sexual energy, but also one of extreme cliquishness. In the cafeteria, like in the ark, the animals came in by species. Chinese students sat together, Blacks, Whites, Koreans, Indians, Hispanics. . . . They all had their separate tables. If there was intermingling it was in the classes, not over their Diet Pepsis and bacon cheeseburgers.

It was easy for me to spot who I was looking for. Anyone over six-foot-four and black at St. Bartlett's was probably on the basketball team. I walked over to a table with two guys that looked like the NBA would be interested in them. One was wearing a Bart Simpson T-shirt that said "Don't have a cow, man," and the other was going it on his own wit. His shirt was blindingly white. They were the only two at the table and looked at me curiously as I sat down.

"Hey, bro, what's cookin'?" the one closest to me said eyeing my cute maroon and gray uniform.

"I caught your practice last night," I answered. "I think you guys are ready for the NCAAs."

They both smiled.

"You know where I can find Jason? I got to ask him something."

"Yeah, he over in SEARS in Nathan 401," the one with the Bart Simpson T-shirt said. "He don't get out till twelve."

"Thanks," I said above the racket. "I'll catch him over there." I got up to leave when the one with the white T-shirt asked, "What choo want wid Jason, anyway?"

"Nothing important. Just about some class he's taking." The big guy shrugged, then went back to talking with his friend as

43

I made it out with my eardrums still intact. A very relaxing place, that cafeteria. Like having lunch on a subway platform.

SEARS is not a place to buy lawn mowers or hardware supplies, at least not at St. Bartlett's. It stands for Supplementary English and Reading Skills. SEARS is what the students call it. Bonehead English is how it's referred to by faculty.

To be placed into the program you have to be performing on an eleventh-grade level or below. I guess that means *Moby Dick*, although it's been a long time. Why kids are admitted to college who can't write a sentence, or read correctly, is something I still don't understand, although people here are always talking about keeping things in perspective. SEARS was the college's answer to this problem, and I had been told it had been waging a good fight for years. The trick was to get students reading and writing about things that interested them, their own lives, rather than things out of a textbook. Close to 20 percent of the student body had passed through Nathan 401 at one time or another, and so it was no surprise that Jason Sanders had been caught in its web.

Perspective, I kept telling myself as I waited outside the classroom. Maybe they were right. Did Sanders really have to know future conditional verb forms to perform on a basketball floor? As I was thinking these weighty thoughts, the door opened and twenty-five students nearly trampled me in their exit from the room. Sanders, towering over all the other kids, was still talking to the teacher. Right away that was a good sign, unless he was trying to sell her tickets to the Wagner game. Except for the double pleats in his pants, there was nothing flashy about his clothes. Where he had invested his money was in jewelry. He wore a heavy gold two-finger ring with the initials "J. S." framing a diamond and a gold chain around his neck the thickness of a pencil. Against his dark skin the gold stood out like splashes of light. I waited politely until he was finished, then intercepted him by the door.

"Got a minute, Jason?" I asked. "My name's Costas."

"You a guard here?" he asked simply.

I nodded. "And also a friend of Hap's. You want to take a detour and ask him?"

Sanders inspected me at the same time I was giving him my once over. Not too subtle, like two dogs sniffing each other's tails. He must have thought I had a trustworthy face because he shrugged and leaned against the door frame.

"Nah, I got a few minutes. What's it about?"

"You heard what happened to Ponzini yet?" I asked. I saw his face stiffen. He was wearing his hair cut flat on top and shaved on the sides, which made his expression even more austere.

"I heard. But it don't effect me till Tuesday morning when I got his class." He straightened up and went through the doorway.

"Hey, I thought you had a few minutes?"

"For basketball. I thought you wanted to ask about that." He was walking fast.

"Not everything in life is basketball, Jason," I answered, trying to keep up with him.

"I got no time for this," he called back.

"You better make some. Next person I'm talking to is Lisa Cunningham."

He wheeled on me and for a second I understood what it might be like to defend against a Sanders lay-up. Here came this mountain at me spewing heat, Mount St. Helens going in for the dunk. Fortunately, he stopped a step away and got himself under control.

"You leave her out of this."

"Hey man, the guy's dead. Questions are going to be asked. You can either talk to me or talk to the police, and I don't think the cops go to any of the home games." I looked up at him without moving. "You got an easier time with me."

Sanders bent down and put his face close to mine, so close that I could smell the after-shave lotion. "She had nothing to do with him, you got that?"

"I got it," I lied. "How about you?"

He stood back up. "I took his class, that was it. I painted pretty pictures."

"Did he like them?"

He was silent for a moment. Finally, he said, "Not much."

"Why not?"

The muscles in Sanders's jaw were working overtime, but he managed to come out with it. "He said my hands had no feeling in them. Funny, right, with me averaging over thirty-two points a game?"

"I didn't realize he was so direct."

"He was an asshole." He turned around and started walking again, but this time at a pace I could keep up with.

"So, I guess you didn't like Lisa modeling for his class?"

"I didn't know about it," he said in a tight voice full of anger. "The first time she did it we were in a tournament up in New Paltz. Last week."

"You two living together?"

"That's none of your goddamn business."

"Sorry, Jason, I guess I could ask a bunch of other people for that answer."

He took a few more steps and said, "Yeah, we are. Since August. So what? You got a problem with that? . . . Black man, white woman?"

"None whatsoever. I'm from Greece, birthplace of democracy. I got a problem with a dead teacher that shouldn't have died when or where he did. You got any ideas about it?"

"Maybe one of his B students wanted an A."

"Interesting," I said. "But I don't think it works. I like this one better. How about an F student wanting a passing grade."

Sanders stopped in his tracks and looked at me. "Who told you I was failing?"

Sometimes long shots pay off. I didn't help him.

"It wouldn't a happened. I was going to pull out of it."

"Good," I said. "Teachers always like to see improvement. Did Hap know?"

"I don't know what Hap knows."

I nodded. "What are you, Jason, a business major?"

"Yeah, management."

"How you making out in the other classes?"

"I'm here, ain't I?"

Some answer. Sure he's here. All thirty-two points a game worth. "Thanks," I said. I could see we were getting close to the cafeteria and I knew I'd have a hard time bringing the interview inside.

"If you get any other ideas, you'll let me know," I said, and stopped at the entrance to the cafeteria.

"Just one, leave her out of it," Sanders repeated and shot me a glance that could have stripped a ball from the hands of an all-American. Then he turned and dove into the throbbing music.

I've seen hot looks like that before. At defense tables. Christ, I thought, this is getting complicated.

ELEVEN

Lately, I've been thinking a lot about the boy I killed. After it happened I spent long hours justifying the whole thing, thinking through my reaction, second by second, replaying the sequence like a film editor trying to see more than what was there, eventually settling for what was before me. I remembered everything perfectly, his hand dipping inside his jacket, the defiant expression on his face, the explosion of sound as my gun discharged a split second too soon. And after each run through I come to the same conclusion: It had to have happened that way, and would again. And yet I see his surprised face float before me at the oddest times, and hear his last gurgled breath for no apparent reason. No matter how I try, I can't shake it. I'd like to say that the boy was unlucky, or stupid, but they all are in one way or another. Hector, my son, has done foolish things, but no one ever killed him for it. And if someone did, what would it matter if it was justifiable? Would I feel the loss any less?

We visited the family after the funeral, Helen and I. I thought maybe it would help them understand what happened, but I see now I was really going for myself. Helen understood and helped me through it. But the parents didn't care if their son had had a shotgun at my head. He was gone and, to a great extent, so was a part of their life.

So I still see him, this Charles Lee, when I'm walking the halls of St. Bartlett's. I see him in the posturing of youth, and in their eager eyes and healthy growing bodies; and I've finally come to understand what the hell I'm doing a year into a job I should have quit months after I started. This is some crazy form of payback, atonement for my sin; this is me helping all the other young Charles Lees make it through, and ultimately, this is me being forced to remember. I was being punished by the police force in their indeterminate suspension, but it was only half the story. The other half was me punishing myself with St. Bartlett's. And the sad part is . . . there was no way out, no way except upward, back on the force.

I thought of this on the way to find Lisa Cunningham, the student with the supple body and a smouldering volcano for a boyfriend. Maybe I could smell the trouble hanging in the air over that relationship like a cloud of swamp gas, or maybe it was just Charles Lee getting even, sending me laughingly into the swamp itself. I figured either way Ms. Cunningham could use some advice, even if she didn't have an interesting perspective on Ponzini's death. And if she did, all the better. I like two-way streets. You get places faster.

It took me most of the afternoon to find her. She hadn't gone to her liberal arts classes all day, so her academic schedule didn't help. I managed to speak with a few of her classmates who made some interesting comments and suggestions as to her whereabouts; but she wasn't in the library, student lounge, or cafeteria. I was about to give up when I decided to try my luck in the studios. I found her behind an easel in one of the empty painting classrooms. In front of her on one of the tables was a still life with a bottle of Coke, some loose oatmeal cookies, a plastic banana, and a Bloomingdale's catalogue. It was not the collection Cézanne might have chosen, but she was hard at work and didn't even look up when I came over. The closer I got, the less I smelled the oils and turpentine in the room and the more I smelled the pungent, fruity aroma of jasmine. I like women who wear perfume just for themselves. I like them more if it's my favorite scent, the one Helen wore the day we were married.

Lisa Cunningham was working with pencils and crayons. From what I could tell, the kid had talent. The cookies looked good enough to eat. I waited patiently another two minutes, but when that didn't work either, I decided to interrupt the creative process.

"I'm impressed," I began. "You're just as good on this side of the easel."

She looked up then and stared at me with the bluest eyes I had ever seen. Ice blue and just as cold. She took me in with a glance and then turned back to the drawing.

"How would you know?" she said.

"I was in Ponzini's class yesterday afternoon, remember?"

"I don't remember anything." She put a few more strokes onto the paper and sat back. "My memory was erased at birth."

"I guess that's a joke," I said, not laughing. "I'm sure you can remember a lot of things; your telephone number, your address, your friends . . . like Jason Sanders."

She put the crayon down and turned on the stool to face

me. Something new had crept into her eyes, a note of apprehension, but she was doing her best to hide it.

"Is that part of your job, Mister Security Guard, to check on who's friendly with who?"

"With whom," I corrected. "Maybe you shouldn't cut all of your liberal arts classes."

She gave me a nasty look, which under the circumstances I guess I deserved.

"Mind if I ask you some questions?" I continued.

"Depends on what they are."

"Good. You tell me if they're not the right ones." I took a seat nearby and rubbed my eyes for a moment. "The first one is, why were you modeling in the first place? From what I understand, you don't need the money."

"Jesus, people are always jealous of something. Who told you that?"

I shrugged. "Common knowledge. Everyone seems to know everything around here. Well, almost everything. Not why you were modeling." I looked at her and waited. After having seen her body, her face was no surprise. There wasn't one element misaligned.

"Experience," she said finally. "I wanted to see how Professor Ponzini would pose me and how he'd have the students draw me." A grin crossed her face. "Then also there's the narcissist in me. Most women fantasize about being naked in front of a roomful of people. I went ahead and did it."

"Most women I know fantasize about putting clothes on, not taking them off. . . . New clothes in particular." I took a breath, and asked Helen silently to forgive me for that one. "I don't suppose your friend Jason shared your feelings?"

"I didn't ask," she said casually.

"Maybe you should have."

"Listen, Mr. Security Guard . . ."

"You can call me Costas."

"I don't need another father, one's enough." She stood up

and leaned toward her drawing with a different color crayon. "Excuse me, I've got to finish this before six tonight."

"I've also found that experience leads to knowledge," I said, not paying attention to her brush-off. "So I was wondering if you had any knowledge about Ponzini. . . . About his death in particular."

She kept sketching, but I could tell I had hit a nerve. The movements of her hands were now more jerky and the lines they drew not so self-assured.

She shrugged. "What could I know? I only modeled for him twice."

"I thought you might have seen him outside of school."

That hung in the air like a lobbed grenade, something you couldn't kick under the rug. She took another few swipes at the paper and sat back down. "Costas, I'm afraid you are mistaken. I never saw him except in his studio here at the college." She looked at me, and her eyes got even colder. Some people are good at lying and others couldn't fib their way into a Shriners' convention. She fell somewhere in between. Her eyes watched me, but the rest of her face looked like it was set in concrete. The mask she offered was so stiff it had to be covering something. I tried a different approach.

"Have any ideas why someone might want to kill Ponzini?"

"President Malloy said it was an accident."

"President Malloy has different concerns than I do. Let's assume for the moment that he was wrong. Should I repeat the question?"

She shook her head. "I have no idea," she said. "I thought everyone liked Ponzini. Maybe he was rough on a few students. . . ."

"Like Jason Sanders."

There was silence in the studio for a moment. Finally, she answered. "Art is not Jason's best subject."

"So I gathered. He was failing it. I suppose you tried to help him." I thought it was an innocent question, but her reaction took me by surprise.

"That's none of your goddamn business. In fact, none of this is your business." She looked down at my uniform. "Even if it is some kind of official investigation by the college."

"No, it's not official," I reassured her.

"Then it's over." She got up and ripped the sheet of paper off the pad. "Jason is a very sensitive guy with incredible athletic skills, and soon enough he'll be the focus of every magazine and newspaper in this city. The last thing he needs is being associated in any way with this Ponzini mess. He's a big man, Mr. Security Guard, but inside he's like a little child and needs to be protected from all the sharks around." She unzipped her large vinyl portfolio and shoved the drawing inside. Then she stood up and turned toward me. Her face looked like she just barely had it under control. "Take a walk sometime into Bedford-Stuyvesant and see where he came from, and how far he's traveled. Then ask yourself if you really want to push him back down there. Leave him alone, and while you're at it, leave me alone too." She turned quickly and threaded her way through the standing easels until she made the door. Then, without looking back, she passed through and I was left in the empty room staring at some stale cookies and a plastic banana, breathing in the lingering smell of African jasmine.

I spent years covering Bedford-Stuyvesant so I knew what she was talking about. Escaping the drugs and street fights is a constant struggle, finishing high school is a feat, and actually going to college is nothing short of a miracle. She was right, but that wouldn't bring Ponzini back, or find his killer.

I got off my stool. Sharks usually swim, but I walked out.

TWELVE

St. Bartlett's doesn't employ me to run murder investigations. I have a job that is supposed to be full-time, so all of this free-lance work I was doing was cutting into my assignments. I checked my schedule and realized that I was already ten minutes late covering the president's little get-together Winston had talked about the night before. When I arrived at the small auditorium on the ground floor of Cameron I was expecting another polite convocation with faculty and administration and trustees and some parents all stroking themselves into believing that they were all working for the common good, something called a decent college education. What I found, however, looked more like a hostile leveraged buyout attempt at one of the Fortune 500.

The president had the microphone and looked like he was going to use it in an unnatural way against the person in front of him. Dr. Malloy was a big guy, an Irishman with a footballer's frame, whose voice carried to the back of any room and whose white hair added distinction to whatever he was saying. Right now, he was talking tough about his responsibilities as president of the college, but the woman in front of him was giving him a run for his money. I felt for the guy. He just had someone die on campus, and now he's got this meeting on AIDS. Not a moment to breathe.

"Please sit down," he said. "We can't discuss anything if people are interrupting all the time."

"You are not here to discuss anything," the woman said to his face. "You've already made that clear. You're here to appease any of the parents who feel they have a right to dictate policy to you."

"Please sit," he tried again, and looked to the rest of the audience for support. "We can't continue like this."

"Sit *down!*" someone shouted from the back of the room, and the woman turned and gave him a vicious look.

"I'll sit," she said after a moment, "like the rest of the faculty members here . . . sitting on their hands for the last year on this AIDS issue." She turned back to face Malloy. "But only after you give us an explanation of why, at a time when compassion is called for, all we get is ruthlessness. And from a man who calls himself a Christian."

"I am a Christian," Dr. Malloy said angrily, "and the Christian thing to do is not jeopardize our students with disease. Also, we mustn't lose sight of who we are and our unique mission. This is a Catholic college endowed to inspire religious principles. The message we would be sending is not one I care to endorse. It cannot look appropriate to the general community at large, and the smaller community of prospective parents and students, to have faculty members, many of whom are priests, advertising their promiscuity. AIDS as a medical problem is one thing, it is quite another to give it entry into our classrooms."

Hands shot up across the floor. There were about eighty people in the auditorium and it looked like half of them had a statement to make.

Dory Stabler didn't wait. He stood up a few seats to the right of where the woman faculty member was. But instead of talking to Dr. Malloy, he faced around to the room behind him.

"My name is Professor Stabler," he boomed. "I am the president of the teachers' union, and I have something to say about this. Prejudice is never pretty in any form, and what I see before me is certainly a clear example of that. Now, understand this, both the union's central committee and our general membership support the right of any teacher to continue in his profession according to his contract with the college."

He got a few catcalls over that but he continued, raising his voice to overcome the static. "Unless you can prove a clear danger to a student by his continued presence, you can no sooner relieve a teacher of his duties than you could if he espoused Marxism or Shamanism. A very wonderful teacher, one who has been at this institution for twenty-four years, is no longer at the college because he was forced to retire this semester by the kind of obscene pressure you are displaying here in this room and to which President Malloy is succumbing." His face was getting red, but he kept going. "And it is obscene, more so than the McCarthy witch-hunts because you are hitting people when they are down. Father Simmons was no pariah. He was a superb teacher, and now he's looking at nothing but emptiness and despair."

"Good, at least he's not looking into the faces of our kids," a woman from three rows behind him called out. She was obviously a parent and obviously just as worked up as Dory. Stabler looked at her with contempt, looked over the rest of the auditorium, then pushed his way out of the aisle and stalked out of the room.

Dr. Malloy motioned with his hands to hold the noise down. He leaned forward and said into the microphone, "We must not let emotions run away with our reasoning. I want to assure everyone that we will provide for those unfortunate few who will have to leave, but I want to repeat, that one condition of employment here at St. Bartlett's, and it's in all the contracts, is that teachers remain capable of teaching. The way

55

I read that is, among other things, that they remain healthy." He looked to his left and motioned to a smaller man with a natty business suit on. "Now Dr. Kehoe, one of our trustees over there, has explained to me exactly what kind of liability this college faces in the event that a student contracts this disease from a faculty member known to be afflicted with it. The numbers are staggering."

"So is your monumental indifference," the same woman faculty member called out. I felt sorry for her. To razz the president of your college took either guts, insanity, or tenure. I assumed she had the latter, but I also had no doubt that she'd never see a sabbatical in her life or another comfortable teaching schedule. While Dr. Malloy glowered down at her, he got some assistance from over on his right.

"Now it's my turn," someone said, and a woman rose from her seat. She was dressed in a combination of clothes that reminded me of an advertisement for a Maurice Villency living room. Everything was in mauves and creams, with color-coordinated accents and jewelry made out of chrome and lucite. The bright blond hair added to her visual statement that surface is substance. "I ain't sittin' down until I say this," she continued. "We pay good money to get our kids educated, not infected. All this other stuff about liability and whatnot don't concern me. We're talking here about the health of our kids. How can we compromise on that?" She looked around once and added, "Ain't that right?"

The room broke out into a lot of commotion and I thought for a moment that Dr. Malloy would ask me to clear the place. After a couple of minutes of asking for quiet, people finally settled down and the president was once again able to speak.

"I think you'll find the question is moot anyway. At this time there are no teachers here at St. Bartlett's with AIDS, so we are only talking about policy here. Now we do have some other things to discuss with you today, so I am going to turn the meeting over to Chester Rooney, our freshmen dean of students, and he will talk about our new student counseling

56

program. For those of you that did not hear it earlier, I made a statement about the unfortunate accident that took place in one of our gym facilities last night and can assure you we are following up with our own investigation. At this time I want to reassure everyone that it was, indeed, an accident." He cast a smile out over the room and motioned to Rooney sitting next to him. Then he backed away from the rostrum and headed to a door in the side of the room with a look of incredible relief. Scattered applause, a few catcalls, and he was out of there.

I hung around the back of the room until the meeting broke up twenty minutes later. Student counseling had always been a joke at St. Bartlett's, and everyone knew it. All the kids wanted was advice on contraception, and there was no way that was going to come out of a meeting with any of the sisters or priests chosen to advise them. Rooney's suggestion was a novel one; it had something to do with computers, but I had stopped paying attention long before he was halfway through. I was thinking that with a little luck I might still have time to catch Hap in his office before he got to the gym floor. There was something I was curious about, so curious, in fact, I was willing to miss my afternoon coffee break. But first I had to check something with one of the secretaries in the registrar's office.

THIRTEEN

Every now and then when the weather is nice and there's nothing around the house for me to do, Hector and I go down to the high school and shoot some hoops. I've never been much for the fancy stuff. Just your basic head fake and jump shot, which usually works if I'm inside fifteen feet. Hector is more for the behind-the-back stuff, reverse lay-ups and twenty-foot hook shots, which constantly mystify me. He allows me to stay close just to make it a game, but at some point, like a world class miler, he'll pull away for a final sprint and break his old man's heart. But his most elusive shot is the alley-oop, which we have to practice together each session, signals and all, for at least ten frustrating minutes. It's something like the aerialist's quadruple flip; we haven't pulled it off yet. He once confided in me that his greatest ambition in life was to do a perfect alley-oop; just one time to fly up high in the air at the precise instant to catch a lofted pass and in one fluid motion slam-dunk the ball through the hoop. I mention this only because as good as Hector is, he still couldn't pull off an alley-oop, which is a move that most good high school players can make. That's because, as good as he is, he couldn't make his high school team. The kids who did were unbelievable. The kids who go on to make their college teams take it even one step further.

Being able to coach a group of athletes like that has always impressed me. It's a little like being both the designer and driver of a precision race car, a job that takes incredible patience and skill. But being head coach of a college basketball team, like Hap, took something else, a great deal of caring. Hap was not working with machines. His raw material was kids, and kids ran amok for reasons other than overheating or material flaws, reasons you couldn't cure with another quart of STP.

Hap's system was one of rigid discipline. He set practice times, and if someone was late, they were benched a game. He set smoking and drinking codes, even eating codes; and if someone broke those, they sat out two games. He set academic codes, which was that you didn't play at all if your grade point average fell below a 2.0. And that was just for openers. There was a whole different set of regulations concerning performance on the basketball floor. The kids playing for Hap knew exactly what to expect if they screwed up, and Hap had a reputation for meting out justice evenhandedly, according to his system.

I found him in his office, a comfortable room next to the gym filled with mementos of his ten years at St. Bartlett's. There were pictures of him and earlier teams holding trophies for tournaments won; pictures of him with graduates, a few of whom had actually made it to the NBA; and a bunch of framed clippings headlining his teams' accomplishments. I didn't have to look to know that the most recent clipping couldn't have been less than four years old. Four years was a long time for a dry spell, especially when the college gave you such a big office.

I didn't bother knocking. Hap was alone and studying a sheet of paper on his desk. He looked up as I sat in the vinyl seat opposite him.

"Hello, Costas," he said with a note of curiosity in his voice. "What brings you into the inner sanctum?"

"Yesterday you gave me some advice about Verne?"

He nodded.

"Well, now Verne's in even deeper with this Ponzini thing. He needs some help."

Hap shrugged. "I don't know anything about it. It happened after midnight as far as I was told, and all of my guys are out of here by eight-thirty."

I shook my head slowly. "Not that, Hap."

"What?"

"About Jason Sanders." I saw his eyes get that kind of mirrored sheen when people go on their guard. "About whether or not you knew he was failing some of his courses?"

Hap didn't say anything for several seconds as he leaned back in his chair. His eyes never left mine. In the vacuum of Hap's office, the sound of bouncing basketballs across the hall sounded like jackhammers on pavement. Finally, he smiled.

"Beware of Greeks bearing gifts," he said. "What are you bringing me, Costas?"

"A question. Did you know?"

He leaned forward and nodded. "Yes, I knew. I know about all of my players. I get midterm warning notices and their last semester's transcript. That's how I run things around here."

"Before I came I checked with one of the secretaries in the registrar's office," I said. "Unfortunately, she wouldn't let me see Sanders's sheet."

"I don't believe it. Finally, someone around here doing their job." He cranked up a smile and just as quickly let it go. "Now, why would that interest you?"

I took a deep breath and proceeded. "Because, Hap, as I understand it, if Sanders flunked on a subject and dropped his average too low, you wouldn't play him . . . unless you turned your back on your own system. I took a look at your schedule, and that would mean two more important games this year . . . and the NITs if you got lucky. With a record like St. Bartlett's has had in past years, I figure there'd be a lot of pressure for Sanders to pass all his courses. Am I right?"

"There's a lot of pressure on all of my players."

"Come on, Hap, this is Costas you're talking to. Quit the bullshit. Sanders is your hot player, without him your team maybe hits another four hundred average. With him you could go all the way. You don't think that makes for a different kind of pressure?"

"Yeah, it does." He took a towel off his desk and wiped his forehead. I hadn't realized that he was sweating even though the room seemed kind of underheated to me. "But we had it all figured out," he continued. "I helped him with his program. He was doing okay."

"You mean he was above the two-point-oh."

"Let's say he was skimming the surface."

"And this semester, you already got the midterms?"

Hap stood up and walked behind his desk to a file in a corner. After a moment of searching, he came out with a folder and dropped it on the desk in front of me.

"Not midterms yet, but early warnings in two subjects. Management Practices and Drawing. I knew about the management course from one he took last semester, he was probably going to pull a D, but I'd figured all along we'd bring up his average by scheduling in a gut, some easy art course. Then, son of a bitch, he pulls that cocksucker Ponzini."

"You talk to him?"

"You're goddamn right I did. After I got his warning notice I went right up there and asked him how he could think of giving someone an F in drawing. I told him to take a look at some of the crap on the walls in the museums around town and asked him how you could be so sure of anything in art."

"Where'd it get you?"

"With a smart-ass lecture on something called the 'golden mean,' whatever the hell that is. I walked right out on the guy."

"Be careful what you say, Hap. He's dead."

"Serves him right. I wish he'd taken up weight lifting years ago." He sat back down and looked at me closely. "I'm sorry, Costas, that's how I feel. An F in his class would have ruined Sanders. He should have taken that into consideration."

"It wasn't an accident, Hap."

"What?"

"He was murdured."

Hap stared at me for a moment as though he hadn't heard me. But he had, I could tell from the way his color all of a sudden turned flat.

"That's not what they reported."

"It was inconvenient, but they'll get around to it."

There was silence in the office for a full minute. "I guess when they do it won't put me in such a great light."

"You said it, not me."

Hap glanced at his watch and stood up. "Christ, the team's out on the floor."

"One more question, Hap. You know anything about Sanders's girlfriend, Lisa Cunningham? He talk about her at all?"

"Costas, I've been here ten years and I've seen all kinds of girls around the players, from chippies to fundamental Baptists. I can tell you who's in it for what from a block away."

"And Lisa?"

"She's one of the good ones. She was trying to help Jason get through. She really worked at it. Why? You got a problem with her?"

I shook my head. "Not yet."

Hap moved to the door. "You want to hang around and watch the practice for a few minutes. We got New York Tech this week, then the big one, Wagner, following a week later."

"No thanks, Hap, I gotta go talk to someone soon as the

shift ends." I followed him out. "And listen, pal, before someone takes you by surprise, you might want to remember
where you were last night when Ponzini was taking his last
breath."

"You serious?" Hap said with eyes as piercing as bullets.

"Dead serious."

FOURTEEN

St. Bartlett's has a hundred bulletin boards plastered around
the campus, each duplicating the announcements on the
other ninety-nine. I usually stop during the day and read over
at least one board to see what's coming up. So after leaving
Hap, I spent a moment in front of one of them. My eyes
traveled over the announcements for the bible studies club,
the Irish students' flea market, the crisis intervention office
hours, the tarot card-reading workshop, the woman's awareness lecture series, and the union health plan claims discussion group. Not much new as far as I could tell. At St. Bartlett's,
crisis intervention meant a lapse of faith, not a dead body in
the gym; and woman's awareness ran to things like undiscov-
ered sixteenth-century female painters rather than experienc-
ing multiple orgasms.

I headed down to the locker and my leather jacket. My eight
hours as a paid employee of the private educational system of
New York was over. Now, as they say on TV, it was Miller
time. Except I was headed over to ask Ray Matthews, one of
the locals who had been in the gym the night before, a few

questions. I wondered how he'd take to some guy asking a lot of nasty questions. I had a feeling it was not exactly what the beer commercial had in mind.

Matthews lived three blocks away from the school on a street that looked as if it had once been a thriving factory block. Now it was full of quiet warehouse space. A few broken bottles littered the gutter. When the St. Bartlett's publicists said their campus was in an urban setting, they were trying their best to be honest. These days, only the uninitiated take urban to mean something out of a Noel Coward movie. St. Bartlett's was a little oasis in a neighborhood that had seen a lot better times but was bravely hanging on.

Matthews lived on the top floor of a small brownstone wedged in between two larger buildings. The front door closed tightly on its jamb, the lobby had no graffiti, and the downstairs intercom was in working order. The place was shaping up to be one of the seven wonders of Brooklyn. I rang the buzzer for Matthew's apartment and told the voice that answered that I was a friend of Verne Newton's. The door released instantly, and the voice told me to come up to 4B. I've been in a million of these buildings before, but mostly with a gun on my person, so walking up the dim staircase seemed particularly unnerving. But the place didn't have the characteristic smell of dank urine, and the hallways I passed had been painted recently. Four B even had a door that had been stripped and revarnished, revealing the original hundred-year-old oak. I knocked and waited.

The guy who opened the door looked like Christopher Reeves in street clothes. He had dark hair, an easy smile, and a handshake that was firm but not crushing. I asked if he could spare me a few moments for some questions, and he motioned me in. A kettle was on in the kitchen, and I could smell something cooking. I took in all the inexpensive but tasteful furnishings in one glance.

"This about the accident?" he asked. It was a good guess

since I had replaced the maroon coat with the worn leather jacket.

"Yes. Verne's kind of in a mess for letting you guys in."

"I figured," Matthews said, sitting down. "He already called this morning. But like I told him, it happened after we left."

"Can I run through it once again? This morning Verne was kind of pressed, so maybe he forgot something." I took a step over and sat down on a wicker chair in front of him. "Like, what time did you get to St. Bartlett's, and how did you get down to the gym, and did you see anyone?"

"Sure. It's no big deal. We got there same time as always, ten o'clock. There were only three of us last night, and Gonzales let us in. We don't shower or anything, just use the weights and the machine. We bring our own towels. We usually leave around midnight and go back the same way we came." He shrugged. "No one was down there, either in the gym or in the weight room. The place is most always empty that time of night.

"Did you ever see this guy Ponzini, the one that died? He ever come down to work out when you were there?"

Matthews hesitated and looked at me closely. Whatever was going on in his head finally got resolved after a few long seconds.

"One time, two weeks ago, maybe it was him. Two guys came down when we were there and kind of acted surprised to see us. One of the guys waited around for maybe a minute then took off. Funny little guy, too. . . . He didn't look like a weight lifter." He laughed. "Had one of those literary sweatshirts you see advertised in *The New Yorker* with old-time faces on it. I remember it said something like 'The Importance of Being Oscar.' " He shrugged.

"So, he left, then what?"

"The guys I go with get along fine sharing the equipment, but this other guy acted pissed he had to share the same breathing space. After an hour of him making comments under his breath, we decided to clear out. Verne told me the next day that some guy had complained to him. . . . The name sounded like Ponzini. That was on a Thursday, so Verne recommended that we just use the place on Tuesdays for a while. We haven't seen him again."

"When you saw him, do you remember if he was lifting heavy weights? . . . Say like pressing one hundred seventy?"

Matthews looked amused. "No way man. If he was doing a hundred I'd be surprised. That's why I told him he was kinda out of order getting so pissed. Like he didn't need more weights than he had."

"You had an argument with him?"

"Hey, with four guys in a small room"—he smiled—"conversation goes on."

"But you left before it got ugly."

"We left. I wouldn't call it ugly, but you can ask my friends. I can give you their names. What he called it you have to ask Verne."

"Yeah, I'd like their names," I said, "and their phone numbers."

There was silence in the room for a moment as he pulled out a pen and scribbled down the information. I looked over the list for a moment. "Last night," I continued, "did you notice anything out of the ordinary? Any weights out of place or unusual arrangement of things?"

Matthews wrinkled his forehead and tried to remember.

"No. The weights were all on the racks like usual, and the Nautilus machine was working fine." He shook his head slowly, still thinking. "Wait a minute, now that you mention it, I think there was a bar missing. The school has six bars, so with the three of us working out, there should have been three left over. I only noticed two." A timer went off in the kitchen. "Listen," he continued, "I teach junior high school. The place where I teach has got the worst athletic facilities in the city. You want to keep in shape there you got to lift garbage cans. I asked and Verne did me a a favor. But the last thing I want is for it to turn into a big hassle for him, or for me. You get what I'm saying? I'm sorry the guy hurt himself, but accidents do happen. A bar dropped on me once and broke a rib. Maybe if we were there we could have helped him, but we weren't." He stood up and took a few steps toward the kitchen; on the way he opened the outside door. "Say hello to Verne for me."

"I'll do that," I said.

He smiled and headed into his dinner.

FIFTEEN

Every night after work I pick Helen up at the Acropolis Diner. Her shift runs from ten to seven, which is Uncle Spiros's idea of an eight-hour day. Greek time. I usually make it okay if I can wake up my old Pacer. When I bought it, back in the seventies, American Motors was a respected car company, and the Pacer was something of a daring design. Now people pass me and give me looks like I'm driving an original Stanley Steamer. I still love its goggle-eyed profile and roominess, but the engine gave up being reliable after its second ring job. Now it's simply a question of what the temperature is outside. Below forty degrees, I'm in trouble, below freezing, and I might as well just take the bus. Fortunately, the temperature this evening was hovering around fifty, so I started the car without trouble, pulled out of the parking lot, and headed up to the Bronx.

Once inside the car I started thinking of Helen. With all that was going on around me at school, my real concern was with the person I had been married to for eighteen years. You take so many things for granted in life that it's shocking when one of them shakes its head and says, Hey, pay attention. Not that Helen would have said it herself. In all those years, she has never asked for anything other than my being honest, which I find easier than providing a new car every couple of years. The other side of the equation is that she is also open about things, which is why I was sitting there in traffic on the Brooklyn-Queens Expressway worrying about her.

Helen has never been sick a day in her life. There have been sniffles and colds and headaches, but they come under the heading of things you cure with an aspirin. She's never been out of work because of bad health. So when she started complaining about a pain in her lower abdomen a month ago we both thought it was some of Spiros's discount eggs he buys upstate. Then the pain went away, and we forgot about it until two weeks later when I came to pick her up at the diner. I found her almost doubled over behind the cash rigister with a look on her face that sent shivers through me. She had been that way for twenty minutes and was trying to ride it out. I got her to one of the larger booths, propped her up against the wall, got her a glass of water, and asked if Dr. Silverman was still eating dinner.

After so many years around the fringes of Uncle Spiros's place, it was impossible not to get to know the regular customers. Silverman was a widower who came in every evening after his office hours for a bowl of soup or a pastrami sandwich. Uncle Spiros's pastrami was probably like the Stage Deli's moussaka, but he came, I think, more for the routine than for the food. He was a man with a sense of humor, an eye for detail, and a generous nature; and every Christmas he gave baskets of fruit to all the employees at the Acropolis. Fortunately, he was still on his coffee at one of the tables in back and he came around immediately.

He examined her, made a few phone calls, and an hour later she was in Montefiore Hospital. The pain went away during the taxi ride, but they kept her overnight while Silverman arranged for a series of tests. That was two weeks ago, and everything had come back negative, everything but the gynecological report from a Dr. Nakaru, who said he was running some samples through again. So we were waiting, and had been waiting for over five days for the results of the second test. It was no wonder I was cursing the traffic and worrying about what would greet me when I made it to the diner and found Helen and Silverman.

The Acropolis is situated on the corner of Broadway and 260th Street in one of the nicer sections of the North Bronx. Spiros has half the block across the street from Van Cortland Park. As good as the location is for a diner, it's even better for a new apartment building, and the developers have been after Spiros for years. So far the numbers they have come up with don't match the numbers in his head, so he continues to place his weekly order for two thousand eggs and a quarter ton of coffee and watches the profits roll in. Uncle Spiros is no dummy. He knows the money boys will someday get to his level, and until they do, I'm sure he figures it's a good way to keep six members of his immediate family out of trouble and at the same time get all that cheap labor. For that reason alone Spiros has always said he won't sell unless he finds a new place to go.

I pulled into the parking lot and turned off the ignition key. The Pacer doesn't give up so easily, and the motor kept chugging along on fumes until I was well out of the parking lot and heading up the front stairs. Hard to start, hard to stop . . . I like the consistency. I saw Helen still behind the register talking to one of the customers on his way out. She had a pleasant smile on her face, but that didn't mean anything. She always has a smile on her face, which makes living with her sometimes very ambiguous. I looked around for Silverman, but he had already left. By the time I walked over the customer had received his change and walked out and Helen was now smiling at me.

"Any news?" I asked, trying to keep it casual.

She lowered her eyes to the cash drawer and fiddled with the money. Not a good sign.

"Nothing serious," she said softly. "Silverman called it a fibroid."

"What the hell is that?"

"Something that has to be cut out. It's like a cyst, I guess, in one of my ovaries."

"I see," I said softly, not really understanding at all. I sank down into the booth next to the cash register. Helen motioned to one of the women behind the counter who came and took over the register, then she sat down across from me.

"When?" I asked.

"In a couple of weeks. It's not an emergency, Costas. Silverman has to set up an appointment for the surgeon. He says it's not a difficult thing."

"Good," I said, reaching out and holding her hand. I felt an enormous weight descend on me, almost as though all the little sicknesses and emergencies Helen had avoided in life had been biding their time and had now decided to drop in one congealed mass. I didn't like things growing inside people that shouldn't be there. "It's not . . ."—I stumbled—"cancer?"

She shook her head but I could tell there was just a little spark of doubt behind her eyes. "No. That's what Silverman says."

"Good." I gave her hand a squeeze and looked into her eyes. "You call Hector?"

She nodded. "He can help me around home. I think I'll be off my feet for a couple of weeks. I've already spoken to Spiros."

That brought me back to reality. Spiros didn't carry any health insurance on his employees, and his vacation policy was as lenient as if he'd been running the siege of Troy. He employed his family, but then he expected them to work their hearts out. Being on suspension from the police force immediately took you off city health benefits. Thank God I had decided to join the union health plan at St. Bartlett's.

70

"And what did my uncle offer?"

"One week paid sick leave."

"That's generous of him after sixteen years without a day sick." I felt as angry as when he had offered me the job washing dishes.

She looked down at the empty table in front of me. "You want a coffee? I'll ask Gloria to get one for you."

I shook my head.

"Spiros wants to talk to you. He told me to get him when you came in."

I looked at her curiously. Spiros never wanted to talk to me. "What about, your leave?"

"No, he asked me before I spoke to Silverman. I have no idea what he wants." She got up and walked into the kitchen area. My uncle had a little office back there where he did his books and, I had heard, his new waitresses, the nonfamily ones. The space was just big enough for a desk and a couch, which was all he needed. While I waited, I looked over the inside of the diner. There is a particular kind of decorating scheme that I could only describe as Greek Garish, to which my uncle had succumbed. If Homer or Achilles had suddenly materialized in this diner in the Bronx for a quick BLT or chicken salad on rye, he would have felt right at home. The entrance had plaster of paris columns with Corinthian capitals, the floor was terrazzo, Greek urns supported the table tops, the lighting came from electric candelabras made to look like oil lamps, epoxy-cast statuary littered the corners of the rooms, and the walls had paintings of the Acropolis in the four seasons. Subtlety in decoration was not Spiros's strong suit. Buying cheap eggs was. Eggs and the hundreds of different items that were needed for his daily menu, which was only slightly thinner than the Manhattan yellow pages. "More is more" was my uncle's motto, in food as in decor.

Spiros made his way through the tables and sat down opposite me. Helen, the good employee, went back to the register while the men talked. I knew for a fact that my uncle was

Greek, but every time I saw him I always thought he looked like a Turk. Maybe I was just biased, but he had that sly look to his face and the darker complexion, and stretching it he couldn't have been over five-foot-six. His head was as bald as an upside-down cereal bowl, but what hair he had left, a two-inch fringe, he cultivated with as much care as the pilgrims did their first crop of corn. There was always the smell of pomade in the air when Spiros was nearby. And yet, for a sixty-five-year-old man, he was in good shape. One only had to look at the waitress turnover.

"I am sorry to hear about Helen's problems," he began. "But this cannot be so serious. Two weeks at most."

"Easy for you to say, Uncle Spiros." I smiled, but the irony was lost on him. "How's business?"

"The food business is good, very good." He leaned closer. "But the real estate business is even better. I think I may be changing locations."

"Is that so? Got an offer you couldn't refuse?"

"Possibly."

I let that sink in. "So where you moving to? Nearby, I hope."

He smiled. "Some of that depends on you."

I felt flattered. I never thought my two cups of coffee a day and the occasional western omelette meant that much to Uncle Spiros. "How so?"

"There's a location I'm very interested in. With the money I get from the sale of this property I can build an even larger place, bigger back room for functions, bigger all around." His gesture took in a space as big as the Parthenon. "It's still in the Bronx, but it's right near Mosholu Parkway and the Grand Concourse, a lot more traffic. Like I said, it's a great location."

"What's the catch?"

Spiros fiddled with the saltshaker for a moment. "There's a school nearby."

"Less than two hundred feet?"

He nodded. "It's some little rinky-dink nursery program the city is running for welfare kids."

"But not rinky or dinky enough to keep you from getting a liquor license. That it?"

He nodded. "Yeah, and I got a deadline to make my mind up on the offer for this place. The developers want an answer by next week, Wednesday. After that they're going for another location."

"So, how can I help?"

"I would like the school to move. There's an empty house across the street I could buy cheap."

"Yeah, well I'd like the Dodgers to move back to Brooklyn. But it ain't gonna' happen. Some things are not in the cards."

He looked at me for a moment without saying anything. Then he continued. "This is. I found out the director of the jerky-ass little school is a woman named Wilson, Mary Wilson. Name familiar?"

I shook my head.

"I did some checking," Spiros went on. "We're talking about a lot of money here, Costas, a big deal. I wasn't gonna let this slip away on account of my not putting in my homework. You get what I mean?" He stabbed at my arm in his friendly way that made me want to break his finger. "This Mary Wilson's been in the Head Start program for a while. So she knows the ropes and could probably swing the move. She only has about twenty kids there."

"Why should her name be familiar?" I asked. All of a sudden something was beginning to gel.

"Her husband works at St. Bartlett's. I think he's some kind of coach. Basketball maybe."

I leaned back in the booth and tried to breathe evenly. So that was it. Spiros had indeed done his homework. More than that, he was applying pressure on all fronts like a good general. My bet was that he'd already tried to talk to Hap's wife himself.

"Think about it," Spiros said. "If she agrees, there could be some money in it for you." He smiled again. "Maybe even a big job at the new place. Banquet director."

73

I felt sick to my stomach. Banquet director, of all things! "Uncle Spiros," I said calmly, "I'm still a cop, believe it or not, and this job you're asking me to do is definitely not up my alley. You're asking the wrong guy." Just then I caught Helen's eye and realized that she had probably overheard the conversation. I stood up and pushed out of the booth. "We got to get home to Hector."

"Whatsa matter? Think about it," Uncle Spiros repeated. "Let me know."

"Let's go," I said to my wife.

We left the Acropolis and made it to the Pacer without speaking. I didn't know what was on Helen's mind, but I was feeling about as comfortable as a nightcrawler in trout season.

"You going to speak to Hap when you see him?" Helen asked innocently, as she slid into the passenger's seat.

"Let's change the subject," I said. "We've got enough to worry about." I started the car and we drove for a moment in silence.

"Okay, but it's no big deal," Helen said with a crooked smile. "It's just a simple and safe operation."

"Sure," I said. As if anything inside a hospital was simple and safe.

SIXTEEN

Hector was waiting for us as we entered our apartment in Queens. I never wanted to raise a child in New York, but I was a cop during the Koch administration at a time when he was "urging" all city employees to live in one of the five boroughs. I took Koch at his word, even though it was probably unconstitutional, and we found this pretty apartment off the Boulevard. We've been there ever since.

Our son was in the living room trying to look busy doing his homework, but if I know him, he had only one eye on his book and the other on the front door. Helen and Hector have this special relationship; sometimes it's like he's the parent and she's the child. No matter how angry he is with her, all she needs to do is sound hurt and he melts. With me he can stay angry all week, but not with Helen.

So now, when he knew she was feeling shaky, he was falling all over himself trying to make his mother comfortable. He'd already set the table for dinner and was asking Helen what she was planning to make because he'd be happy to do it for her. I could see this sickness thing definitely had its up side. I left the two of them planning the meal and went into my little office. Lord knows, with what had happened that day I needed some time to think.

I call it an office, but it's really a large closet I converted with shelves, a small table, and a swivel chair. There's no window, no telephone, just a space to be alone. I carved this place out early on when Hector's nighttime crying tore at Helen's heartstrings, and she would bring him into the bed with her to quiet him down. Hector doesn't cry anymore, but I haven't given up my space. There's something about the blank walls that is calming and forces my mind to make associations that aren't obvious outside. But sometimes just looking at the flat painted walls doesn't work, and I go to my baseball cards.

I started my collection twelve years ago when Hector was five. I was looking around for some way the two of us could communicate, not as father and son, but as friends. Rather than buying the standard current cards, I took him to a local card show and introduced him to the baseball stars I grew up with in the forties and fifties. The first card we purchased was a 1951 Bowman Gum "Allie" Reynolds for four dollars. Hector insisted we had to have it when he found out Reynolds was part Indian; his kindergarten class was studying the Mohawks. At the time it was cheap enough, today it would be six times that.

Then came Whitey Ford, Mickey Mantle, Bob Lemon, Early Wynn, and a bunch of others over the years. Along the way I lost Hector, I think when he discovered girls, but I kept it up as a hobby. I've even made some money at it when I discovered the joys of trading. The one I'll never forget was unloading a 1935 National Chicle Company Schoolboy Rowe and a 1934 Goudey Gum Company Lefty Grove for a 1914–1915 Cracker Jack Company Bullet Joe Bush. The deal netted me a cool five hundred dollars when I cashed in the World War I card at the next show. But sometimes I get more joy out of just looking through the old cards than dealing them, especially when I need some perspective on things current.

76

I closed the door behind me and brought down the 1941 Gum Incorporated book and flipped through the pages slowly. I stopped at Joseph Edward Cronin of the Boston Red Sox only because I remembered that, like Pete Rose, he had also been a player-manager. Then I started thinking about gambling and that led me to basketball, and before I knew it I was thinking of Jason Sanders. See what I mean, associations. But I was particularly thinking about Sanders's diamond ring. I'm not much of a judge of fine diamonds, but if that rock was real I'd bet my Ted Williams rookie card it had to be over ten grand. Now where does a kid out of Bedford-Stuyvesant get that kind of money?

While I was on the subject, I thought, what about Ostyapin and Howell Tandy, the two guys I found arguing about tenure the night before Ponzini was killed. Certainly that had to be investigated. But the NYPD in the person of Mr. Dass Dougherty was obviously not picking up the ball. That left me and Verne, and to be truthful I'd seen Verne in better form earlier in his career. I looked around the tiny space and put the card book back up on the shelf. Costas Agonomou versus Dr. Stanley Malloy and his board of trustees. That was a good one. And this while my wife was facing surgery? I could almost feel my peptic ulcer getting ready for some fun. I shook my head then pulled out my little penknife and rubbed its slick black side. No genies appeared, but it made me feel better. Hell, for all I knew maybe the weight did slip from Ponzini's hand and he died of natural causes. Yeah, I told myself, and maybe I'm Joe DiMaggio. I couldn't forget about the missing bar Matthews had told me about.

After a few more minutes, I moved out of the small space and closed the door behind me. The smell of cooking came at me from the direction of the kitchen, and I went to investigate. There comes a time when the question of personal responsibility takes second place to the question of "what's for dinner?" That moment had arrived.

SEVENTEEN

Verne didn't look much better the next morning when I came in for work. A newspaper was sitting on his desk, and he was reading a small article buried inside. He looked up when I walked in, but his face didn't change. I could have been a student asking for a lost book bag for all he seemed interested. I signed the register, then came over and sat down next to him.

"You look terrible," I said. "You need more sleep."

"I need something, but it's not sleep." His eyes lowered to the desk drawer. "You find out anything yesterday?"

"Yeah, I found out that Ponzini complained to you about those guys down in the gym. How come you never told me? At the very least I'd say that was interesting. People more creative than me would say it was suggestive."

Verne didn't say anything for a moment. Then he closed the newspaper and leaned back.

"Ponzini was a son of a bitch."

I waited for more, but that's all he said.

"You want to elaborate, Verne? I mean, let's not try to make it difficult here for poor Costas. I'm only trying to help you. Remember, you told me yesterday that you really didn't know the guy."

He shook his head. "That hasn't changed. The first time I met him was about nine months ago when he wanted to move a wall of lockers out of his classroom into the adjoining hall to give him more space. The issue landed on my desk since it was narrowing the hallway and posed a potential safety problem. I told him he couldn't do it." Verne fidgeted with a pencil. "He was pretty abusive when he found out, but on those kind of things this office has the last say."

"And after that?"

"Maybe three weeks ago. Like Ray said, Ponzini came charging over here after he found them in the gym. I can't exactly say the man was a prince." He continued fidgeting with the pencil while he looked into my face. But I was trying hard to concentrate on something else, something he had just said. He knew I was working on it also because his eyes had that defensive look. I've known Verne too long not to pick up on his signals. Finally, I got it.

"You son of a bitch," I said. "I remember. You moved the lockers a couple of weeks ago. They're in that hallway now. Underneath the clock."

Vern sighed and dropped the pencil. "I reconsidered the safety hazard and decided the hallway was wide enough after all."

"After Ponzini threatened to go to Malloy when he found Matthews and his friends. The guy was playing hardball, right?" I looked at my friend closely. "You shouldn't have done it, Verne. You were just digging the hole deeper. You should have just told Matthews and his friends that their free ride was over."

"Maybe," Verne said. "I thought it was easier just to move the goddamn lockers. Then no one gets hurt."

"But your self-respect. I can't believe you let some pumped up art twit pull you around on a nose ring. You're really slipping buddy." I shook my head in anger. "You shouldn't have done it." I said again. "Goddamn. He was a calculating, blackmailing, son of a bitch."

"To a lot of people it looks like," Verne added.

"All it took was one." I got up and went over to pick up my walkie-talkie. I still had to do my opening rounds to check on all of our people.

Verne stood up and walked next to me. He watched as I strapped the carrier around my waist. He shook his head sadly. "You're right, Costas. It was stupid of me. Couple of years ago I never would of let that happen."

"You're getting too mellow, Verne. In our line of business that's fatal. Now, how about from now on we pretend we're being honest with each other. We got enough problems second-guessing Dougherty, Malloy, and a loose murderer."

"Sorry," Verne said and went back to his desk.

"Okay," I said. "I'll see you later."

It took me over an hour to make the morning rounds and check on all the security people we had posted. Normally it's just a matter of seeing that they're where they are supposed to be and double-checking that they know whatever special is happening that day. It also gives me a chance to chat with them and find out anything of interest. They are, after all, the eyes of the college.

With all that, I finally got to Gregor Ostyapin during the morning coffee break. Sometimes the studio teachers skip this ritual because they're swamped with students needing their help, but on the days when he was teaching, I never failed to see the big Russian sculptor outside his studio around ten-thirty, always with a brown, foul-smelling cigarette dangling from his lips. Even though the door to his studio was closed, there came from within a steady hammering noise as zealous students continued assaulting their pieces of rock. The expression on his face told me that Ostyapin was obviously enjoying his brief moment of freedom.

"Professor Ostyapin?" I said, walking over. The professor part was pure flattery. Around St. Bartlett's, instructors were usually called by their first name. The big bearded Russian nodded and a small flake of marble fell from his eyebrow to the ground. He peered at me curiously through the smoke curling up from the crooked cigarette.

"Have you got five minutes?" I asked. "We're trying to get some background on your colleague." I hoped the *we* was vague enough to inspire his confidence. The fact that I was wearing my uniform didn't hurt.

"I see you two nights ago, yes? In Tandy's office?"

I nodded.

"No problem. I give you ten minutes if you want. The longer outside from this room the less my heart is breaking. Is criminal what some of them do." He pointed over his shoulder in the direction of the noise. "Maybe we start them on concrete instead. A lot cheaper."

As I watched, he took a drag on the cigarette and blew smoke up toward the ceiling. I noticed his hands for the first time. As big as he was, his hands were disproportionately huge. Each one could easily have lifted a bowling ball upside-down without using the holes. Imagining them swinging a hammer was not a pleasant image.

"I guess you knew Ponzini?" I started. "You were in the same department."

"I knew Vincent. He was good painter." Ostyapin peered at me through deep-set eyes and a hairstyle that hid most of his forehead. With his beard framing the bottom half of his face, he reminded me of the mad monk Rasputin.

"I'm sure he was. We're more interested in what he was like as a person." I smiled politely.

"He was . . ." His voice trailed off as he heard from within the sound of a big chunk of stone hitting the floor and then someone curse. Ostyapin closed his eyes for a second. "He was good teacher also."

"So I gathered. His student evaluations were over nine-point-two. His classes were always closed. But you know students, they can be fooled."

"About life, maybe. About teaching, no."

I let that sit for a moment. The noise of hammering framed our conversation like a chorus. "So you liked him?" I asked finally.

"Please, do not patronize. I am aware you overhear discussion with Tandy the other night. You know I think Ponzini as a person is a shit."

I had to smile. The Russian, like any true sculptor, had a knack for cutting to the heart of the matter. "Why, because he was taking your tenure recommendation? That's not his doing. You should be angry at Tandy."

Ostyapin took another puff. "You really think Tandy recommended him because of student evaluations? Or maybe because he is on health committee. Is big joke. Tandy is recommended him because Ponzini pays him for this." He rubbed his forefinger and thumb together. "Much money."

Maybe I'm naive, but I found this hard to believe. Besides, it's not the first time someone pissed off at losing tenure stirred up some muck. "How do you know this?" I asked.

"I know." Ostyapin dropped his cigarette on the floor and mashed it into the linoleum. Somehow he made even this little gesture seem menacing. "I can't prove it, but I know."

Sure, I thought, like Stalin knew about Bukharin. I changed the subject. "Correct me if I am wrong, Professor, but doesn't Simmons's tenure line still have to be filled? Otherwise the department will lose it?"

"This is so," the sculptor said in a low voice.

"And presumedly you are next in order?"

He didn't answer for some time. His eyes narrowed as he leaned down toward me. "I do not like this suggestion. The thought is totally decadent. I do not kill for success, I work for it." He looked at his watch and stood up straighter. "Now is time for me to go back into this madhouse and see what tragedy has taken place during past ten minutes. I can deal with foolish students, Mr. Agonomou. Foolish security guards are different matter." He turned and put his hand on the door knob.

"One last thing," I said raising my voice. "You told Tandy that Ponzini was screwing around with some of his students. Is this also something you knew but couldn't prove?"

He turned the knob and pushed on the door but hesitated before walking in. A dozen pairs of eyes looked up beseechingly from a dozen misshapen hunks of stone. He didn't move for a few moments while he studied their faces.

"Look at them," he said softly. "So innocent."

"I asked a question Professor Ostyapin."

He sighed heavily and turned his face toward me. "No, this I cannot answer," he said. "I am their teacher. It would not be right."

"Who knew?" I pressed.

"Ask someone without any honor," he said, and started walking slowly into the studio. "Ask Tandy."

EIGHTEEN

For someone without any honor, Tandy certainly could have chosen a better job. Short on prestige or perks, a chairman's job at St. Bartlett's was thought to be mostly schedule-making, fund disbursements, and student recruitment, and had as much to do with power as a pencil had to do with megabytes. Not that there weren't deals that couldn't be cut with other chairmen on the curriculum committee for added courses, or deals made with deans for questionable equipment, or deals made with individuals to hire them on one course tryouts; but that was mostly nickel-and-dime stuff. Truly dishonorable people looked for career patches that were more fertile. From what I gathered, Tandy did his job creditably. While he was notoriously abrupt with his secretaries, he always produced the figures and schedules and bodies and programs that were required of him. Consensus was that he was not overly creative, but then again, that was nowhere in the job description.

I found him in his office talking on the telephone. I knocked on the open door, then took a step inside. With all the discussion of buying and selling and earnings ratios, he must have been talking to a stockbroker or financial advisor. I was impressed. The only time I ever got near financial independence was when Publishers Clearinghouse congratulated me on my opportunity to win a million dollars. Tandy frowned at me and cut the phone conversation short.

"Yeah?" he asked coldly.

I could see that the secretaries' underground sheet on Tandy was essentially correct. Long on ego, short on charm. I'd have to take a hard line with him. I pulled over a chair and sat down.

"I've got to ask you some questions about this Ponzini thing," I began. "Dr. Malloy wants to get a fuller briefing." I was taking a big chance throwing names around, but I figured if I didn't I'd never get a thing.

"I already spoke to Dr. Malloy yesterday. Now what does he want?" He looked at my uniform and frowned. "And why wouldn't he have someone from his office do the questioning?"

"This is a security matter, Professor Tandy. You think maybe the bursar would be better qualified?" That quieted him for a moment. "First of all, did you know that Ponzini was using the weight room to work out?"

"I knew only because he chose to tell me. I don't usually

check up on the private lives of my teachers. He told me he worked out a couple of nights a week."

"Alone? Or did he usually go down with someone else?"

"I have no idea. He told me maybe a year ago, and I just forgot about it."

"Do you know if he told anybody else?"

Tandy shook his head. A little smug expression came over his face and stayed there. "I only know about his performance here as a teacher."

"Okay," I nodded. "Ponzini's performance was acceptable?"

"More than acceptable. He was a fine artist and one of our best teachers. I recommended him for tenure."

"To replace Father Simmons." I looked in a little notebook I had stuffed in my jacket pocket. I always like to carry a notebook. It's good for reminding myself to pick up a quart of milk or loaf of bread on the way home and for intimidating people under questioning. It works wonders, especially if I make little notes every now and then. I put down a check mark, then looked up. "Simmons retired, right?"

"Not exactly. He was asked to retire."

"Not a good teacher even though he had tenure?"

"He also had AIDS."

I nodded. "Of course, I remember." I leaned back. "And with Ponzini you wouldn't have that problem."

Tandy chuckled. "No, Ponzini was not a drug user or gay. He was heterosexual, very heterosexual." He smiled pointedly.

"Did he ever try sleeping with one of his students?" I asked. That brought him down pretty quickly.

"Isn't this getting pretty far from the poor guy's accident in the gym?"

"Only if you're convinced it was an accident."

Tandy peered at me now through narrowing eyes. "Is that what this is about?"

"Maybe. Maybe Dr. Malloy is just curious about what kind of man Ponzini was." I waited. "Did he?"

Tandy shifted uncomfortably in his seat. He looked down at his hands for a moment, then looked back up. "Ponzini was a good-looking guy," he finally said. "It happens with some of the teachers."

"This is off the record," I said and put the notebook back in my pocket. "Can you give me a name? You understand, President Malloy is very concerned about this. He doesn't want the wrong idea to get out. . . ."

"I could give Dr. Malloy half a dozen names," Tandy said abruptly. "Things always leak out. But I don't think it would be right."

"I only need one," I said. "The last one. That makes it easier." I smiled at him and waited. He looked down once again at my uniform and my badge, then nodded.

"What the hell, the guy's dead anyway. Lisa Cunningham was mentioned." He shrugged. "There's nothing definite though."

And this from a man who claimed he didn't check up on the private lives of his teachers. Ostyapin had him pegged as neatly as the secretaries, just from a different angle. The man was a real prick.

"Thanks," I said. "I have to ask you a couple more questions about this tenure thing?"

"What about it?" He looked down at his watch. "I've got a meeting in ten minutes."

Hopefully not with Malloy, I thought.

"Now that Ponzini is dead, who gets it?"

"There are a few possibilities. The dean and the president have to approve."

"But you select, is that right?"

He nodded.

"How often does that happen? That you get a guaranteed tenure line?"

"When someone in the department retires or dies. In our department, not too often, maybe every five years."

"So there'd be a lot of pressure to get it on the part of your eligible faculty."

"You could say that," Tandy said.

"Enough to maybe eliminate one of the competition?"

There was silence for a moment while Tandy looked into my eyes. The man didn't have to be all that creative to see where this was heading. Especially since he knew I had been a witness to his argument with Ostyapin. He shook his head softly.

"I think you're way off base."

"Then how's this?" I said. "What if someone paid to be guaranteed a tenure line. Stepping up from an adjunct instructor to assistant professor has to be worth close to fifteen thousand a year. So what if there was just a lump-sum payment of say ten thousand dollars for the appointment. Then say the person who made the bribe kept proof of it as a bargaining chip so when he wanted something in the future he could always threaten to use it. Does that work any better for you?"

Tandy got out of his seat at the same moment his fist slammed into the desktop. His face was a shade of color somewhere between catsup and steak sauce. I was just trying it on for size, but hell, looks like I had hit a nerve.

"Get the hell out of my office," Tandy said. "I don't know what you're trying to do or suggest, but for the record, I never took any money for any appointments I initiated. . . . Ever. You tell that to Malloy or whoever is calling your shots. Never! Now, as far as I'm concerned, Ponzini's death is just like the president reported it, an unfortunate accident. That works the best for me." He brought his hand back up but it was still balled up into a fist.

I'll bet, I thought, and got up also. Tandy was at least half a foot taller than me and built like a boxer. I didn't like the idea of becoming his private speed bag and took a step backward.

"All just theories," I said. "There's no need to get excited. Maybe it was an accident."

Tandy started to come around his desk, then stopped. I realized that he was not looking at me, but over my shoulder. I turned slowly and saw a student standing in the doorway. Lisa Cunningham didn't move. She regarded the two of us, then finally took a step inside.

"Yes, Lisa," Tandy said evenly.

"I won't be modeling anymore," she said. "In case Professor Ponzini's replacement asks who his model was. I thought you should know."

"Thank you."

She nodded, then turned and walked out. I recognized the fragrance of jasmine that hung in the room after she was gone. Tandy's eyes didn't leave mine, but they had lost their aggressive look. I shrugged and turned toward the door where Lisa had exited.

"Easy come, easy go," I said. "Students have peculiar agendas."

"What I said before was off the record," Tandy growled and sat back down behind his desk.

I turned and walked out. Lisa Cunningham was nowhere in sight. As I slowly walked away from Tandy's office I heard the rotary dial of his desk telephone clicking as he placed a call. Seven digits would probably be to his financial advisor, four would be in-house. I listened, but the fifth digit never came. I could only think of one person Tandy might call, Dr. Malloy. Now wouldn't that be cute?

NINETEEN

Halfway down the hallway my walkie-talkie squawked my code numbers. The little pesky thing was more of a nuisance than a help, and I usually turned it so low I missed half of my checks. Verne was constantly getting on my case about my poor communications response but if they kept at it I usually answered. Around St. Bartlett's there weren't many emergencies anyway. I lifted the black electronic marvel out of its holster around my waist and reported in. Verne's voice came back loud and clear.

"Come back to base," he said. "A call just came in."

"What about?"

"Back to base," he replied, and I knew I wasn't going to get anything over the airwaves.

"Ten-four," I answered. Now what the hell was this? I looked back up the corridor to Howell Tandy's office. Damn, I couldn't have been more than a half minute walking away and I was already on the carpet.

I started on my way back toward the security office thinking that maybe chairmen had more power than I realized. I turned out of Nathan and down through one of the corridors in Cameron where I almost bumped into Winston Taylor fixing the lock on the personnel office. The door was open and Eric Westman, another of my poker buddies, was watching Taylor's progress. Normally I stop to chat when I see them, but right now I thought I'd better keep going. Except Eric took four quick steps out into the corridor and called my name. I stopped, and he came the rest of the way.

"Costas, you got a minute?"

I turned back and looked at him. I was about to say that I was kind of in a rush, but there was something about his expression that made me stop. I'd never seen a frown on Westman's face, but today he made up for all of that.

"Sure, Eric, what's up?"

He pulled me over to the side of the corridor to let people pass and lowered his voice. "I didn't tell Verne yet, but last night we were broken into. Winston is fixing the lock now."

"What?"

"Someone forced the door open. They didn't pick the lock, they snapped it. It took a lot of force. Take a look." He pointed and I could see that not only was the lock damaged, but the door was sprung a good half inch out of alignment.

"Why?" I asked. Of all the places to break into, personnel was the least promising. There was no cash like they had in the bursar's office, no expensive equipment . . . just a lot of files and a few computer terminals.

"I've had the girls check on what was missing so I could give a full report to Verne. They just finished."

"So?"

"Nothing. Looks like the burglar just broke in to get a look at something." He hesitated and leaned closer. "I don't know why, Costas, but you seem to be real interesting to someone."

"Me?" I felt the blood drain out of my face.

Westman nodded. "Of all the files, yours was the only one pulled out. The drawer was still open. Nothing else broken, nothing missing as far as we can tell. As soon as Winston finished with the lock I was on my way to tell you."

"What the hell . . ." I said. "What could they lift from my file? My police record?" I shrugged. "My height and weight?"

He shook his head. "You got a listed telephone?"

"No. . . . It's unlisted. I never liked any of my old collars to get funny ideas."

"So this was the only way to get your address. Maybe that's it."

I made a fist and hammered it into my other open hand. "Shit!"

"Why'd someone want to go to all that trouble to get your address, Costas? Why didn't they just ask you?"

"Maybe they wanted to send me a surprise bouquet of flowers. How the hell do I know?"

"Great secret admirers you got." He started to turn back to his office. "Listen, do me a favor and report it to Verne, will you. I'll have one of the girls make out a written report later today."

I nodded and turned back down the corridor. Things were certainly heating up. I sure as hell didn't like the implications; but then, I told myself, look on the bright side. If you had any doubts Ponzini was murdured before, forget them. No one risks breaking into a locked office for an address unless they're desperate . . . or stupid. Worst of all, maybe they were desperate and stupid and then there was no telling what was coming next. Either way, I didn't like it.

I turned into the security office two minutes later fully expecting a rampaging President Malloy hovering over Verne, but he was the only one there.

Verne lifted a piece of paper from his desk and handed it to me. "Helen called. Said there was some good news. She's at this number. I didn't want to blab it over the intercom for everyone to hear."

I looked at the paper but there was nothing familiar, certainly not the Acropolis Diner. Then I remembered she was going in for a second opinion this morning to some new doctor that Silverman had recommended, some guy over in Riverdale. I felt lousy that I had forgotten.

"You can use my phone," Verne said and pushed it closer. Normally I don't like broadcasting my conversations with Helen, but I was too anxious to hear what she had learned to go two floors down to the pay phone. I dialed the number and got some receptionist. In another few seconds Helen was on the line.

"So what's the good news?" I asked.

"Laser surgery," she said with some emphasis. "It's something new. This doctor is only one of the few people who does it."

"Laser surgery?" I said and saw Verne's eyebrows go up.

"He's calling Silverman right now to discuss it. I don't think they need to cut into my stomach at all."

"When will you know?" I asked.

"Tonight. Then we can discuss it."

I hesitated for a moment. "Listen, Helen, find out everything you can about it," I said. "Sometimes these new techniques are risky."

"Don't be such a worrier, Costas. I'll see you later. I thought you'd like to know."

"Good-bye," I told her. Then, "I love you." I hung the phone up slowly.

"Laser surgery?" Verne's eyes questioned mine.

"Woman's stuff. I'll know more tomorrow." I sat down and told him about the break-in at Westman's office. Verne just shook his head.

"Could be anything. We get break-ins now and then for petty cash."

"Verne, come on. Someone was after my address."

He sighed and leaned back. His eyes answered me, but all he said was, "So what're you gonna do?"

I looked at my watch. "I've got one more little errand to do, then I was thinking about lunch. That okay with you?"

"Go ahead. Then after lunch you can check the library and maybe take off early." His eyes narrowed. "I'm sure Helen could use the company."

I smiled. Verne was at it again, looking out for his friends.

"You get anything from Matthew's buddies?" I asked.

"Nothing more than you did. I spoke to all of them on the phone. This idea of yours that he was murdered is not going anywhere fast."

"I wouldn't say that. I've got six distinct suspects with six different motives, each one better than the next. I'd say that was promising. And someone's anxious enough to find out where I live to commit a crime. . . ."

"Six suspects?" Verne shook his head. "Who are they?"

"Three students, two teachers, and one basketball coach."

Verne looked at me carefully. "You're kidding?"

"I wish I were. I think it's time for me to start paring the list down."

"I think it's time," Verne said, "for you to call Dougherty."

TWENTY

The little errand I had to do brought me back to the weight room. There was now a big sign posted that said Facility Temporarily Closed. Very amusing. Dougherty had not even deigned to use his yellow plastic "Crime Scene" tape. He wasn't conceding an inch.

I took out a ring of keys I had for the internal doors and found a master that opened the lock. I flipped on the lights and closed the door behind me. Nothing had changed. There was still the fingerprint powder scattered around and the 175-pound bar with the blood stain. But I wasn't interested in that one. Matthews had said there had only been five bars when he was there, but I seemed to recall six when I visited the day before. I hate discrepancies, especially in "accident" investigations. A quick check told me that my memory had been correct. Six heavy steel bars were scattered around the floor with different amounts of weight on their ends. One had as little as eighty pounds and the others ranged up in size depending on how many disc-shaped cast-iron weights had been threaded onto the bar. One of these hadn't been there when Matthews had been working out, but which one? I looked carefully at each of them until it jumped out at me. There was only one bar that had the weights strung on in a random pattern, some lighter weights closer to the center, some closer to the ends. In fact, when I totaled the two ends, they didn't match. One side carried seventy pounds while the other had only sixty. I knew that one thing weight lifters did was even the distribution so the bar is raised evenly. I bent down, unscrewed the end clamp, and very carefully started removing all the weights. The first end looked clean enough, but when I started taking off the other side, I could see a faint smear. The weights had neatly covered it. When I got them all off I examined it more closely. It definitely looked like the discoloration might be blood, but someone had hurriedly tried to wipe it clean. It would need examination by a laboratory. If this was the murder weapon I had no doubts the other end had also been wiped clean of fingerprints, but what the hell, I'd put that in my request too. But not to Dougherty, not yet. I knew this chemist, David Beller, down at the crime lab over on Clinton Avenue. I'd gotten friendly with him on several of the cases I'd worked on where I needed some expert advice. He had two things going for him; he knew his stuff, and he was fast. I had one thing going for me; he owed me a favor.

TWENTY-ONE

Helen usually packs me a lunch from the diner so I don't have to be gouged by the cafeteria prices. It's one of the perks of working for Uncle Spiros although it's one I'm not sure he's particularly aware of. That gives me the freedom to take my lunch break wherever I want, and after coming back from the Clinton Avenue Lab, I felt like eating outside. The smell of all those sharp chemicals was still lingering in my nostrils. Beller had told me to call him in an hour for the results, so there was not much to do but wait.

St. Bartlett's has a few little spots of green with benches, and I headed for my favorite, the one next to Nathan Hall. Normally it's empty since it's near one of the administration buildings, and administrators, I've found, prefer artificial light and enclosed spaces. But today someone was already there; Jeanette, the president's secretary, was getting some sun and taking glimpses at a paperback book called *Deadly Desire on the Delta.* I sat down and smiled her way. I'd spoken to her a few times since I'd arrived on the job when I found her staying late in her office to do some work. She was one of those black women with lots of style, someone who could impress you one minute with her Katharine Gibbs efficiency, and then unnerve you the next with her down-home black colloquialisms. She was in her forties but had a face that was real easy to look at. I unpacked the tunafish sandwich and thermos of coffee and began my lunch. I'm not one to start a conversation with someone so intent on literature, even if it is a piece of trash; so I was just sitting there, thinking about Verne's suggestion and eating the day-old sandwich when I heard Jeanette's book slap shut. Then I felt, rather than saw, her slide down to within a foot of where I was.

"Costas," she began. "What're you up to these days?"

I thought the question was innocent enough so I just shrugged and said, "Nothing Jeanette, just doing a job."

"The hell you are. You're getting a lot of people all bent out of shape, including my boss. You're giving him more of his migraines."

I stopped in midbite. "How's that?"

"And Hap too. Asking a lot of funny questions. You've only been here a couple of months and already you're causing trouble."

"Jeanette," I said, "it's been close to a year, which as far as I'm concerned, is just about a year too long. But while I'm still here, don't go telling me how to do my job. Besides, what are you, our own gossip columnist? I can understand the president's office, but how the hell do you find out what's going on in Hap's department?"

"Honey, ain't nothing goes on at this place that I don't find out about sooner or later. We secretaries stick together. Don't you know information is power?"

"And today's information is that Malloy is pissed?"

She looked surprised. "Well, what do you expect, going around suggesting Hap and Tandy and God knows who else might of had a hand in Ponzini's accident. Course you're stirring up something." She leaned back against the wooden slats of the bench and lit up a cigarette. "You ever hear of Middle States?"

I shrugged. "Nope." I finally took the bite from the sandwich.

"Well, honey, hacks have got the taxi and limousine commission, restaurants have the board of health, and colleges, leastwise in the Northeast, have got Middle States. They look over our shoulder and see if everything is being done right. If it is, they give us their seal of approval. If not, they don't, and we lose our accreditation . . . and federal grants, charity donations, and probably half our students. Very simple. They make a study every five years and this year it's our turn. They're coming onto campus for two weeks starting next month and let me tell you it's not some namby-pamby rubber-stamp organization. You should see some of the questions they ask." She took another puff and flicked the ash in front of her. "So it's no mystery why Malloy is particularly sensitive right about now. He can deal with an accident that was the fault of the victim. He's having a hard time dealing with suggestions that an accident was premeditated, and other members of our faculty were involved. A real hard time."

"I know. He convinced Captain Dougherty." I thought about that for a moment. "You know what's puzzling is how Malloy got away with that. Didn't Ponzini have a wife or family to put pressure on the police? All your boss has to do is say it was an accident and so be it?"

She shook her head. "The way I heard it, this school was his life. He was active on union committees and things. That and his painting. As far as I know, he had no family and no one's complaining." She paused. "No one except you."

"Someone has to."

"Be careful, Costas, Malloy has a lot to lose. The college has a lot to lose."

I took a swig of the coffee and recapped the thermos. After

a moment I turned back to her. "Jeanette, can Malloy get into the personnel records without permission?"

She looked at me strangely, like the question just floated down to her from Mars. She thought for only a moment and said, "Yes, and Eric Westman, the head of personnel. Anybody else needs authorization from the person whose records are being read."

"Thanks." I mulled that over for a moment, then leaned closer. "So, if you know everything that's going on around here, Jeanette, do you think it was an accident?"

She smiled, tossed the cigarette down and ground it out with her toe. "I'm willing to believe it was an accident. This is a fine school, I wouldn't want to see anything damage it. Take this as a word to the wise. Verne's days here are numbered as it is. Dr. Malloy's looking around right now for a replacement. Keep up your questions, and you'll go down with him." She stood up, brushed off her skirt. "And of all people, you got to pick on Hap. It ain't right."

"Neither is murder, Jeanette. And you can tell your boss that." I felt my face redden.

She took a hard look at me, then turned and walked away. I was left to finish my sandwich in peace. But what peace is there when you've just been threatened? Or for that matter when some creep risks getting arrested to find your home address? I thought again about what Jeanette had said and about Verne's suggestion and the more I thought, the more convinced I became. Hell, this was starting to get personal, and I didn't like that at all. Pride goeth before the fall they say, but in this case, the fall was turning into a headlong plunge. It was time to get a little official help.

I took a look at my watch and saw it was time to call Beller at the lab. I found a quiet pay phone in the basement of Nathan and waited patiently until I got him on the line.

"Well, you were right," was the first thing he said. "You always did have a nose for blood."

I felt a great deal of relief. "Did it match Ponzini's?"

"Yeah, I got a copy of that report. Matches perfectly. Not only that, but under a microscope there was evidence of skin and cartilage tissue. Minute, you understand, but enough to indicate that the bar had been used to hit someone, probably in the face. There's also some indication that an attempt was made to wipe the blood away but they must have been in a real hurry. The sample looks pretty recent, I'd say between one to three days old. Does that fit?"

"Like a glove," I said. "What about fingerprints."

"Not much luck there. There's a lot of smudging. I couldn't get anything clear. Destroying prints with a rag is easier than eliminating microscopic traces of blood." He took a breath. "I hope what I got is what you wanted."

"You're a prince," I said to Beller. "Save all the information. You'll probably be getting a call from Dougherty later today. And thanks . . . I owe you one."

"Nah, let's call it even," Beller said. "I know you got your troubles these days."

"This will do a lot to get me back. Thanks again." I hung up the phone slowly. Getting Dougherty to change his mind had just become a hell of a lot easier. I still needed a little extra pressure on my side, but I had an idea now where to get it. Somewhere at a gallery down in Soho. The last thing I wanted to do was to go to Dougherty with my hat in my hand. Then, if everything went right, I could finally get to see Helen. Funny, I thought, how it's always the most important things that come last.

TWENTY-TWO

Captain Dougherty's precinct was located on Nevins Street about ten blocks from the college. It looked like many of the other precincts in the city with its dusty brick exterior, its light green cracked plaster walls, and its overpowering aura of fatigue. I'd been in so many station houses that they all looked the same to me anyway. I walked up to the woman duty officer and flashed my biggest smile.

"Captain Dougherty in, Collins?"

"Yeah." She looked at me peculiarly. "Good to see you back, Costas."

I shook my head. "I'm not quite there yet." I nodded toward the rear. "Can I go on back?"

She thought for a moment, then nodded. "Sure."

I found Dougherty's door and pushed it open. Dass was hunched over his desk reading the daily UF-61s, the crime reports. He put his finger on the paper to keep his place and looked up.

"Agonomou," he said after a moment. Then with a nasty grin he added, "Sorry, we're not hiring today."

101

I didn't even give him the satisfaction of a grin. "You get the call yet from Franco Castori?"

Dougherty's expression darkened, and he took his finger off the page. I guess he realized he was in for an extended conversation. Either that or he was getting ready to punch me.

"Yeah, he called. How'd you know?"

I let that pass for the moment. "He's a big name, Dougherty. One of the biggest gallery owners in the city. One of the media's experts on art. You know what I mean. He burps and they print it. Now, you still backing off on the Ponzini investigation?"

"Why, just because some society type calls up and wants to know what happened? If I let everyone who called up make the decisions this department would be a three-ring circus. Besides, I never backed off on it. We investigate all accidental deaths. Some of them just have a higher priority, like the accidental deaths with bullet holes in their brains."

"Funny," I said. "I thought the ones with the higher priorities were the ones the press got a hold of. There are plenty of murder cases over in Bed-Stuy with bullet-riddled brains that are languishing in some police file drawer." I pulled over a nearby chair and sat down while Captain Dougherty watched me.

"So, how come you knew that Castori called me?" he repeated.

I shrugged. "I thought it might be a good idea to speak to Ponzini's dealer. Castori hadn't even heard that his client was dead. Imagine how surprised he was."

"You should tell him to read the obits closer. Besides, I wouldn't exactly say he sounded surprised. Pissed off would be more accurate."

"Of course. I told him the reason he hadn't heard anything yet is because you guys are handling this like Ponzini had a heart attack. Castori is not the kind of guy to let one of his artists just fade out of sight when there is some publicity in the offering. He told me he is going to demand a full investigation." I smiled and sat back. "So I figured he might have called. My guess is that he's sitting on all of Ponzini's unsold works, which maybe just doubled in value. The more press, the better it is for Castori. Anyway you look at it, it's about time someone besides me put on a little pressure to find out what happened."

Dougherty leaned forward. "Listen, pal, let me tell you something. I walk into a case I can figure right away which way it's going to bounce. And I don't mean only about who did it, but whether it's worth all the effort. Half our unsolved cases we know who the perp is but the DA tells us we don't have a case. So I say, why break our hump if the guy is gonna walk anyway? Throw a scare into him, maybe, but that's about as far as you go with it. You should know that, Agonomou, you were a cop."

I corrected him. "I still am."

"Sure, sure." Dougherty smiled weakly. "Whatever."

I let that pass. "You still got to try," I said. "You might put it all together."

"Only on the ones that look good. This one stinks. I can smell them." He leaned back in his chair and studied me closely. "And so if no one gets a hair up their ass, we take the bullshit cases kind of mellow, you know what I mean? Concentrate on the ones where we can get a conviction."

"Would it stink so much if I gave you the murder weapon with Ponzini's blood and tissue on it? And I don't mean the one you dusted for."

His eyes narrowed and he leaned forward. "What is this, just a wild guess on your part?"

"Not so wild. Call up Beller over at the lab. It was a different bar in the weight room, the blood was at one of the ends, covered by the weights. Beller says it's a perfect match. Now, if you can work up a scenario where that adds up to an accident, I'd like to hear it."

Dougherty didn't say anything for a full minute. The phone started ringing on his desk but he paid it no attention. Finally,

103

he leaned forward and asked softly, "Agonomou, how come you're so interested?"

"Because I'm still a cop," I answered. "And I want to stay one." I hesitated. "And because of Verne. This murder goes unsolved, he loses his job. And make no mistake about it, this was a murder. I can show you why and give you six suspects."

"You know, Agonomou, when you were a cop——" He corrected himself. "I mean when you were on active, I remember you had the same reputation, a lot of motion, a lot of spinning wheels"——he straightened up and made a circular motion with his finger——"a lot of friction. Now what would I want with six suspects? How about you give me just one?"

"I'd like to but I can't. I need your help, Dougherty. I've gotten to this point but I can't focus it further without asking different kinds of questions, breaking down alibis. I start going around without my badge asking 'where were you on the night of March third between midnight and three?' and they'll just laugh in my face. But you can ask that. That's your job. You also bring a certain authority to the investigation that I lack. Little maroon uniforms don't carry much weight."

Dougherty sat there thinking for a few moments. The muscles in his jaw were working on something, tobacco or gum, or just plain nerves. He fingered the sheets of paper on his desk absently, then finally laid a palm down on the stack of them.

"With all due respect to your president, what's-his-name . . ."

"Malloy. And he's not my president."

"Malloy, maybe there's something more here after all. Besides, this guy Castori, thanks to you, could become one big pain." He leaned back in the chair and his eyes took on a more friendly look. "You know we did spend the whole day there. We talked to over three dozen people."

"Not the right ones."

"Not the right ones!" He threw his hands up. "Shit, who's to know the right ones? That's what I mean, you could spend a year there and still come up empty. That place has got over four thousand students and five hundred employees."

"But I know," I said simply.

"You know. . . . Great!" He shook his head resignedly.

"Come on, Dougherty, the thing is still fresh. It only happened three days ago. I'll give you everything I know."

After some time, he continued, "I suppose I could go back there and ask some more questions. I'm not guaranteeing anything."

"You got to be serious about it, Dougherty. I want real answers."

Dougherty stood up and pointed a finger. "Goddamn it, Agonomou, don't try and tell me how to go about doing an investigation. You give me your thoughts on the matter, and I'll try to keep you up to date. I just want to get one thing straight first."

I stood up also. I hate looking up to anyone who's pointing a finger at me. "Yeah, what's that?" I asked.

"We get something out of this. It's a police investigation, not some little jerky-ass operation conducted by the school's lost-and-found service."

I had to smile at that one. He sure was watching out for his own ass. And if nothing came out of it you could bet I'd be drawing all the heat, just like Jeanette called it.

"Sure," I said. "Like it was from the very start; a thorough, no-holds-barred police investigation under Captain Dass Dougherty." It was hard for me to keep the sarcasm out of my voice. "Maybe just a little credit to me with Chief Barnet if it works?"

He took a breath. "Maybe." Then, "Shit, Malloy will not be happy."

"Murders are never convenient," I said. "Now, you got a pencil, I got some names."

TWENTY-THREE

They were talking soccer when I arrived at the Acropolis around six that evening. It was an obsession with my uncle and his countermen. They all had roots in different parts of Greece, and so a day without an argument over some local soccer team was like a day without bread. This evening the discussion was over the winning goal that Haridopoulis had scored for Salonika to win the division semifinals in Athens. Since my sports heroes ran to Bobbie Richardson and maybe stretching it, Don Mattingly, it was definitely not the kind of conversation I could participate in. They could have been talking Greek as far as I was concerned, and in fact, they were. I got Helen and was about to leave the restaurant when Spiros saw me.

"So, I think Helen is feeling better today," he said, walking over. "This is good."

For him to break off in the middle of a soccer argument took more than a pleasant discussion of my wife's health. But I played along. "I don't think she's out of the woods yet," I said.

He nodded and patted Helen's shoulder. "Helen is very

strong woman. You need an extra couple of days off, you just tell me, don't even ask."

"Spiros, this thing could take weeks," I said. His eyes narrowed, but he made an effort to stay casual.

"Sure, sure. These doctors, all they know is cut, cut. My advice is get another opinion and drink a lot of ouzo. Cures anything." He turned away from Helen to lean closer to me. "Did you speak to Wilson's husband yet? I got to get moving on this thing."

"I got so many things on my mind right now, Uncle Spiros," I said, "I don't think I'll be able to get to it. What was it you wanted me to tell him again?"

He looked exasperated. "She moves her little fucking school program and I'll buy the building and give them some money to fix it up. What could be better." He flashed a tight smile. The son of a bitch probably had the tax write-off angles already figured. Besides, the numbers on his deal must have been staggering for him to offer to relocate Mary Wilson's twenty kids. He lowered his voice. "And for good will I'll throw in another ten thousand for your friend, the coach. For his basketball program. . . . You understand. Good for everyone."

I grabbed Helen's hand and turned toward the front door. "Uncle Spiros, you realize you're talking to a cop. You ought to be careful with that stuff."

"Just think about it. Let me know." He winked at me then turned back to his discussion of soccer. I got to give him credit. The man doesn't know the meaning of the word shame.

On the drive back Helen talked to me about the laser surgery. I admit it was hard concentrating what with all that had happened during the day, but I think I got it all.

"So what do you think?" she concluded, as we were pulling onto our block.

Whatever I was going to say stuck in my throat. Hector was on the front steps of our building holding a towel up to his forehead. I knew our towels and none of them had a white-and-red splotchy pattern. Besides, I could see the blood dropping onto his blue T-shirt. Helen gave a little scream when she saw him and instinctively opened the door. I slammed on the brakes and skittered to a stop angled into the curb. Within five seconds we were both next to him.

"I was just waiting for the police," he said innocently. "I called them over ten minutes ago."

"Are you all right?" Helen said gently, pulling the towel away from his forehead exposing a three-inch cut going up into his scalp. "Christ, what happened?"

I examined the cut and saw with relief that it was only superficial. Scalp wounds bleed a lot and sometimes scar, but we weren't talking life and death here.

Hector pointed behind him to one of the front windows of the apartment. For the first time I realized that the glass was shattered in the center as though someone had thrown a baseball through the pane. Except it was double-glazed. One of Bob Feller's hundred mile an hour fastballs would have had trouble making it through.

"I was doing my homework at the dining room table," Hector said, "when the window exploded. A big piece of glass flew right at my face and I ducked, but I guess I wasn't quick enough."

"Jesus," Helen said and turned to me. "I heard about these drug shootings with their innocent bystanders, but I never thought they'd get to our neighborhood."

"It wasn't a shooting, Ma," Hector said. "It wasn't a bullet."

The way he said it, I was afraid of what was coming next. Maybe I already had guessed it. In the background I could hear a police siren and then out of the corner of my eye I saw them turn down into the block.

"It was a brick," Hector continued. He looked at me with the bloody towel framing his face. I could tell that, cleaned up, his face would have had the most curious expression on it.

Two cops pulled in next to my car and started to get out.

One of them took one look at Hector and went to his radio to call in an ambulance.

Hector shook his head. "Why us, Pop?"

Helen also turned toward me, but I knew she wouldn't buy the simple answer.

"Just some local vandalism, Son. I'll take care of it." The policeman walked up and for the next ten minutes we filled in his report. Hector hadn't seen who had thrown the brick so there was no one to search the streets for. When the ambulance came, the police left. Helen and I rode with Hector to the hospital, held his hand as he was getting stitched up, and then took a cab home. Helen cleaned up the broken glass, I put some plywood over the open window, and Hector went to bed with a splitting headache. An hour later when he was asleep, Helen turned to me with the expression that had been simmering for the last three hours.

"What the hell is it?" she asked.

"I thought you wanted to talk about your surgery?"

"I want to talk about why my son has twenty stitches in his head."

So I told her.

TWENTY-FOUR

Helen didn't like it at all, but thank God she didn't press. She must have realized that I was fighting no less than a battle to retain my self-respect, a battle that somehow might get me back on the police force and help me get on with my life the way I had planned it. In the eighteen years I'd been a cop I'd been threatened before, that was not the hard part—Hector's wound was. And to give her credit, the decision to not demand that I stop must have been impossibly difficult for her. But she made it, and I went on with what I had to do.

Because of the way Dass had originally played it, Ponzini's studio was not sealed with some rookie cop keeping watch. I had lifted Ponzini's address from the Manhattan telephone book and after explaining things to Helen, I thought I'd take a drive downtown. Thirty minutes later I was standing outside his building in lower Manhattan.

I suppose the landlord had been notified, but so far there was nothing to indicate that Ponzini was dead and not just taking a trip somewhere. The place was in a loft building down in SoHo, one of those big-windowed, cast-iron factory buildings that twenty years ago were producing safety pins or foam rubber shoe inserts. Neither the outside door nor the one into his loft gave me any problem. I'm also good at opening locked car doors, but that's another story.

I emerged into the open space of his loft and softly closed the door behind me. I had brought a decent flashlight with me, and holding the light low to the floor, I looked around. From the look of the equipment neatly stashed around, Ponzini was either selling a lot of paintings or moonlighting as a drug dealer. His stereo set looked like it could power a Grateful Dead concert and his television screen would have done nicely in one of the art houses in the Village. He had enough CDs to fill four large shelves, and a bookcase that sagged under the weight of all the matching black components whose function I could only guess at. I figured I was looking at a whole year's worth of my salary in electronic gadgetry. And that didn't even include two other bookcases filled with the kind of expensive art books one normally sees on coffee tables. This was not the loft of some struggling painter. Even the furniture looked expensive. But to be truthful, the place was a working studio. Paintings in different states of composition were propped against a side wall, and one entire end of the loft held his paints, unstretched rolls of canvas, and racks of completed work. The floor in that area had enough splatters to guarantee that Ponzini, for whatever else he was into, was definitely a working artist. Off to one side I spotted the bathroom and the kitchen area, and far to the other end of the loft was an enclosed area made out of sliding screens. I walked over, slid one to the side, and entered Ponzini's bedroom.

What I saw was asking too much, even from someone who enjoyed a good laugh now and then. The headboard was one large mirror and by the bed was a control panel of switches that probably changed the track lighting overhead to any number of possibilities. Another television and VCR were at the foot of the bed, which itself was round and covered with

111

satin sheets. It looked like Ponzini had bought the Playboy myth with a vengeance. The only thing lacking were a dozen bunnies from Smalltown, U.S.A., but I figured he had a ready supply at hand from St. Bartlett's. I flashed the light around the room, but there wasn't too much else of interest; a set of hand weights in one corner, a bureau and closet. I poked around for a few minutes before I came back to the night table with all the control buttons. With the kind of layout Ponzini had, there had to be one final item, and what better place to find it than in the night table? I didn't have to look too far. Right on top was the address book and in it I found over forty names. . . . All of them women's. After each name was a date, or a series of dates, and sometimes a little comment. The man may have been a good painter and a good teacher, but his address book showed he was a sleazeball with a big ego problem. There were a lot of old entries, but also a few newer ones. I was only interested in one in particular, and there, under the C's, was Lisa Cunningham's telephone number. There was a date of a week earlier, but he had left off writing any comments about his recent success. The whole thing would have stood up in a court of law about as long as it would have taken a defense attorney to jump to his feet with an objection, but I had other uses for the information. I slipped the book in my pocket and went once again into the loft area.

Ponzini had a desk next to his expensive leather couch, and I figured I'd give it a toss. That's one of the only nice things about being suspended. I wasn't playing by the same rules. No warrants, no rules of evidence to worry about, no constraints. I opened all the drawers until I came to something interesting. Most of what he had stashed were letters from Franco Castori about clients or about upcoming shows or reviews of shows. There were also some bills for supplies and a few sales invoices from Castori's gallery, certainly not enough to account for all the luxury I saw around me. He also had a folder of personal bills, which I glanced at. I noted that for a man who dressed in blue jeans he certainly bought expensive jewelry. There was a two-month-old bill from a jewelry store called Cipriotti's for a three-carat marquise diamond purchased for seven thousand dollars. I pocketed the bill, put the folder back, and went to the bottom drawer. Nothing much there but a collection of old roll-book inserts from past classes. These were paint-flecked lists of names with spaces after them for attendance, project records, and midterm and final grades. There was a stack of them about forty deep, which I was idly flipping through when I came to the bottom one, one that was very different. First of all, it had no paint; second, it had no names, only a series of six-digit numbers down the left-hand side; and third, over the line of columns were penciled in months, not days. There were ten sets of numbers and all of them had check marks for the fifteen months that the sheet recorded. All, that is, except one. The third one from the top had check marks up until June and then for the past eight months they remained blank. A pencil line had been drawn through the number and the check marks. This was curious, I thought, even more curious when I turned the heavy sheet over and saw the little handwritten table. Next to each of the six-digit numbers was a dollar amount ranging from three to six hundred dollars. This was obviously a payment record, but of what and from whom were not evident. What was obvious was that Ponzini had meant to disguise it by both putting it in code and putting it on an innocuous roll-book insert with a stack of others. I didn't have time to puzzle out the code, so I folded it and stuck it in my pocket along with the address book. In the dim light, I was starting to get spooked by the groans and creakings from the old loft building. I closed the drawer quietly and took a last look around the space.

For the first time, I actually looked at the paintings closely. They were mostly figure studies of female nudes and all of them displayed to me, a bona fide member of the art-ignorant public, a mastery of the sensual. The women all looked like whores posing for the officers of the Seventh Fleet. But then

113

what did I know about art? I did know when I was pushing my luck on time, so I turned off the flashlight, closed the door behind me, and made my way back to the street. I was home by eleven-fifteen and in bed ten minutes later. Helen was sound asleep in her flannel nightgown in our double bed under JC Penney white-sale plain cotton percale sheets. In a world full of track lighting and satin, it's nice to know that some things remain classics.

TWENTY-FIVE

I didn't need an alibi from Lisa Cunningham, I needed an explanation. I'd let Dass worry about finding out if she had the opportunity. With a little luck, I'd find out about the motive. I caught her the next morning as she was entering the school from the main parking lot. Classes didn't begin for another twenty minutes, so I offered to buy her a cup of coffee in a nearby diner. She started to refuse when I brought out Ponzini's little address book and waved it in front of her. I don't think she had any idea what it was until I told her. She made a grab for it, but her hands weren't as quick as her boyfriend's. I slipped it back in my pocket and made the offer again. Five minutes later we were facing each other across a small table. Turns out she takes her coffee black, which somehow didn't surprise me. A strong smell of jasmine drifted my way, which did a lot to cut the odor of fried bacon, sautéed onions, and hash browns.

"Where did you get that?" she demanded after the waitress had brought over the two cups.

114

"From his night table," I said. "I guess you were too busy to see it." She flashed me a look that could have sliced through a boiler plate. Normally, I wouldn't have started off laying down my high cards, but I only had ten minutes.

"What do you think you're trying to prove?" she said. "That I was at his apartment? Just because my name is in his book." She tried to laugh but it came out forced, like extruded lumps of hard clay. She was trying to be brave, but I knew I had her.

"I'm not trying to prove anything, Lisa." I took a sip of my coffee. "Just because your name is in his book with a date under it. . . . Hell, that wouldn't even stand up in kid's court. Anyone reasonable would know that he could have just penciled you in for his own amusement." I took another swallow and pushed back in the booth. "But that's not what he did, is it? The date he wrote happens to coincide with when Jason was up in a tournament in New Paltz." She started to say something, but I raised my hand. "Let me finish and this will go a lot quicker. Just drink your coffee and listen. And don't worry, so far this conversation is just between the two of us." I waited for a moment, then continued. "So Jason's up in New Paltz and you decide you want to model for Ponzini's class. Now that was kind of sudden, wasn't it? I asked myself, how come a nice girl like you would do something like that?"

"Sounds like you have a prejudice against art."

"I have a prejudice against a female showing herself off in front of her fellow classmates. I don't understand that. I told you that the first time we talked. It doesn't make sense unless she wants to get something more out of it. So I guess what I'm asking now is, why? Why did you get involved with Ponzini if you're still living with Sanders? And why did you lie to me when you told me you'd never seen him except here at school? Little questions like that give me insomnia."

She took a gulp of her coffee and looked up with the same angry eyes. "I don't have to tell you a goddamn thing."

I shook my head. "Okay, Lisa, apparently you don't understand. I thought you were smart enough that I didn't have to spell it out. I'm not going to go to the police with Ponzini's address book because they won't know what to do with it. I'm going to Sanders with it. When it comes to love, no one is reasonable."

The color drained from her face and I could see her hand tighten around the coffee cup.

"You bastard," she said.

"Life is rough," I said. "It's up to you. Last night someone threw a brick at my son over this. I figure this is a lot less violent." I leaned forward and drained my cup. She looked away like dogs do when they know they've done something bad and have to stay and face the music, and then I saw the tears on her cheeks. I waited patiently through the next two minutes while she searched through her handbag for a Kleenex, then wiped her eyes, then blew her nose. I waited because I knew she was going to tell me. And I also knew, for some strange reason, that I would never show the book to Sanders, even if she never said a word. She swung her head around and looked at me full in the face. When she started to talk, it was in a different voice, one not so defiant. It sounded like a young girl talking, young and hurt.

"I met Jason in our junior year at high school," she began. "We were at different schools, but we were both working in this program at the Y helping with kids. I was teaching art and Jason was working in the gym. He had a nice way with the kids, who all looked up to him like he was as big a star as Patrick Ewing. By that time he already had a name in city basketball. We just kind of drifted to each other." She looked down at the cup and played with the handle. "Last year, when we were seniors, we spent a lot of time together. He came to depend on me to help him with some of the things that he couldn't understand. Things were happening very quickly, offers from all over to play in big basketball programs, and his mother just had no idea. She was so deep into Jesus and her fundamentalism, she didn't want to hear about anything else. It was all secondary to her. Jason wasn't saved and as far as she was concerned, everything else was meaningless."

"He have a father?" I asked.

"His father had died years before, shot at some bar over an argument about a woman. I was the only one he could talk to. His friends were all into drugs or just hanging out on the streets, so he knew that their advice was worthless. And I guess I also represented something unattainable in his world. A white woman. I was like a symbol even though I came from a working-class family." She took a deep breath. "But then he did things for me that were so sweet, so out of character for that wasted community he comes from, that I suspected he was falling in love with me. And I let it happen, I encouraged it. I told him he should go to the same school I had chosen even though there were better basketball programs around. So I guess I must have been in love with him too, because I knew what I was doing and where it would lead."

"A St. Bartlett's subsidized apartment."

She nodded. "One of the many benefits of his coming here. We moved in in August." She looked up at me and her eyes started to tear again. "And everything was working out just fine until Ponzini started giving Jason a hard time in his class. He decided he was going to fail him, and that would have kept Jason out of playing basketball. Ponzini didn't care, he didn't care about all the struggles Jason had gone through just to make it to college, he didn't even care that the team would suffer, he just wanted his pound of flesh and he was going to get it. Jason went to plead with him, which must have been so very difficult." She paused. "But Ponzini wouldn't change his mind. It was an impossible situation. He had Jason over a barrel. And the funny thing was, I've seen Jason's work and it really wasn't so bad. I didn't understand it." She raised her coffee cup and finished what was left. Then she put it down softly and looked back up.

"And that's when you decided to model for Ponzini," I asked softly, "with the ulterior motive of convincing him to change his mind?"

She nodded and a hard look came over her face. "He had a reputation with women. I thought it would work. I just couldn't let Jason know."

"And did it work?" I asked.

She didn't answer for some time and I was getting worried that I'd lost the flow, as they say in basketball. Finally she leaned forward and shook her head.

"No. After I modeled the first time he invited me to his apartment. When I got there I came right out and explained the deal, but he wouldn't agree to anything." She smiled. "So I didn't either. It was awkward, but I'm not foolish enough to give something away before I get paid. I waited another few days to let him think about things, then agreed to model again. That's when you saw me. I was sure I could convince him the second time. Only I didn't get a chance. We had an appointment for later that night, but he never showed up."

"Because he was dead."

"Because he was dead," she repeated. "I can't say I'm sorry. It saved me a lot of grief. I didn't know how I was going to live with myself afterwards."

"Sometimes you make sacrifices for people you love," I said. "And sometimes you go even further." I looked at her closely. "Did you kill him?"

She laughed and this time it sounded genuine. "Do I look like I could lift more than thirty pounds over my head? I heard the bar that fell on him weighed close to two hundred pounds."

"If he was killed that way," I said. I looked at my watch and saw that it was time to go. "One last thing," I said. "If I were you I'd try to remember exactly what you did after you left his class that night. I think the police will be asking a lot more questions from here on." I dropped a couple of dollars on the table and stood up. "You want me to walk you back?"

"No," she said. "I want you to tell me what you're going to do with Ponzini's address book?"

I smiled. "St. Bartlett's still has a few men with principles."

"Thanks," she said and stood up. She started for the door, then hesitated and came back. "I didn't kill him," she said. "But I would have."

"I think I believe you," I answered. "Let's hope the police do."

TWENTY-SIX

On the phone Jeanette had been evasive, but after I pressed her in the name of truth and justice, she admitted that Dougherty had indeed talked with her boss in person earlier in the morning. She guessed he was now somewhere on campus, because Malloy had asked her to get the teaching schedules of Hap, Tandy, and Ostyapin. I've got to give him credit. When Dougherty gets his teeth into something he usually does a pretty thorough job. It's getting him to take the first bite that's the hardest.

Most colleges have library buildings or, at the very least, a library wing. St. Bartlett's had the bottom three floors of Diamond Hall, so named for one of their wealthier alumni who did something significant with a silicon chip. The top three floors were devoted to specialized computer laboratories and the business faculty. Most of the students stayed in the bottom half. Tuesday and Friday mornings I usually check on the library, which may be the single most active place for larceny in the whole school. The director of the library reported that for every ten new books they buy, three wind up missing after two years. While they can't prove it, they suspect that by far the largest number are stolen in the evening during the continuing education classes. In fact, we caught one person two months ago who admitted he was taking a class in twentieth-century psychology just to get a student card so he could steal books from the library. It was not a bad tradeoff; the class was only one hundred dollars and we found over two hundred of our library books in his apartment. At five dollars each on the resale market, he was getting his money's worth.

Verne places his men right by the checkout desk to give potential book lifters second thoughts. I come by to check on them and make a few passes through the reading room just to show my face. I do my best to look alert, but all those books around are an incredible diversion. When I arrived for my regular check, I made my pass through, then went to one of the empty reading cubicles. I figured I needed some time alone to work on what Lisa had told me.

It was a slow morning, Fridays usually are. There may have been seven students in the large reading room, and three or four faculty members. No one was checking in or out. I closed my eyes and started playing back the Cunningham conversation in my head when my walkie-talkie started to buzz. Even though I keep the volume on low when I'm in the library, I can usually hear things when they come over. The buzzing and humming continued interspersed with static for another ten seconds. I pushed a few buttons, turned a few knobs, then remembered with a sick feeling that I had forgotten to recharge my unit the night before. They usually are good for twenty-four hours, but I had been careless and had let mine run down. Just then the librarian came over and told me that Verne was on the phone and needed me in a hurry. I slipped the useless walkie-talkie back in its holster and followed him. When I got on the line, Verne's voice came through so loud I figured he must have been shouting.

"Where the hell were you. I was calling for maybe two minutes."

"Sorry, Verne, I got to come in for a new unit. Mine's out of power."

"Never mind that, we just got a report of smoke in the equipment room next to Diamond 603. Check it out. Right away."

"Okay," I answered, and dropped the phone back in its cradle. Then I took off for the sixth floor. I wasn't surprised. We get a lot of smoke reports on campus, but they rarely point to fires, just smoldering cigarettes, carelessly discarded.

There's a custodial equipment room on almost every floor of the college and most of them look exactly alike. Against one wall are steel shelves that contain all the janitorial supplies including toilet paper, rolls of paper towels, soap, floor waxes, and powdered cleansers. Against another wall are the wheeled slop buckets, the vacuum cleaner, and the floor polisher. Finally, on the third wall are all the hand tools, mops, brooms, brushes, and bags of sponges and rags. This made it possible for the custodial service to go from floor to floor without having to worry about moving a load of equipment around. The rooms are like large walk-in closets with one bare lightbulb coming down from the ceiling.

When I hit the sixth floor I turned toward 603 and immediately spotted the problem. The door to the equipment room was open, which was not unusual, and a wraith of smoke was making its way out. It didn't look too serious, so I stepped inside and flipped on the light switch. Nothing happened. I looked up, and in the light from the corridor I spotted the lightbulb still in the middle of the ceiling. Then I felt, rather than heard, someone move into the doorway behind me. I started to turn instinctively, but I was too late. Whatever he used caught me at the base of my skull and was swung just hard and accurately enough to stun me. I felt myself being pushed inside, completely disoriented. The only thing that was clear to me was that I had been set up and was in some

121

kind of danger, from someone clever enough to unscrew the lightbulb.

My senses came back one at a time. The first was my sense of smell as the acrid fumes pinched at my nose. I coughed but it wouldn't go away. Then I blinked. I thought for a few seconds that I was blind until I realized that the door had been closed behind me. The only thing I could see was a thin strip of light coming through at the bottom, which I concentrated on, trying to stabilize my balance. I felt for the handle, but the door wouldn't budge. Of course, they lock from the outside. Another sense kicked in as I heard the incessant sound of the fire alarm bells only five feet on the other side of the door. Smell, sight, and hearing all confirmed that I was in a shitload of trouble. I was all alone in a locked, unlit, smoky closet, and by an unlucky chance, my walkie-talkie was dead.

I banged on the door and shouted, but then I realized with a pang of fear just how thorough my attacker had been. The alarms had not gone off automatically, they had been called in so that the entire building would be cleared of students and faculty. Anyone who might have heard me was now six floors below and out on the street. That meant I could be in the closet for up to fifteen minutes until the fire department came. I turned back into the closet to see where the smoke was coming from. I figured, where there's smoke there's fire, right? Wrong. Nothing showed up in the darkened interior of the closet. Then I realized with a renewed stab of fear that this smoke wasn't just any smoke, it had that characteristic sharp, oily smell of synthetic fabrics or plastic, that toxic smell you're always reading about when a plane goes down. Forget the fifteen minutes, five minutes would be deadly. What a clever son of a bitch, whoever it was. I hadn't been hit too hard so that the whole thing would look natural. Verne would report that I got his call to investigate the smoke and that I must have gotten trapped in the closet. These things happen all the time. A simple, little perfect murder.

I banged on the door again, and again nothing happened.

Then the smoke started biting into my eyes, and I had to stop and cover my face with my arm. The adrenaline was pumping through my body, and with each pulse it was telling me the same thing. You're about to die if you don't think of something. Think of something! Christ, under the circumstances, even breathing was a luxury, thinking was next to impossible.

I scrambled onto my stomach and put my lips next to the opening at the bottom of the door, but when I sucked in I got mostly smoke. I could imagine what it looked like from the outside, a doorway with smoke pouring from underneath. Any clear air couldn't be found for at least a foot beyond the door. I was still choking from the lungful of smoke when my foot kicked out and hit something. The slop bucket. In the last half minute, my eyes had started to adjust to the dim light and I could see finally that the smoke was coming from over in the corner where a little pile of material had been stacked up. Quickly, I turned over the slop bucket and put it on top to cover it, but the goddamn bucket had a handle on the top and it wouldn't go flat to the floor. Smoke continued to flow out of the one inch crack between the bucket and the floor.

The alarm bells were still ringing and driving knives through my brain. I knew what the street in front of the building would look like with all the students waiting impatiently for yet another stupid fire drill to cease and let them back in to finish their classes. Funny, I thought, to die in a custodial closet with all the mops and brooms. I knew I must have been losing it then, because I started to cry and lay with my back against the door just looking through the dim, smoky interior at the mops. I had probably only been locked in for under a minute and already the toxic smoke was getting to me. I thought of Helen once, then Hector, then through my tearing eyes, spotted the vacuum cleaner.

It wasn't even one of the industrial ones, simply a small cheap canister type vacuum cleaner that the janitors used to clean up the shavings from around the pencil sharpeners and the chalk dust from the blackboard shelf. It sat against the wall about a foot away with its electric cord neatly coiled around its handle. But I wasn't looking at the cord so much as the suction tube that came out of it and snaked against the wall. I rolled over and gave it a tug, but it was connected to the machine and in the dim light I had no idea how to remove it. Then I remembered my little black penknife, and I fished it out of my pants pocket.

I put my arm over my mouth and sucked in a lungful of the smoky air, coughed again for a few seconds, then opened one of the blades. I figured I had maybe another thirty seconds before I had to take another breath which I feared might be my last. The smoke was burning my lungs, and my body, like a drowning man's, was bursting to gulp in quantities of fresh air. I kept my teeth clenched to keep from breathing and started cutting with the knife on the plastic tubing. In ten seconds I had it free from the machine and I crawled back the half dozen feet to the door with it. But I could see a problem right away. The ribbed hose was an inch and a half in diameter and the crack under the door was no more than a half inch. With my fingers I forced the cut end flatter and just managed to squeeze it under the door. But now it was a struggle forcing the hose thinner so the ribs could clear under the door while I pushed it out. I must have cut my finger on the knife or the metal edge of the door because around the hose I saw some blood. But I struggled to keep pushing it out, almost rib by rib, until I figured it was at least two feet outside.

I was way past my thirty seconds and my chest felt like it was exploding, but I knew I had one last thing to do. The rest of the hose was still coiled inside the closet, about five feet of it attached to the metal handle, I knew it was all filled with the same deadly smoke I was choking on. I looked around for my knife but in the move to the door it had skittered away. God, to die for want of a simple blade! I put my face flat to the floor and looked toward the vacuum cleaner and finally spotted it. I grabbed for it, then plunged the blade into the plastic a foot inside the door and furiously cut my way around the outside.

124

I was maybe five seconds from passing out when it separated and I lunged for the open end with my mouth. The air I gasped in wasn't the freshest air I had tasted, but compared with what I had inside, it was sweet and only mildly acrid. I didn't choke and that in itself was a blessing. I took three more gasps of breath and lay on the floor heaving, afraid to remove the hose from around my mouth even for a cough.

The smoke was so thick around me now I couldn't open my eyes, but I kept my mouth pressed into my homemade snorkel and tried to breathe evenly. A minute passed, then another, then I heard some footsteps coming down the hall, then voices. One of them was Verne's. I remember shouting into the tube. Verne told me later that it came out the other end like a voice from one of those cheap horror movies, like from the far end of an echo chamber. I called for help three times. The next thing I know the door started vibrating with loud noises as something was swung repeatedly at the lock. Five, six, seven blows, and then the lock finally gave way.

"Like a Cajun barbecue," Verne also said later. "When we pulled the door open all I saw was smoke coming at me in a wall, and you lying on the floor. You had me scared to death." Apparently he dragged me out, dragged me down the corridor, and made sure I was breathing okay. Only then did he move off and try to put out the smoky fire.

"Leave the lightbulb," I croaked after him.

"What?"

"The lightbulb. Don't touch it."

"What the hell for?" he called, still moving toward the smoky closet.

"Fingerprints," I said, then passed out for good.

TWENTY-SEVEN

I woke up in the ambulance with an oxygen mask on my face. Verne was right beside me and stayed with me until I was resting comfortably in a hospital bed forty minutes later. By then I had been checked over by some resident and declared to be out of any immediate danger although he recommended that I stay at least one night for observation. Verne took off back to the college and it gave me a chance to try and figure out what the hell was going on, besides the fact that someone had just tried to kill me.

Verne had told me that Clarence had taken the fire alarm both times and that it had been a man's voice on the other end. That let Lisa off the hook, something I had already suspected. Also Ostyapin, since Clarence had reported that the caller had no particular accent. That left Tandy, Strickland, Hap, and Sanders, although Hap wouldn't risk a break in at personnel to find out something he already knew. He'd been to the house one time for dinner only a month earlier. Ditto for President Malloy, if I wanted to entertain that farfetched notion, since he could have gotten my address by walking into the personnel office and looking for it. I was coming to a lot of dead ends, inching closer to what I was fearing might be the ultimate irony: that none of my suspects had killed Ponzini. I decided to give my brain a rest for a few minutes.

I must have gone right to sleep, because when I woke up the sun was already down in the sky and there were two new people in the room. Helen was sitting next to the bed holding my hand, and Dass was pacing back and forth by the far wall. I guess I must have looked pretty awful, because the police captain made a face and left off with any of his usual wise-cracks. He pulled a second chair over and asked how I was.

"Well, I'll never eat smoked ham again," I offered, and looked up into Helen's smiling but worried face. "I'm okay," I added. "Just a little smoke inhalation."

"Polyethylene terephthalate," Dass said. "Cut up soda bottles dipped in isoproponol. Not very healthy. You're lucky to be around."

I gave him a dirty look. I had been all set to tell Helen it was just some smouldering electrical insulation that had gotten out of hand, but now that option was gone. Helen's worried look deepened. I squeezed her hand and asked if she could let Captain Dougherty and me talk for a few minutes since I was sure he had to go back to the precinct. It was obvious that I didn't want her around to get even more worried, but it was equally obvious that she was not about to leave the room. She got up and pulled the chair over to the wall and sat down.

"Go ahead," she said tightly. "Now's not the time to keep things from me."

I nodded and Dass leaned forward.

"You get anything this morning?" I asked.

Dougherty shook his head. "After I saw you I had a nice little chat with Charlie Strickland. Talk about weird students, that one's right out of *The Rocky Horror Picture Show.*"

"Don't underestimate him, he's not stupid, just in need of a stage and a few footlights. What time did you speak to him?"

"I caught up with him about ten minutes after I saw you,

and was with him for about half an hour. Over in this place they call Flagler Hall."

"Until when?"

I guess my voice rose a notch because Dass frowned, looked straight ahead, and finally said, "I guess till around ten-forty-five, give or take a few minutes."

"As best as I can figure it I was hit around ten-thirty, so that definitely eliminates our friend Strickland. I'm sure Verne logs in all the alarm calls so we can double-check." I propped myself up in bed a little higher and felt a stab of pain at the back of my head. I put a hand back there and felt the bandage. So, one less suspect. We were moving right along.

"Verne speak to you about the lightbulb?"

Dougherty nodded. "Unscrewed three turns . . . wiped clean. Very efficient. And the fingerprint boys tell me that the outside handle was the same way. You didn't by any chance get a glance behind you, maybe even just for a height determination?"

I shook my head, but this time I made sure it wasn't rubbing the pillow. "Nothing," I said. "Whoever it was came from the empty classroom across the hall. I didn't hear anything. I guess I was too concerned about the smoke."

"Who wouldn't be?" Dass said, and leaned back. "This afternoon I also spoke to Cunningham, Ostyapin the Russian sculptor, and the basketball coach. The three of them were in classes when you were playing fireman. Each has at least ten witnesses to back them up. So, let's see, that leaves Sanders and Tandy." He looked at his watch. "I think I'm calling it a night. I'll be back there in the morning." He stood up. "What happens, Agonomou, when those final two come up with alibis for this morning, or for the night Ponzini was killed, what then?"

"It has to be one of those two," I said with a lot more conviction than I felt. "No one's left."

"Sure," Dougherty said, "nice and neat, just like in the movies." He headed for the door. I watched as he walked out and then as Helen drew her chair nearer. She sat down and grabbed my hand again.

After a minute she said, "I thought I was the one supposed to be in the hospital bed?"

"Yeah, well, I guess my script read different. What're you gonna do."

TWENTY-EIGHT

Hap came in to visit the next afternoon and cut my options in half. In a pleasant conversation we had over what the hospital laughingly calls lunch, he told me that his number one star, Mr. Jason Sanders, had been with him the previous morning from ten until eleven. They had been talking strategy with six other members of the basketball team. They had New York Tech on the schedule for that evening and it was almost as important as the Wagner game. These two last games of the season had significant consequences for Hap, the players, and the school. Winning them both would most likely guarantee an invitation to the NITs, which by itself could mean several thousand dollars in alumni booster money. Hap's job as a consequence would no longer be on the line for at least two years. As a result, Hap told me he had decided to put in an extra strategy session with his offensive team in the morning.

"You sure about the times?" I asked.

"Damn sure. It was the only hour I could arrange with everyone's schedule. Why? What're you getting at?"

I shrugged. Verne and I had decided not to tell anybody the

real reason I had been trapped inside the closet. We didn't want that kind of news to leak out and send a panic through the faculty and students. "Just curious," I said, and tried to change the subject.

"So, how did you do last night?"

"Sanders was hot and we won, eighty-eight to seventy-six. Only one more game to go."

How's it look against Wagner?"

"Can't tell. If everyone stays healthy we got a chance. But we haven't beaten them for over six years. They are a much better team than New York Tech. It should be a hell of a game."

I took a sip of coffee, made a face, and put the cup down on my night table. "Even the coffee at the St. Bartlett's cafeteria is better than this stuff. I got to get out of here."

"When are they releasing you?"

"I'm out of here this evening even if the doctors say no. You think you might be able to come by after school and give me a lift home? Helen's going to be tied up at the diner."

"Of course, no problem," Hap said.

"You still remember how to get to my place?"

"Once I've been someplace, I never forget."

I smiled up at him and a new thought crossed my mind. "How is Mary? She still running that preschool program?"

He nodded. "She could be better. They're yanking her around."

"How's that? I thought she was the boss of what she did."

"Costas"—he shrugged—"you know this city is two-thirds bankrupt and one-third bullshit. That doesn't leave much room for healthy employment. They're consolidating her preschool program with another one over in Astoria. She's going to lose her title and add on another half hour to her commute."

I made a face. "When's that going to happen?"

"Maybe in a month. They haven't made the announcement yet."

Now, how about that, I thought. Either Spiros had a lot more political power than I imagined, or this was one tidbit of information that was worth its weight in western omelettes. But what the hell to do with it? "Sorry to hear that," I said.

"Thanks." Hap grinned, then pressed my shoulder. "See you later, around six, okay?"

"Perfect."

He slowly turned and went out the door. I guess it was a fair trade. He took away Sanders as a suspect but gave me something to use with Spiros. That still left me with Tandy, the art department chairman. But something in my gut told me that that was all wrong. Tandy taking a bribe? . . . Maybe. Ponzini looked like he had the dough. But murder? And would Tandy be foolish enough to leave a paper trail of the payment so that Ponzini could blackmail him with it? Not likely. But stranger things have happened. And a tenure line was nothing to sneeze at. I looked at my watch and realized that it was a long time until dinner. Dougherty had told me he'd set up a meeting with Tandy in the afternoon and could call afterwards. I was looking at a couple of hours of dead time.

I turned to the night table and saw the stack of mail that Helen had left that morning when she came to visit. I guess she thought it would do me good to look at catalogues of clothing for twenty-year-old weekend rugby players. Or maybe she figured the bills from Con Edison and MasterCard would take my mind off more intellectual concerns, like who was trying to kill me. What the hell. The stack wasn't big and the models in the JRT catalogue were the next best thing to the ones in Victoria's Secret. I pulled the pile over and started flipping through.

Usually my mail comes in three categories. Stuff to toss, stuff to pay, and stuff to enjoy. The percentage runs around 60-35-5. Occasionally, I get letters from friends, but as far as I'm concerned, the postal department is running nothing more than an advertising and bill-collecting service. I am constantly amazed at their dedication to forging through wind, rain, sleet,

131

snow, and gloom of night just so they can get to my door and deliver the latest circular from Figi's Fruit of the Month Club. I was throwing envelopes into the wastebasket by the side of the bed, mostly unopened, when I came to one I recognized. This was from the health insurance company that covers my family through my employment at St. Bartlett's, one of the many perks of working for Verne. I'd gotten a few of these in the last year, mostly for Hector's dentist, so I knew the envelope. I slit it open and looked at the computer-printed information. It was a claim summary for Helen's first series of tests from a Dr. Nakaru at Montefiore Hospital. I looked at the charges, what the insurance company was going to pay, and made the quick subtraction that would also wind up as a subtraction from my bank account. My finances are as fine-tuned as a race car, so getting hit with a medical bill of over one hundred dollars is something like running out of gas at the Indy 500. Still, there was loan money around, and Helen's health was not an optional luxury. I was about to stuff the report back in the envelope when something caught my eye. The form had been sent to me, but under "address of employer," in clear type, was Vincent Ponzini's name above St. Bartlett's College, 227 Dekalb Avenue, Brooklyn, New York. Ponzini? I brought the paper closer and peered at the name. This certainly was a hand from the grave. Then I remembered that Ponzini was on the union health committee, actually, he was the chairman of it, so of course he would get a copy of all the claims to coordinate with the policy.

I put the paper down on my lap and stared straight ahead. In front of me was a picture of two kittens playing around a bowl of fruit, which had been annoying me for the past twenty-four hours, but right now I wasn't seeing it. I hate coincidences, and I especially hate meaningful ones. As far as I'm concerned, there have been two bona fide coincidences since the beginning of recorded time. Moses' being spotted in the bullrushes by the pharaoh's daughter, and the time I caught Helen's brother cheating on his wife in a restaurant in Long Island City.

Ponzini's name on the form fell under a different heading, one labeled "coincidences, highly suspicious." These things happen I guess; someone has to be the coordinator of benefits for the union, but that he also is the victim of a murder that I was currently investigating was just a little too cute. At the very least it opened an avenue of investigation that I had not thought of. Ponzini as coordinator of benefits. . . . I let my mind wander over the possibilities that that entailed until I remembered the roll book with the numbers and check marks I had lifted from Ponzini's place. I had left that at home in my office. Up until now it didn't make any sense, but now . . . Suddenly the phone rang on the night table. It was Pete Howser, my poker-playing, AIDS-phobic college purchasing agent calling to see how I was doing. He had heard about my accident and wanted me to know he was thinking of me. Sweet. He also wanted to know if I was going to make the game Tuesday night, because if not he wanted to bring his brother-in-law. We have a rule in our game that you can only bring in an outsider with permission from at least three of the regulars, and that under no circumstances could you do it if it meant more than six players. Howser had been trying to get his brother-in-law in for the last few months, and I guess he thought he saw an opportunity.

"Thanks for your concern, Pete," I said. "I'm feeling fine. I'll see you Tuesday night."

"You sure you don't want to take the evening off?"

"No, I'll be there. Everyone else coming?"

"Yeah." He sounded disgruntled.

All of a sudden I had a brainstorm. It hit me like a cloudburst on a dry Mexican arroyo and made me realize that raw creativity can be a frightening thing. I guess half my mind was still working on the Ponzini coincidence. "Pete," I said. "I'm glad you called. You're always buying all sorts of things for the college, right; you ever have to buy a safe for anyone? I'm thinking of getting one for my house for papers and valuables and stuff. You know a good place I could pick one up?" I waited a beat. "Anyone around St. Bartlett's ever put in a requisition for one?"

Howser thought for a few moments and said into the phone, "Hold on for a minute, Costas. Yeah, we've got a couple over the years. One for the bursar, I know." I heard the phone land with a thud on his desk, then some drawers being pulled out. In a minute he had slapped a folder on his desk and I heard papers being shuffled around. Finally, he came back on.

"Yeah, here it is. Banning and Company, safes and security systems. Looks like we've bought four since I've been here. Like I said, one for the bursar, one for food services, one for the college bookshop, and one for the union office. They're all probably too big for your house. Why don't you go down and see one when you're out of the hospital?"

"Union office?" I said. "I didn't know they handled any cash."

"Not for money," Hauser said. "I remember that one. It was more like a file-and-safe combination. The health committee asked for that two years ago. For confidential records. Probably be easier for you to see the one in food services. They're always there."

"Thanks, Pete."

"You want the address of Banning and Company?"

"Let me take a look first." I hung up and lay back into the pillows. Very interesting, I thought. Now, how do I get into it?

TWENTY-NINE

I have always been good at talking my way out of things, so I had no trouble signing myself out of Kings County Hospital at 5:30 P.M. after convincing a twenty-seven-year-old, tired-looking resident I was healthier than he was. Before I had cornered the young doctor, Dass had called with the results of his Tandy conversation. I wasn't surprised. It was almost as though St. Bartlett's was an alibi factory. Tandy had been in a meeting with Chester Rooney, dean of students, during the time I was being attacked; a fact Dougherty was able to confirm with a simple call to Rooney. Besides that, on the night Ponzini was killed Tandy had been at a gallery opening in SoHo until ten o'clock, and then afterward out drinking with three friends until about two-thirty. Dougherty had asked point-blank if Ponzini had made any offers to him regarding his tenure, to which suggestion Tandy had reacted as shocked and angry as he had with me. The whole thing had been a dead end, Dass said, along with my five suspects he'd interviewed. If he hadn't confirmed Beller's work on the second steel bar, I have no doubt he would have walked on the whole thing right then. As it was he didn't sound too happy. I reminded him, just for the record, that someone had tried to kill me.

"Hey, when you were a cop they were trying that all the time. You never got so uptight about it then."

"I'm still a cop," I reminded him, and hung up. But I figured Dougherty was trying to tell me something, and not too subtly. The message, handle it yourself, was just the kind of send-off I needed leaving the hospital.

When Hap came a half hour later I was dressed and ready. I felt as good as one could after taking in a few lungfuls of toxic smoke, kind of like the Marlboro man after an all-day shooting schedule; but otherwise, none the worse for wear. Hap drove me home and delivered me into the hands of my son with a set of instructions including the recipe for chicken gumbo and the warning that I was not to leave the house until Helen got home. Hector took it all in and then the two of us said goodbye to Hap. I turned to him and smiled.

"Hector," I began. "We are now about to see how good an education you've received in our fine city schools. Let's see how practical all those A's you got in math and algebra are."

"What? I'm making you some soup."

"Come with me," I said. "First we have to wrestle with some numbers."

We both went into my little office and I fished out the roll-book insert I had taken from Ponzini's desk. I explained what I thought it was to Hector and why the numbers were so important. I had spent maybe a half hour looking at them earlier, but had drawn a blank. It was some kind of code, but putting letters to the numbers didn't seem to work, even for initials.

"Your turn," I said. "Let's see what you come up with."

Hector is a good student. Unlike his old man, who thought a hypotenuse was a large animal with small ears, my son actually enjoys playing around with x's and y's. When he saw the list of numbers, he got out a piece of scrap paper and started scribbling. I watched him for ten minutes before my eyes began to waver onto my baseball-card books. By then he had three sheets of paper completely covered with lines of letters and figures and he was starting to mumble to himself. I stood up, stretched, and was about to pull down the book with the Ted Williams rookie card when Hector said, "I think I got it. Take a look at this." I dropped back down into the seat and leaned forward. Hector had broken the numbers down into their six individual columns and above each he had written how many times each digit had occurred. As I looked at them, Hector pointed out that in the first column only zero or one appeared; in the third column, only zero, one, two, or three; and in the fifth column, only a three, four, or five. I raised a skeptical eyebrow.

"So?"

"Don't you see it," he said excitedly. "They're dates. But special dates because they all occur between 1930 and 1959. I think they're birth dates. Say your birthday is May 15, and you were born in 1950. The number would be 051550. My guess is that they're birth dates of people who are currently between thirty-one and sixty."

Goddamn! I looked down and did see it. Ponzini had coded in the birth dates of people he was getting money from. A minute after Hector had figured it out, I was on the phone.

Seven o'clock on a Saturday night most single young men are getting ready for an evening in the greatest party city of them all. I didn't really expect to get Winston on the first call, or even the second, but by the fourth I was getting pretty impatient. I was about to hang up and try again the next morning when I heard the receiver being lifted and then Winston's voice on the other end.

"Whoever it is," he said without waiting for a greeting, "you better be of the female gender and have a naughty suggestion for this evening. Otherwise I'm jumping right back in the shower."

137

"You're fifty percent correct," I said.

"Costas, my man," he laughed. "I was kind of expecting someone else."

"I take it you're free then later tonight."

There was a pause, then Winston cleared his throat. "My man, everything in life is relative," he said. "If you mean free free, the answer is no. If you mean can I arrange to not go to the two parties to which I was invited, not drop by the Limelight around midnight to eyeball the out-of-town scene, and finally, not to call up a little action I have stored two blocks away in the incredible unlikelihood of my not scoring by then . . . well then, yes, I guess the answer is I am, or could be, free. Only trouble is I'm in the process of taking a shower and I hate to waste it."

"Forget the goddamn shower. I need a big favor, Winston. Can I meet you in front of your building at ten."

"Where are we going?"

"St. Bartlett's."

"Jesus, Costas, don't you and I spend enough time there?"

"Ten o'clock," I repeated. "And bring your keys."

"Which ones?"

"All of them."

After that, I had one more phone call to make. While Hector went in to put some soup on the burner, I dialed Verne's number. I was going into the college to do something pretty illegal, and I wanted some assurances that my back would be covered if I got caught with my hand in the cookie jar. I wasn't expecting a St. Bartlett's-gate, but I didn't want to take any chances either. Verne's wife, Delores, answered and we had a two-minute get-together before I asked for her husband. She was a little reluctant at first. She told me he was taking a nap, but I told her to put him on, awake or not. I needed to talk to him more for his own good than for mine. I waited, and in a minute Verne's sleepy, deep voice came down the line.

"What's the matter, Costas," he said. "It can't wait? You still in the hospital?"

"Verne, who's on tonight?"

There was silence for a moment, then he said a name I didn't like. I had forgotten it was Saturday, and the weekend security chief was strictly a regulation man. That meant he might not look the other way if one of the guards spotted some activity later that night.

"Call him up," I said. "I got something for you to tell him."

This time there was an even longer silence on the phone and finally Verne came back on.

"Guess you haven't heard," he said slowly and with great difficulty, "that I am now officially a lame duck."

"What? Malloy canned you?"

"After next weekend I go down. Son of a bitch told me the fire was the last thing. 'Sf it was my fault."

"Shit, Verne, he can't do that. He doesn't have anyone yet to be head of security."

"Not 'cordin' to Jeanette. The Monday after the Wagner game he's gonna make an announcement. He got someone coming in, guy from Philadelphia." He stopped talking for a moment and I heard the clink of ice in a glass as it was tilted. Then I realized it wasn't a nap he'd been taking, just a little hair of the dog.

"So whatever the hell you're doing for my sake, it's too late," he continued.

"We got a week," I said, "and besides that, this whole thing has gotten bigger than just saving your job. Someone threw a brick through my window and then tried to kill me. You may be giving up, but I'm not." I took a breath. "And I need you to call up your guy and tell him you're sending me in to get something out of the union health office. I don't want a hassle."

I heard the clink of the ice again, then Verne put the glass down. He sighed so heavily I was afraid he had gone to sleep.

"Okay," he said finally. "Jus' be careful, Costas. You're getting someone goddamn angry as it is."

"Good," I said. "Angry people make mistakes."

"Wrong," Verne said. "Angry people make victims."

139

THIRTY

It took me all of an hour to argue my way out of my house. Convincing Helen was hard enough, but Hector took his instructions from Hap so seriously I thought he was going to lock me back in my office and throw away the key. Not being from the old country, I don't usually pull rank on my family, but this was one time I did. It got to the point where I looked at Hector, pointed my finger and said, "I'm the father around here, you're just the son." It stuck in my throat on the way out and the look Helen gave me was withering, but it seemed to work. Hector turned away like a hurt puppy and went into his room. The last thing he said before closing the door was, "Next time do your own homework." Great. At least the kid has a sense of humor.

"I'll be back before midnight," I told Helen. "Don't worry."

"First Hector's in the hospital, then you. Of course I worry. It's just like when you were on the force."

I smiled and put on my coat. "Tell Hector I'm sorry for coming down on him so hard. I'll see if I can get him a ticket for the Wagner game." I left them and went out into an evening that was cold and dry.

Winston was waiting for me outside his apartment building when I drove up. I motioned him into the car and found a parking spot. I left the motor running as I went through the drill. I needed Winston for two things. One was to get into the locked union health office, which, on the surface of things, was stretching my job description to the breaking point. The second thing was to get into the safe, which was clearly a criminal act. I thought I might need a strong moral argument to convince Winston to go along, not realizing that he loved a good caper as much as he loved his womanizing. All the time I was trying to appeal to his sense of justice when the whole time he was responding to the simple challenge of it. He agreed to get me into the office, but told me he had his doubts about getting into the safe. He didn't have a key to it, but then he winked. "I've been picking locks since I was a kid in Bedford-Stuyvesant. Just tell me you're not stealing anything."

"I told you Winston, I just want to look at something. Besides, you're the maintenance man. Anyone comes in, it's your job to fix things around this place."

"On a Saturday night?"

St. Bartlett's at night has its eerie side. All the lights are still on, but the halls are empty except for a few maintenance crews that move along their rounds like zombies. The union health office was over in Cameron, which was locked, but Winston found the key and in a minute we were inside. The door to the union health office was just as easy. It was a little room with two desks, one bookcase full of forms and pamphlets, a computer, and the safe. The office's function was to advise faculty and staff about their benefits, help them file claims, and recommend doctors and dentists to those who needed suggestions. The one full-time secretary was always busy with paperwork, but the union's health committee overviewed the operations. The head of the committee directed his members in their work, but his most important function was to act as liaison between the health insurance companies and the union members when there were any problems. Consequently, he had access to everything, and for the past several years that role had been Ponzini's. Most faculty viewed it as a thankless job. Now I wasn't so sure. I had brought Ponzini's little roll book with all the scribbled numbers in what I now knew was a birthday code. I was hoping I could find some answers in the locked files.

I started in on the desk cabinets while Winston walked over to the safe. It was not a wall safe like in the movies, hidden behind a painting with a combination lock and full of jewels. It was the size of two filing cabinets, with heavy steel-plate sides. Inside were the drawers on rollers that contained information on all the claims and payments for everyone under contract for the past three years. The whole unit stood against one wall and had a locking mechanism that looked sophisticated, but not impossible. Winston looked at it then started in with some keys. In a moment he shook his head.

"I got to get some things from my shop," he said. "No way I can do it with a key." He slipped out of the office and disappeared down the hall. I started going through the desk drawers, but couldn't find anything of interest. Blank stationery, lists of addresses, paper clips, pens, an old *Playgirl* magazine, bottle of nailpolish remover . . . the usual. I was still working on the desk when I heard footsteps and figured Winston had come back. But it wasn't Winston's voice that greeted me.

"Costas, what are you doing here? You on tonight?"

I smiled up into Clarence's face and shook my head.

"Verne asked me to get something out of this office for him." I got up and walked over. "Everything quiet tonight?"

He nodded and took another step inside. Just what I

needed, someone watching as we picked a safe. He walked inside further, found a chair and stretched out his legs.

"Clarence," I said, "I don't think Verne would like to know you were sitting down on the job. This is a big place."

"Ain't it though?" he said, but made no move to get up.

"How'd you get in? I thought the door was locked."

"It was. Verne got Winston to come along and open it. Now do me a favor, I got some work to do and it would be a lot easier if I didn't have to carry on a conversation at the same time. You know how Verne is when he wants something done."

"I guess I do," Clarence said, and finally stood up. "If you need me for anything I'll be around."

"Thanks," I said, and watched as he trudged out of the room. A minute later Winston returned with a small canvas bag and started in on the lock. He was deadly quiet as he worked, one ear to the metal while his hands played with a set of long picks. Three times he thought he might have sprung the tumblers, but each time when he pulled the handle the door remained shut. We had been inside the union health office over half an hour without any luck when he stepped back a fourth time and gave the door a tug. The plate metal door levered out ever so quietly and Winston looked up at me with the broadest grin I'd ever seen, even broader than when he won a seventy-dollar pot the first night we ever played poker. He stepped back and waved me forward with an exaggerated bow.

"I'm also available for birthday parties and weddings," he said. "Not that I do this for a living. Sometimes there's a legitimate reason to get into a lock, even here at St. Bartlett's." He packed away his picks hurriedly and looked at his watch. "Just close everything when you're finished; it all locks by itself. Sorry, but I got to run. I can still make the first party. You can thank me Tuesday night. Remember your word. . . . Nothing leaves the premises."

I nodded and he turned, leaving me alone with the open safe and eight drawers of papers. I'd never make it home by midnight, that was clear. Maybe not even by 3:00 A.M. I picked up the phone on the desk, dialed Helen at home, and told her not to wait up.

"Everything okay?" she asked.

"Couldn't be better," I answered, and turned to face the mountainous task waiting for me.

THIRTY-ONE

But I wasn't starting from scratch. I had a little toehold, somewhere to start. I realized that the most significant person was the one who no longer was paying the monthly install- ments, the one whose check marks on Ponzini's fake roll book stopped sometime in June. And if I could find who that was, and something about that person, it might unlock all the others. So the first thing I did was to look in the files for a list of people who were no longer at the college. The top drawer of the files had a compilation of who was covered under the contract and who had dropped out of the plan over the previ- ous semester. St. Bartlett's is a big place, and including faculty and staff, the list of drops ran to over thirty names. But I was looking for someone special, someone who had a birthday on October 21, 1931, and I had a hunch who it was. I was coming up with a lot of secretarial staff leaving for better paying jobs, when I finally found him, Father Roger Simmons, the retired art teacher. I pulled his folder out and began reading through.

I already knew Simmons had AIDS, but if I hadn't, it was clearly spelled out in his folder, if only from the drugs he was taking. There was only one use for AZT that I had read about, and from the multiple prescriptions Simmons had been getting it was obvious he had tested positive for this terrible disease for over a year. I slowly closed the folder and put it back. It did not take a genius to realize now what Ponzini had been into. Blackmail, but blackmail through his position as health coordinator of sick people, dying of AIDS, addicted to drugs, whatever, and afraid to lose their jobs at a college that cashed them in once their condition became known. Very pretty. The files had been confidential to a very few individuals, not even people in the administration were allowed to look in them, which made the knowledge contained inside so potent . . . and, to a bastard like Ponzini, so valuable. I looked at the list of numbers and understood finally that one of these people being blackmailed had probably had enough. I had nine birth dates and over a thousand folders to go through. I looked at my watch. At the rate of one every twenty seconds I might just be able to make it through by daybreak. Too bad Winston had gone. I could have used his young eyes. I brought the first drawer over, sat down at the desk, and started in.

By 5:00 A.M. I had all of them but one. I had their names, their departments, their addresses, and their medical conditions. I wasn't surprised to find that it was not all AIDS. One person in the counseling department was being treated for alcoholism and another in the science department had been undergoing treatment for epilepsy, all of which were presumedly being hidden from their department heads and the administration. But the other six names *were* of people positioned throughout the college being treated for positive HIV tests. Some were staff, one was in the library, and three were classroom faculty. So much for Malloy's statement in front of the parents that there were no more teachers at St. Bartlett's with AIDS.

Light was beginning to come streaming through the windows, and I realized I had to leave. Besides, my eyes were seeing spots where there were none and birthdates where there were social security numbers. It was clearly time to go. I closed the safe, cleaned up any traces that I had been there, and made an exit. There was still one name I hadn't found, 031739, but I couldn't risk being caught. The odds that the last name was the murderer were ten to one, long odds by any standard, and I already had a bunch of people to talk to.

As I left Cameron, a few students were already out jogging. My body felt like a lump of kneaded dough, and all I longed for was my bed. Thank God it was Sunday morning. But I felt I was getting closer to the answer of who killed Ponzini. I also felt because of what he had been doing that I was getting further from caring.

THIRTY-TWO

It took me all of Monday to set things up. I arranged everything like one of the sting operations we used to use on stolen-car rings. The nine new suspects were coming in to meet with Verne separately on Tuesday morning in response to an innocuous letter I delivered to them with Verne's signature. The news of his forced retirement had not yet been released by Malloy, so there was no resistance from any of the invitees. When they got to Verne's office on Tuesday, the plan was for him to grill them, no holds barred, until one of them broke. This was right up the old detective's alley, especially since he had a very sensitive button to push on each one of them. It was his last chance, and I figured under the circumstances, Verne would put on a bravura performance. My role was to make sure they arrived and to keep a watch on the outside door of the security office and handle all the little things that might divert the interviews going on inside.

Tuesday arrived with a bang. The Wagner game being only two days away, the student council athletic committee had placed huge banners around the campus the night before spurring the team on to victory. Now that they had a chance to go all the way to the NITs, the student body was enthusiastically responding. A huge rally had been called for Wednesday night and already some of the kids were wearing old T-shirts with Beat Wagner scrawled on them. It was no secret that American colleges did better infusing school spirit than they did infusing knowledge. I had never seen, for instance, any banners waving over St. Bartlett's cheering the pre-law students on to success before the LSATs and ditto for the pre-med students before MCATs. No, only basketball got the kids and teachers crazy at St. Bartlett's, and that was probably not the best atmosphere in which to conduct a murder investigation.

But in they came, the nine people who Ponzini had been blackmailing, each figuring they would be talking to Verne about security in their offices and classrooms. They came totally unprepared for the barrage of questions a very sober, 220-pound, black ex-linebacker was hurling at them in an attempt to save his job. Ponzini had had a large stream in which to pan for gold. There came from the office the sounds of arguing and of defiance, and also the sounds of silence; but by five o'clock, Verne had seen them all. The last one, a little man from the German department who I remembered had been diagnosed as HIV positive and was currently on AZT, left as pale as the others. I felt sorry for all of them having been pressured by Ponzini and now having to face Verne and the results of their payoffs.

But if any of the people Ponzini had been blackmailing had

killed him, it was not something they confessed to in Verne's office. After the last one had left, Verne called me in and we went over the results. I could tell from the look around his eyes it had been a frustrating experience.

"Nothing," he said. "Not even one goddamn admission that anything had been paid to him. I did my best. I pushed all the right buttons, but I couldn't shake a thing out of them. And all of them complained that I was way out of line and that they were going to report me to the union and Stabler."

"Big deal," I said. "I'll speak to him tonight at the poker game."

"Looks like they all hated the guy," Verne continued, "but no one actually said they had paid him any money. Some people had some bad things to say about him, one guy thought he was involved with gambling, another one knew about his interest in young girls."

"I guess they're still worried about their jobs, so all they have to do is stonewall you. I'm sure we'll never be able to trace any of the payments." I walked over to one of Verne's windows. There was a silence in the room. Finally, Verne broke it.

"You had a tenth number?"

I nodded. "031739. March 17th, 1939. I ran out of time to track it down. I'll see if I can go in later tonight after the game at Winston's. Not that whoever it is won't give you the same evasions. Trouble is, your nice, sunny security office at St. Bartlett's is no match for the basement of a Brooklyn precinct house to get information from reluctant witnesses."

"Shit, I can't break their arms. So, what do we do now, give all the names to Dougherty?"

"Oh, he's going to love that." I laughed. "By the time he decides to do anything with them, you'll be long retired." I shook my head. "No, I have to speak to someone who's not afraid of losing his job here . . . because he's already lost it. Roger Simmons. He's the only one that will talk straight." I turned back from the window and looked at my watch. "He lives somewhere in downtown Manhattan."

"Go now," Verne said. "I've got enough men today to cover for you. I'm putting a few extras on up until the Wagner game."

"Oh, that reminds me. I promised Hector I'd get him a ticket for the game. Maybe you could pick up an extra one before they get scarce."

"You're already too late. I could sell the four I got for fifty dollars each."

I smiled. "You mean the three you got." I winked at him and headed for the door. "I'll let you know if I get anything."

THIRTY-THREE

I had gotten Simmons's address from Eric Westman, head of personnel. The apartment was in one of those brownstones in the Village that had resisted gentrification through the sheer determination of its rent-controlled tenants. There were probably half a dozen yuppies in the neighborhood who had designs on the property only to see their hopes dashed when they looked over the rent roll and the life expectancy of their future tenants. Simmons was one whose expectancy would bring a smile to any developer's face, and he looked a lot less healthy than when I had last seen him nine months earlier. He was a man in his late fifties, with a head so angular he looked like a Peter Arno cartoon character. He was wiping some paint off his hands with an oily rag as he ushered me through the open door.

His apartment was dark, with furniture that looked like it had been handed down a dozen times. The rugs on the floor were worn to that state where you have to worry about tripping when you walk on them. I could see another room to the left, which had started life off as a bedroom but was now being used as a painting studio. Except for the wall by the front door, which had a bulletin board with postcards and notices, the walls both in the back bedroom and in the living room held wonderfully luminous small paintings. There were so many that it was difficult to see any clear wall between the frames. They were all of the same style and had as subject matter mostly scenes of Central Park or of rolling farm land. I had heard that Simmons had been one of those painters at St. Bartlett's who had a loyal following not with the students, but with other teachers. It was he they looked up to when they talked about dedication and hard work, not the Ponzinis who made it fast and whose work then began to show signs of wear. The paintings I saw before me still looked fresh, and seeing so many of them, I felt at one moment both privileged and sad. It was obvious that Simmons was not having an easy time selling them and that his job at St. Bartlett's had been what had supported him for most of his life. All this I absorbed in one quick glance before I sat down on a chair that might have been in use during the Spanish-American War. Simmons sat down on a couch that had a throw over it and immediately a cat came and curled up in his lap. His slender fingers stroked the cat's fur as we began to talk.

"How are you?" I asked.

He waved the question aside as though I had asked about the weather. But now, as I looked closer, I saw that his face had an unnatural color to it, the color of someone who has been in the ocean too long. His lips looked bloodless in the low light but still managed a tight smile.

150

"I'm okay," he said. "I recognize the uniform, but what brings you over here to see me?"

"Vincent Ponzini." I sat back in the chair. No use beating around the bush, I thought. His eyes flickered and his hand stopped stroking the cat, but in an instant he was back to normal.

"Yes, I had heard that he had met with an unfortunate accident. I think he was a talented painter."

"But not quite as talented as he was in other fields." I paused. "Say, like in blackmail."

The word filled the airless space like the stench of a dead pigeon in an atrium. No one wants to do anything about it but you can't just ignore it. Simmons took a deep breath, looked closely into my eyes, and said, "Yes, you are right, he was a talented painter, but quite a master at blackmail. I am only sorry that I had to find out the hard way." He looked down at his cat and rubbed a finger between its gray-green eyes. Then he looked up. "But how did you know? He told me he was very careful with the information."

"Let's just say, not careful enough. You were not the only one. He left a record."

Simmons nodded, "I suspected there were others."

"But you were the only one to stop paying him. That took a lot of bravery."

The artist looked around his cramped, dark apartment and smiled thinly.

"When you are sick, bravery is no longer a luxury, it becomes a necessity. Time becomes compressed and tolerance becomes intolerable. I could no longer look at myself in the mirror. Every dollar I was giving him to keep quiet about my disease was like another stab wound"—he looked back at me—"and my body was suffering enough. In June I told him no more. He threatened to leak it to President Malloy and I just laughed. I knew he would go through with it, there was always the possibility of him getting my tenure line, but it was the most uplifting moment I've had in the past two years. I almost cried I was so happy."

"Happy?"

"Yes, in a strange way. This disease is so horrendous it leaves you gasping in terror. There's no meaningful victory back, there's just delay. Beating Ponzini was a blessing."

I didn't say anything for a moment. I wanted to ask whether he had really beaten him, but I thought that would be a cruelty. Instead I asked the next best question.

"Did you kill him?"

He smiled. "I thought of it. Many times. But I'm also a religious person, and the closer one gets to dying, the closer one gets to God. No, I didn't kill him."

Why did I believe him, this sick man, sitting there waiting to die? Maybe it was the gentleness he showed the cat. He looked into my eyes and saw my speculations, then placed the animal on the cushion next to him. He stood up, and turning behind him he searched for a minute on the wall, then pointed to one of the paintings. It was the only seascape and showed a rocky and fractured coastline; a rough windswept piece of land as hard and brittle as any on the Maine coast.

"I painted that the last year I was teaching. There's a lot of anger in that painting, don't you think? Certainly a lot of violence. I think I got my frustrations out in my work. I hope I did anyway, and not on my students."

"But that's all you did?" I was surprised. "You didn't tell anyone? Even afterward when you had already lost your job? You just kept it to yourself and your canvases?"

Simmons sat back down and reached over to his end table for a box. Inside was a pack of Marlboros, which was half-empty. He tapped one out, lit it, and inhaled deeply.

"One of the only nice things about this disease is that it started me smoking again. God, how I missed it all those years I stopped." He took another puff and leaned forward. "No, I did do something about it. As I told you, I suspected I was not the only person this evil man was blackmailing. He had access to everyone's medical files, and certainly there must have been others like me with things that they didn't want known. After I lost my job, I went to the union and told them. They were very sympathetic, but there was little they could do."

"Could you be a little more specific? Could you give me a name? Was it one person or a committee?"

He hesitated for a moment. "One person," Simmons said, finally. "The president, Dory Stabler."

"And he told you they couldn't do anything?"

"He told me Ponzini was on the board of the health committee through the general voting of the membership. Replacing him without proof of what he was doing would cause an uproar in the union. And you know Dory, it's always union first with him. He suggested that I try and get the proof, but there was no way. Ponzini had only taken cash. Besides, by that time it was too late. The information had already been leaked about my disease to Malloy and the students on campus." He took another puff of the cigarette and watched as the smoke coiled up to the ceiling. "Stabler was very decent after the information broke out. You may remember he organized a little protest rally for me with the fine arts students but it didn't amount to much. Between the lack of enrollment in my classes for September and Malloy's pressure, I was convinced the best thing to do was to retire. It's certainly given me a lot of time for painting."

"But you miss the teaching."

Simmons crushed out his cigarette and turned the palest, saddest expression on me I think I had seen in a long time. "No, I miss the students," he said. "I miss them very much." He stood slowly and walked over to the bulletin board I had noticed as I came in. He looked at it for a long time without saying anything. I focused more closely on all the postcards and realized that each of them was a notice for another show of artwork. Over one hundred notices from shows his students had been in over the years and were continuing to have in galleries in New York and elsewhere. They had all kept in

153

touch with him after graduation, suggesting, if not as much as admitting, his influence on their work. He sighed, turned, and came back. "Besides painting, they were my life," he said softly. "But life ends, doesn't it?" He wiped some moisture away from the bridge of his nose, and for a long moment, no one spoke.

"I can't say I'm sorry about Ponzini," he added. "For the longest time I didn't understand the injustice of this awful disease. It seemed like the best, most creative people were succumbing while the others, the Ponzinis of the world, weren't being touched. But I know that's wrong. It carries off all kinds, the good and the bad; and in the end, Ponzini got what he deserved. There was some small satisfaction in that. But I couldn't bring myself to do it." He looked over at me again and this time his eyes seemed like lasers piercing into my heart.

"There's something else," he said softly. "I can show you." He leaned back to the end table and opened a drawer. Slowly, as though he were withdrawing a piece of antique crystal, he withdrew a revolver. It looked very out of place in this gentle man's apartment.

"I acquired this last summer after one of my hospitalizations," he continued, in a voice just above a whisper. His eyes held the instrument with a mixture of wonder and curiosity. "I purchased it because I didn't know if I had the strength to see this disease to its horrible end." He hesitated. "Even though that action would be against my religion." His mouth trembled lightly at the corners. Then he turned his piercing eyes back on me. "And in all the time I had it I never once thought of using it on Ponzini, although I had many occasions." He smiled lightly. "It appears my patience paid off. Someone did the job for me." He leaned back toward the table and laid the gun back in its resting place. I watched while he closed the drawer almost reverently on this, his ace in the hole. "I show you this," he concluded, "in case you doubted that I did not kill him." He straightened himself up on the couch. "Was there anything else you wanted to know?"

I kept looking at the end table with its lethal contents, then finally shook my head and stood up. "No, I think I've covered it." I started to head toward the front door when a thought struck me. "Oh, there was one other thing. Maybe you have an opinion on Howell Tandy and the tenure thing. That was just starting when you were retiring."

He chuckled. "But of course, there was never any question in my mind that Ponzini paid for it. Or I guess you could say that I did, indirectly, after all those months of paying Ponzini. It's exquisitely ironical isn't it? But once again, there wasn't a way anyone could prove it. Vincent had a knack for finding people's weaknesses. Of course, with Tandy, it wasn't hard. The man's a spineless jellyfish. When things got sticky around September with my enrollments, Howell just walked away from it. As chairman, there were things he could have done to help, classes he could have juggled, but he chose not to get involved. There's no love lost between Tandy and me. If you ask me, Ostyapin should have been given my tenure line; but of course, I had no say in the matter." He sighed and started walking to the open side door.

I nodded, then withdrew a pencil and wrote my number on a pad of paper on a table near the front door.

"You can reach me here if something else comes up," I said, "something you remember." When I looked back up he was already on his way into his studio. I would have liked to see the painting he was working on just to see the difference between it and the violent, rocky seascape. I was sure he had come to a certain peace with his situation and was back with his rolling landscapes and park vistas. But to be truthful, I was afraid to look. I passed out of the apartment and closed the door softly behind me. Then I walked down the stairs and headed back to Brooklyn.

THIRTY-FOUR

I can't say there was much interest in the poker game that evening at Winston's. It seemed like everyone there had ten things on their minds, the least of which was deciding whether to hold 'em or fold 'em. I was waiting for everyone to go so Winston and I could make another run at the health office for the tenth name. Howser was mumbling incessantly about the injustices of affirmative action, Dory Stabler had his head full with union problems, and Rooney and Westman could only talk about the Wagner game. It seemed like we were all somehow disoriented, and the betting reflected it. Most of the hands went for small change, with the biggest pot of the evening going to Winston holding a jack on a high-low game. A jack! Sometimes we have a Tuesday when one of the players is off in La-la Land, maybe because of an argument at home, but to have a night when six guys are sitting there like sticks was unusual. I wasn't the only one to notice it. Chester Rooney, a man who as dean of students is paid to be perceptive, looked around and shook his head.

"Hey, did we come here to play or what? You guys are

about as much fun as a convention of Lutheran ministers. Stabler took that last hand with a pair of queens? No one's paying attention here."

"Sorry," Westman said, "I should have stuck."

"Goddamn right you should have stuck. With a possible flush showing, no less. Chances are one in four you hit it."

Westman shook his head and flipped his cards into the middle. "Mea culpa," he said.

"And that's another thing they'll have me doing." Howser interjected out of nowhere. "Not only buying supplies and services from minority businesses, but also transacting all the business in Spanish." He shook his head.

"Mea culpa is Latin," Westman corrected him.

"Latin, Spanish, it's all the same, just another minority group heard from. You know what I think?" Howser continued. "I think affirmative action stinks. It's going to ruin our lives, and I'm not afraid to tell anyone that."

"Well, that's one thing we don't have to worry about here," Winston said pointedly. "This is a bona fide affirmative action poker game." His smile lit up his dark face. "Now deal."

"No, it ain't. No Chinese, Koreans, Hispanics, or women," Hauser said. "Thank God." He started dealing out a hand of seven-card stud. The betting started to pick up around the fourth card when Stabler dropped out. He waited through the hand, then stood up and went over to close the window. "Kind of chilly in here, don't you think?" he said to no one in particular.

"Nah, it's just your cards," Rooney said. "Wait until next hand."

"Latin was my worst subject in school," Westman said, as though emerging from a dream. Eric had the habit of conversing the same way a great chef cooks a six-course meal; things simmered until done concurrently with a half dozen other items. Every now and then he'd go back to stir something up without the slightest doubt it was the fitting thing to do at that precise moment. So he now gave Latin a stir just because it had stuck in his head and the evening was slowing down. Latin and Catholics.

"I'm just sorry they made it a mandatory subject here. After all, this school is only seventy percent Catholic and the liturgy was pure mumbo jumbo when they said it in Latin. I'm glad Pope John had the courage to change that."

"There's Catholic and there's Catholic," Rooney said, flipping his ante into the center of the table. "More specifically, there's Irish Catholic and then there's the infidels. Now this here"—he motioned out Winston's window in the direction of St. Bartlett's—"is mostly Irish Catholic, from the lowliest lab assistant right up to the president himself, Stanley Malloy, born on St. Patrick's day and proud of it. He'd no sooner change the Latin requirement for the B.A. than he would permit condom vending machines on campus. Ecumenical? Ha." He laughed and picked up the deck of cards. "Don't hold your breath. Now who's in?"

We all flipped in our antes although I was slow sliding mine over. Westman buried his head in his cards and only emerged when it was his turn on the third round and folded. I couldn't concentrate on the cards before me even though I had two pair. Stabler took the hand with three kings and sat back with a smile.

"That make you any warmer?" Winston asked.

"Not really." He started stacking his chips in neat piles.

"Anyway," Rooney continued, going back to an earlier subject, "Malloy is more interested in the outcome of the Wagner game than in anything else at this point. I've never seen him quite so excited. Maybe he thinks it will help him with the Middle States accreditation."

"Everyone is excited," Howser said. "We've got this five-thousand-seat gymnasium donated by some fat-cat boosters eight years ago when the teams were hot and from the moment we open its doors we pile on one losing season after another. The Wagner game last year drew only fifteen hundred people. And now I hear tickets are being scalped for fifty dollars. A few more games like that and the president will have enough money for a new computer graphics lab."

I looked down at my watch. It was getting on toward ten o'clock and I knew the game would be going on for another hour at least. If it had been only me I would have left and tackled the health files, but I needed Winston to get in, and Winston was the host. Besides, it was my turn to deal. I picked up the cards and called for a game that even the girls in the Oxbreath, Indiana, Tupperware league would have enjoyed. High-low, iron cross, red jacks wild, auction the option card. Normally the game takes ten minutes to explain and another ten to play, everyone's so busy figuring out their moves as well as everyone else's. We'd played the game before, so I just started a brief summary of its highlights as Dory Stabler got up to go to the bathroom. When he came back he passed by the couch and picked up his sweatshirt and draped it over his shoulders.

I started by dealing the five-card cross in the middle of the table with the sixth option card to the side, then proceeded to deal four cards to each of the players. The highlight of the game comes at the end when the cross is finally exposed and you outbid each other to change one of its cards with the hidden option card. Then you match up the four cards from your hand with either the vertical or horizontal row to select your hand. I had a pretty good hand using two cards from the vertical row, one of which was the ten from the center spot. It gave me a queen-high straight, so the last thing I wanted was for anyone to change it.

I started bidding for the option card just so I could change one of the other cards that I didn't need in the cross. Stabler and Rooney were bidding against me while the others watched, not really caring who won the auction. We'd gotten up pretty high, and the pot was probably the biggest of the evening when Stabler made a bid I figured would be his last, then laid his cards face down on the table and proceeded to put on his sweatshirt. Rooney shook his head, and it was my

159

turn to bid. But as I looked at Stabler, I couldn't bring myself to say a thing. I wasn't looking at his face, but rather at the face on his sweatshirt, the horse face of a nineteenth-century dandy with eyes like glass aggies. I had a feeling I knew who it was. Everyone was looking at me to continue the bidding, but all I could do was stare and shake my head at his sweatshirt. The room had closed in around me and all that existed were my thoughts and that face. I saw Stabler reach for the option card and then flip it over the ten in the center making it a five and making my hand worthless, but of course that didn't matter now. I just had to get it confirmed.

"Is that Oscar Wilde?" I asked, even before Dory had a chance to collect his winnings.

"Yes," he said. "My favorite writer."

It was now ten-fifteen and I had just lost over one hundred dollars. Luck sure has a funny way of working when it's on your side.

The door hadn't fully closed on the last person to leave before I was urging Winston to get on his shoes and coat so we could go back into the health records. He grumbled a bit about cleaning up first, but I didn't give him a chance to get started. In five minutes we were downstairs and heading back into the empty corridors of St. Bartlett's. It took much less time for Winston to get the safe open in the union health office, but this time I told him to stick around. I didn't think I'd be much more than a few minutes since I already knew where to look.

The drawers had been arranged alphabetically in three categories: faculty, staff, and administration. The night before I had made it halfway through the administration files before I had been forced to leave. Now I went directly to the drawer with the M's and lifted out Stanley Malloy's file. "Born on St. Patrick's day," Rooney had said. And there it was, Malloy's birthdate, 031739. The last number in Ponzini's little list of people he was blackmailing. I opened the cover sheet and started reading through, wondering what I'd find that had been sensitive enough for blackmail. It didn't take long to spot. Back in the summer of 1988 there was an entry for Malloy's treatment at the Withers Clinic in Manhattan, the same Withers "Drying Out" Clinic that made it into the *Post*'s page 6 along with every sports star and celebrity that went there. It looked like he had been there for two weeks under the care of a Dr. Kamber and had been making semiannual visits to Kamber's office ever since. It could have been anything, barbiturates, alcohol . . . I suppose one can live in a state of truce with an old addiction. God knows I've known many ex-alcoholics that have done it, but to do it and keep it secret as Malloy had done was real talented. Malloy had covered his bouts of addiction somehow—I remembered rumors about his migraine headaches—to the extent that no one at the college had a clue that their president was an addict. Fortunately for him, because that kind of information at a place like St. Bartlett's would be all the board of trustees needed to crank up a search committee and start looking for a replacement. But Ponzini had found it—I suppose he scoured the files for that kind of dirt—and had been cashing in on it regularly.

But Malloy hadn't killed him. I knew that now. He had been content to pay his monthly dues and leave it at that. He was either unimaginative enough, or just too scared to upset a system that was working with only minor inconveniences. No, someone else had decided to pull the plug on Ponzini and now Malloy, like the nine others, had been pulled in to the web of suspicion. I closed the file and returned it to its place in the drawer, then swung the safe back until it relocked.

"You find what you needed?" Winston asked.

"I think so."

"Good. Let's get out of here. Even the maintenance crew can get in trouble for being in places they're not supposed to be." We made an exit and worked our way down and out the side door we had left unlocked. We walked back the two blocks to Winston's apartment and to where I had my car parked.

161

"Need some help with the cleanup?" I asked. "Six guys all night for poker can leave a hell of a mess."

Winston shook his head. He turned to go into his building, then stopped and looked back. "Listen, Costas, I don't know what the hell you're after in those files," he said, "but be careful. You don't want to upset what we got here. It's a good place to work. I'd hate to see everyone suffer because of something one person did."

"I'll remember that," I said, and turned toward my car. I got in, started it up, then headed out for home. The Pacer struggled through its warming-up phase and by the time I had hit the Brooklyn-Queens Expressway it was pretending to be a real car. Small wonder, I thought, and leaned back tiredly into the upholstery for the drive home.

THIRTY-FIVE

"I'm going in Thursday afternoon, tomorrow," Helen said over breakfast the next day. "The surgeon had time on Friday, and a room opened up at Montefiore so Silverman thought it best to get it over with. He said I'd be in the hospital a couple of days and then I should stay off my feet for a while. You think maybe you could drive me? If not I could take a bus. . . ."

That's my Helen, modest to a fault, and practical. "Of course," I said, and poured myself a cup of coffee. Unfortunately, the Wagner game was Thursday night and both Hector and I were going, he as a spectator and me on duty. I made a mental note to arrange to have one of our neighbors keep her company in the hospital for a couple of hours after we had to leave. She'd accept that, just as long as I was there the next morning when she closed her eyes before going into the operating room.

"You tell Uncle Spiros yet?"

She shook her head. "He was gone when Silverman told me. I'm going to let him know this morning."

"You nervous?"

She shrugged. "A little."

"Why don't I call," I said. "Sometimes it's better coming from someone else. You know what I mean?"

She nodded.

I looked at my watch. "He should be there now," I said, and dialed the Acropolis Diner. After three rings Uncle Spiros picked up. He had his abrupt voice on, the one he used for early morning take-out orders.

"Acropolis Diner, what you want?"

"Three dozen eggs," I said, "poached on matzos, topped with sautéed olives." That stopped him.

"Who is this?" he asked.

"Your nephew, Costas. I got your attention?"

He grumbled a yes.

"Helen's going into the hospital tomorrow. She will not be coming back to work for maybe three weeks. I will be paying for the hospital bill, you will be paying her salary." I let that float for a long moment. "If you have a problem with that, you can find yourself another cashier." I winked at Helen, who had just clutched the tabletop. "We have a deal?"

"One week, like I said before," my uncle shot back. "I can't go around giving three free weeks here, two free weeks there. She already gets a paid vacation. I do it for her, I got to do it for all the other ones."

"Spiros, she's not been sick a day she's been working for you, not a day. In sixteen years."

"Look, Costas. I understand you got your problems, but I

think I'm being generous. Anyone else around here they get sick they don't get nothing. So don't go around threatening. These days it ain't easy to find jobs."

I took a breath. I couldn't believe the little son of a bitch. I wanted to wring his neck.

"I'll tell you what," he said after another moment. "You are family, after all. I'll make it eight days paid. But don't tell any of the other people, I don't want it to get around. And now another thing, you speak to that guy Wilson yet? I delayed on my end. Friday's the new deadline on my signing the agreement. His wife willing to move or what?"

I had almost forgotten. It's a good thing I wasn't standing in front of him, because he would have seen the smile cross my face.

"Forget it," I said. "She's not moving. Not for her husband, not for you, not for money. You better turn down the deal."

I heard him sigh over the phone.

"You sure?"

"Yeah, I'm sure. As sure as you were about Helen's extra two week's pay."

"Hey, Costas, don't take it personally. It's only a policy."

"The answer is Wilson's not moving. You better look around for a different location, that's all. And one more thing. When Helen gets back, she has to take it easy." I looked over at her. "I know sometimes she cleans off the tables if the other girls are busy, but her job's being the cashier and that's all. I want you to understand that. At least for a month until she heals."

"Yeah, yeah." Spiros said dejectedly. He must have still been thinking about the lost opportunity to move his diner. I was glad there was some justice in the world. All Spiros had to be was a gentleman and say, "Sure, take the three weeks, take four if you need them," and I would have told him Mary Wilson's whole goddamn school was leaving. Now when he found out it would be too late for his option, and to tell the truth I didn't care what he'd make of it. One thing was sure.

164

He was still going to the bank every week, depositing, not withdrawing. That's more than I could say. I hung up the phone and faced Helen.

"Eight days paid and light duty when you return. I tried, you heard me?"

She nodded. "So, we'll just have to watch the extras this month, cut down on the nonessentials, like food."

That's my Helen, modest and practical.

THIRTY-SIX

Jeanette looked at me cross-eyed as I pushed my way into the president's suite. Outside of the glass-enclosed inner sanctum she could be a friendly individual, but as Malloy's secretary her duties included being watchdog over who got in to see him and who just left a calling card. The president was a busy man, and in Jeanette's eyes there was no earthly reason why he'd want to take time out to see a lowly security guard. She told me so. I didn't have a calling card, but I did have a name to drop, Dr. Kamber.

"He's in with the deans," she said, without budging or showing any emotion.

"Tell him," I persisted. "He'll thank you."

"Costas, you sure are a ball breaker," she said finally. "Have a seat."

I went to one of the couches and dropped down. The waiting area was large enough to have a coffee table with a bunch of magazines, two side chairs, a large green plant that looked like it belonged in some Brazilian jungle, and a large Xerox machine. Jeanette eyed me and shook her head, then went back to some typing she was doing. I waited a few minutes, then got up and paced. I hate waiting scenes, especially when they precede meetings that are bound to turn ugly. I had come to see Malloy for one purpose only, to save Verne's job. I kept my eyes away from Jeanette as I paced and finally wandered over to the Xerox machine.

It was one of those big jobs that can copy anything any size and shuffle the Gutenberg Bible into neat stacks according to chapter and verse. As I looked at it, I noticed a bunch of supplies in a plastic box on a small table next to it. More out of boredom than anything else, I leaned over and looked at them. There was a bottle of toner, some special cleaning tissues, and a can of something called film remover. As I was about to turn away I saw the Highly Flammable caution on its side and picked it up.

"What's this?" I asked Jeanette.

"It's for cleaning the glass of the screen," she said. "Takes off fingerprints and stuff. Put it back."

And burns plastic to a crisp, I thought, as I looked closer. Isoproponol, the label read. I sucked in my breath.

"Everyone around the college uses it?"

"No, most of the other secretaries just use windex. But you know, this is the president's office. I get what I want right away." She smiled.

I shook the can and noticed that it was almost empty.

"Looks like you'll need some more soon."

She frowned and was about to say something when the door opened and a bunch of men walked out of Malloy's office. I waved at Rooney, who smiled back at me, but the other ones were just faces to me, faces on a security circular posted at all the entrances. These were the big shots on campus, the ones not required to show an ID. In a minute they had all left, and the room was empty again.

"I'll call now," she said, and picked up the receiver. Try as she might, it was hard for her to keep the skepticism out of her voice. It was too bad she had no idea how powerful an effect the name Kamber had on her boss. After talking to Malloy, she looked up at me with eyes that no longer looked skeptical, only curious. Then she waved me in toward Malloy's door. I slipped the can of film remover into my pocket and walked in.

There was a lot of smoke in the room from the previous meeting. Malloy sat behind a large mahogany desk reading some report, but I could tell he was not concentrating. His eyes flicked up to mine, then he raised his head.

"What is it?" he growled abruptly. I guess he was trying to build an impregnable wall between us, but that's hard to do when you're starting out in mud. I sat down without asking and watched him for a minute. I had an idea where I wanted to wind up but I was willing to get there as leisurely as I needed. It was a technique Verne had taught me with some of our tougher, more self-assured collars, a technique that only worked if you were patient. I watched him, then repeated Kamber's name.

"Who's that?" Malloy said, but I could see his eyes flicker behind the wisps of smoke still trailing through the room.

"You tell me," I said.

"I don't have to tell you anything," the president of the college said. "You're only a security guard."

I looked around the room at a bunch of framed photographs, each one meant to show what an important man I was talking to. There was Malloy with Governor Cuomo, Malloy with Cardinal Cooke and then with Cardinal O'Connor, Malloy with Koch and Mayor Dinkins and even Malloy with Karl Malden. There were a bunch of other ones with people I didn't recognize. I was impressed, impressed enough to ask whether one of the pictures was with Patrick Conlon, the chairman of the board of trustees of St. Bartlett's. Malloy didn't say anything, he was still building his wall.

"Because," I added, "I'd like to know what he looks like before I meet with him."

That displaced a few of his stones. He leaned back in his chair and said with just too much confidence, "You're kidding yourself, Agonomou, Conlon would never let you in."

"Conlon reads his mail, doesn't he? Conlon takes phone calls from the other board members asking about their mail? I don't see the problem. It's his job to listen to reports about his top employees. Especially from people who are members of the New York police department, not from crazy students or annoyed parents."

"You mean suspended from the New York police department, don't you? Suspended because of some fuck-up." Malloy's face was getting red, which was a good sign. But then again, so was mine.

"Yeah, you've done your homework," I said angrily. "You can throw all the accusations around you want, but you still can't run away from your years of addiction." I took a breath. "I have no idea what it was, pills or alcohol, but I don't think that matters. I don't think Conlon will care, even if he thinks that you've done a pretty decent job of being the president. Especially now with the Middle States review staring you in the face. It won't matter, just like it doesn't matter how good a teacher you are in this place if you happen to have AIDS." I let that sink in for a minute. Malloy was watching me carefully, not moving so much as an eyelid. "And if he needs proof, and Dr. Kamber won't cooperate, there's always the Withers clinic. It will come out, somehow. You've kept it hidden for three years, but your time has finally come. Even with all the money you paid Ponzini, it had to find a way out."

Malloy swiveled in his chair and faced behind him. He looked out the window that looked into the central quadrangle of the college. I could see students walking the paths between the buildings, could see the gray sky promising an afternoon of rain and cold. Malloy must have been seeing the same things, but he didn't say a word. For all I knew he had his eyes closed. Finally, after a long moment he said, "How'd you find out?"

"Does it matter?"

"I suppose not," he said. "I had a feeling you would. Dig deep enough and something was bound to show up."

I could feel my temples pounding as the blood rushed up to my head. I slowly lifted the can of film remover out of my pocket and placed it on the desk in front of me. The son of a bitch had tried to kill me. He turned back and saw the bottle and smiled.

"No fingerprints," he said. "Don't bother even trying to find any."

"Nor on the light bulb or the brick," I added.

He frowned. "What brick?"

Then I remembered. Whoever threw the brick had to break in to the personnel files to get my address, something Malloy didn't need to do.

"You didn't try to scare me off by throwing a brick into my apartment?"

He shook his head. "You must be a very popular man, Mr. Agonomou." He turned back to the window and shook his head. "I don't suppose you'll believe this, but I was only trying to scare you in that closet. I looked to see that you had your walkie-talkie. I couldn't believe it took that long for Newton to get to you."

"My radio was out of power. It's funny, isn't it? It's always the little things that kill people. A patch of ice on a road, a faulty pilot light on a gas heater, a dirty hypodermic needle, stupid little things"—I glared at the back of his head—"and stupid little people. I was five seconds away from being history."

"You're a lucky man." He turned back. "I'm sorry it went so far, but quite frankly, I'm even sorrier that you didn't heed the threat. This college has always been very important to me, and I did, and would do again, almost anything to stay here."

"Including killing a member of your faculty?"

He looked at me strangely. "I didn't kill Ponzini. You can't think that I—"

"It's a natural. He was blackmailing you about the Withers thing. Maybe you were as ruthless with him as you were with me. Maybe he wasn't so lucky."

"I told you I thought you could call and get help right away. Besides, Ponzini and I had a working relationship, one I could live with. There was no reason to upset it."

"What if a jury doesn't buy that."

His face went white and for the first time I could see that he was really scared. A man can live with being kicked out of a job, can always find something else, but falling from the heights of the presidency of a college to a jail cell on a murder rap, now that was true Greek tragedy. Too bad it wasn't going to happen.

"I didn't kill him," he said in a voice now somehow louder and more insistent. "I couldn't have—"

"Why, President Malloy? Because you couldn't lift that heavy barbell and drop it on his face? You look strong enough to me."

"Because I was . . ." He looked around his room once quickly, took a deep breath, then continued. "Because I was home in bed, inebriated, unable to move. Dr. Kamber was there." He looked at me in pain. "Because it was the week I fell off the wagon after almost two years of fighting. I couldn't have killed Ponzini, I couldn't even walk." He wiped a sleeve across his mouth in a gesture I'd seen many times from Verne.

"You were an alcoholic," I said slowly, filling in a missing piece.

He nodded. "I controlled it for many years, did my drinking at night. When I slipped, my wife and Jeanette covered for me with an excuse about migraine headaches. But Jeanette didn't know about Kamber or after eighty-eight, the clinic. Fortunately, it happened during the summer when the college was on its break. After that I was seeing Kamber on a periodic maintenance schedule . . . for two years. I thought I had it licked."

"What happened?"

"I don't know, pressure, this Middle States review thing. Maybe it was just my body calling out. It happened, and fortunately Kamber helped me get it under control again." He shook his head. "But I didn't kill Ponzini."

"And Kamber is your alibi." I chuckled softly. I could see the irony of the situation was not lost on Malloy either. "I'd say you have a problem."

He looked at my little maroon jacket with its gold-plated zinc badge over the breast pocket and said in a voice barely above a whisper, "Maybe we could work something out."

The man was consistent to a fault. Ponzini was dead, but Malloy was willing to replace him with a new blackmailer, one of his own making. Of course I couldn't claim complete innocence; after all, I'd done the legwork. I leaned back in the chair and examined my options.

Malloy was right about one thing. I could never make his attempt on my life stick. There was simply no evidence. And if he was willing to stave off a murder indictment by exposing Kamber and his addiction, what would I have gained? He'd be relieved of the presidency by the board of trustees, but not before he had announced Verne's replacement. Then there'd be some new president, and who knew what he'd be like? I had to admit even to myself that I liked the idea of working in a place where the boss owes you, even if it's only informally. Everything seemed to be pointing in one direction. I leaned forward, put the can of film remover back in my pocket, and said, "Maybe we could."

A little smile crossed his face, as though he had just pulled the filler on an inside straight. What the hell, the man had been paying Ponzini for years. To him this would be like switching banks on a mortgage. . . . Just a new address on the check is all.

"How much is it going to cost me?" he asked.

"Nothing." I smiled. "But that doesn't take you off the hook. First of all, I want you to get Gonzales's job back."

171

He looked surprised. "The little guard that was on duty the night Ponzini died?"

"Yeah. The one you had fired. The one who's bound for more brushes with the law after trying so hard to make it the right way. He gets his job back." I stood up and walked over to one of the pictures on the wall, the one with Malloy and O'Connor.

"Is that all?"

"One more thing," I said. "The most important. Verne Newton stays on for as long as he wants to. No announcement on Monday about his replacement."

Malloy frowned. "I've already made a commitment."

I shook my head. "No one gives a shit about a commitment from an ex-president. Break it."

The silence that followed was only broken by the sounds of typing coming from Jeanette's desk outside. I watched Malloy as he went over in his mind the kind of embarrassing excuses he'd have to make. But to save his neck I knew he'd work it out.

"That's all?" he said.

I walked back and nodded. "We have a deal?"

He stuck his hand out and smiled. "Done."

I looked down at his hand, the same one that tagged me alongside the head and then locked me into a smoke-filled closet. Sometimes you bend your principles for friends and relatives, but as far as I'm concerned you go only as far as you can live with. I looked at his empty hand again, nodded, and said, "Okay," then turned and walked out of his office.

"Good meeting?" Jeanette asked as I passed by.

"Couldn't be better," I said. "Your boss is a real prince." I started to move away again, but not before dropping the can of film remover on her desk. "Oh, by the way, you'll be needing some more of this." The last I saw she was shaking the can and looking at Malloy's door. Let her figure it out. For all she knew, he'd drunk half the can.

THIRTY-SEVEN

The brick still bothered me. I certainly would have liked to know who threw it and ruined the symmetry of my son's hairline. Besides, I realized I had another problem. Dougherty and I had initially based our elimination of Lisa Cunningham, Charles Strickland, Gregor Ostyapin, and Hap as Ponzini's murderer because they had classroom alibis for the attempt on my life. Now that Malloy had taken the blame for one and not the other, the four were back in the running as murder suspects. My head was spinning with possibilities. It's a good thing I had a strong idea who Ponzini's killer really was.

I could see from the address on the bill I had lifted from Ponzini's desk that Cipriotti's jewelry store was in downtown Brooklyn on Fulton Street, about ten minutes away. I figured I could extend my coffee break by a few minutes and make it there and back without anyone noticing. The day was wet, but it was warm enough for the Pacer to cough into life after only two minutes of grinding on the starter motor.

I think I've been inside two jewelry stores in my life; once when I bought Helen her engagement and wedding rings, and once when I bought her a tenth wedding anniversary pearl-and-amethyst pin. There's something about the inside of a jewelry store that reminds me of an undertaker's parlor, solicitous men bowing and scraping and sympathizing with your every need all the while calculating just how much dough walked in so as to head to the right casket or showcase. Cipriotti's was no different. The salesman that drifted over studied me with as much proprietary interest as a first-year medical student examining his corpse. Fortunately, my overcoat was hiding my security guard uniform or else he would have left me to wander unassisted in the forest of plastic Hong Kong watches.

"Can I help you?" he asked pleasantly. He looked terribly expectant, waiting for an answer that could lead to anything from a ten-dollar to a twenty-thousand-dollar sale, a once a year coup. In my case the response was even more unexpected.

"I'm trying to track down a diamond," I said, and removed the invoice from my pocket. "The man who purchased it died and the estate is trying to trace it. The invoice indicates it was set in a ring but doesn't mention what it looked like."

The salesman took the paper and studied the writing. After a moment a broad smile crossed his face.

"You remember it?" I asked.

"I certainly do. A three-carat marquise, VSI with an H color for seven thousand dollars. This is not a large store and we don't get too many stones like this in. But the ring itself was quite unusual."

"Why is that?"

"Well, there's not a big demand for expensive stones to be set in two-finger rings. We call them ghetto knuckles, and most of them are sold to kids under twenty. It usually takes all the money they have in the world. But this one was different. This middle-aged white guy walks in and buys one of our more expensive loose stones, then tells me the person who's getting it will come in to talk about how he wants it set. A day later this black kid comes in, picks out our most expensive ghetto knuckle, tells us how he wants the stone set, then a week later he comes in to pick it up." The salesman looked at me with a sly grin. "You know in this business you don't ask too many questions, especially about gifts. Christmastime we get these lawyers coming in from the courts nearby buying two pieces of jewelry, one very conservative and another as gaudy as they come. The wife comes in to have the conservative little seed-pearl bracelet sized, you never ask her how she liked the big pair of gold topaz earrings."

Fascinating, but I didn't want to get sidetracked. "Did you get his name?" I asked.

The salesman shook his head. "The ring was being paid for by the other guy, I didn't need his name. As I recall he had some initials mounted next to the stone. I suppose I could ask our engraver what they were."

"I'd appreciate that."

"Just a minute," the salesman slipped through a back door to the workroom. In a minute he was back.

" 'J. S.' That's what he put on it."

"And was this kid by any chance very tall?"

He looked at me, and the grin slowly slid from his face.

"That's him," he said. "About six-foot-five, at least. A lot of man." He winked.

I lifted the invoice from the top of the counter. "Thank you. You've been very helpful."

"No problem. Hey, you sure I can't interest you in a nice pair of cufflinks? We got a special on this case over here. . . ."

I looked absently over in the direction he was pointing, but my mind was somewhere else; on the ring Jason Sanders was wearing when I spoke to him a week ago, a two-finger diamond marquise ring with "J. S." engraved on either side. More important, I was trying to figure out what that meant. I left the store and walked to my car a half block away, and by the time I was behind the wheel I thought I had it.

The ring was not a gift to a lover, as the salesman had wanted to say, but a payoff for some service Sanders had performed. It didn't take too much imagination to know what that was. Basketball stars have had a long and ignoble history of shaving points for gamblers to cash in on the spread. Given Ponzini's character, I didn't have any trouble seeing Sanders getting caught in such a scheme. Always, the difficult part in all these deals is recruiting the players, and I could see that Ponzini had found a novel hook. He threatened to flunk Sanders, a move which might have derailed his career. But that would only work for as long as Sanders was taking his course, so Ponzini had to shift after a while to some more tangible positive reinforcement . . . say like a seven-thousand-dollar ring. So far so good, but what about Lisa Cunningham? I started the car and pulled out of the space and headed back to the campus.

I focused on Lisa, a girl who's nobody's fool. She sees the ring, figures out it's from Ponzini, and realizes that her boyfriend could wind up in real trouble, compared to which an F in Basic Drawing would look like a Christmas present. She talks to Jason to try and make him understand, but by then the hook is pretty deep. So she tries, with her body, to bribe Ponzini into giving up Sanders. From the beginning it was not only about him passing the course and being able to play, but also about Ponzini stopping his expensive rewards; the diamond rings and God knows what else in the future that, when discovered, would send Jason right from the basketball court to a jail cell. That was the part she never told me. Just a hint of shaving points and Jason's future would be ended. I suppose in her mind it was worth the sacrifice. But of course it hadn't worked. Ponzini was into a good thing and wasn't about to stop just for an evening with Lisa. But I still didn't think she had killed him or thrown the brick. I had seen the

176

forced and ruptured door lock into the personnel office, and it looked like something a Sumo wrestler might have had trouble doing. After Ponzini had been killed she sought help in keeping the scandalous information hidden, and it was a natural who she turned to. Someone strong, with good aim and a great outside shot, someone like Jason Sanders.

THIRTY-EIGHT

I had saved Verne's job, which was only one reason I had started this crazy investigation. Now the cop in me couldn't leave off closing the book and wrapping things up. I parked the Pacer in my normal spot and made it into the college via Cameron Hall. I already knew where I was going and what time the head of the union would be in his office between classes. I found Stabler sitting behind his desk with a danish and a steaming cup of coffee hunched over some papers he was correcting. He was wearing a bow tie, which made him look more scholarly, although I'm sure the effect was lost on his students. His hair was neatly combed and all in all he looked like one of the pictures on his wall, one with the name F. Scott Fitzgerald under it. There were other pictures too, a rogue's gallery of literary figures, few of whom I recognized. Needless to say, Stephen King was not one of them, nor was Ludlum or even Clancy, two of my favorites. I guess this was to set the tone for the conduct of business, which, as Dory explained it one evening during a poker game, was nothing more than making a stab at literacy out of the dark miasma known as high school English. Dory was always the optimist, always expecting more than people had. It was a nice trait, but one that led invariably to disappointment. In Dory's case I could see it in his eyes as he waded his way through the pile of typed paper that had been turned in. He once said there was no one at St. Bartlett's who used more red pencils than he did and watching him for a minute or two I could see why. It looked like blood had been let out of pages of non sequiturs, misspellings, dangling participles, and grammatical errors.

"I'll be with you in a minute, Costas," he said, and slashed some more at the paper in front of him. My glance went back to the wall. Beside the photographic portraits of writers there was another picture, one that was far more significant. It was over his filing cabinet in the corner of the room, a small seascape of the Maine coast, painted with energy and feeling. I didn't need to look at the signature to know who the artist was since I had seen another painting just like it. Roger Simmons's oil painting glared at me from the wall and filled in the final missing piece of the puzzle. Of course it was all conjecture, but breaks in investigations come from the flimsiest of guesses and here was one that almost hit me between the eyes. I knew Stabler had killed Ponzini, now I knew why.

"You were lovers, weren't you?" I said softly. "You and Simmons."

He lifted his head and followed my gaze to the painting over the cabinet. Then he looked down at the desk in front of him. He didn't say anything for a long moment, then he slowly recited,

> "Lo! with a little rod
> I did but touch the honey of romance
> And must I lose a soul's inheritance?"

He looked up at me and smiled thinly. "Oscar Wilde, one of the early martyrs to gay-bashing. Yes, Roger and I were lovers.

We spent last summer in Bar Harbor together. It was a few months before everything collapsed here at school."

"Because of Ponzini?"

He nodded.

"And so you decided to kill him."

Stabler took a breath and placed the red pencil back in the cup he kept them in. He was very deliberate in this action, moving slowly enough to give him time to frame his answer.

"Had it been for that, I don't think so," he finally said. "But Ponzini's greater sin was against the union of fellow teachers that had elected him to a position of trust. He used being the head of the health committee for extortion. He betrayed his friends over and over again, and he did it under the guise of an organization that I deeply believed in and was the head of. And even after I knew, there was nothing I could do to stop him."

"Except kill him."

"Yes. It was the only way. And then there was what he'd done to poor Roger. Together, I took it as a mandate."

I pulled the only empty chair in the room closer and sat down across the desk from Stabler.

"And you thought you'd get away with it?" I asked incredulously.

He looked surprised. "Oh, but I have. You yourself know there's no evidence. I'm actually quite surprised that you managed to figure it out." For the first time a little smile broke across his face. "Pray tell, what led you my way?"

"Oscar Wilde," I said. "The sweatshirt you wore last night at the poker game was the same one you wore another evening when you were with Ponzini in the gym. I suppose that was a trial run, or perhaps you were going to murder him two weeks before you actually managed it. One of the men you bumped into that night described it."

"Clever," Dory said. "I should have taken some advice from my mentor. Wilde said that a man cannot be too careful in the choice of his enemies. . . ." He looked at me and the smile

179

faded from his lips. "I should have chosen someone less observant, someone like Captain Dougherty. He bought every story I handed him." He got up and came around the desk slowly. Stabler was a smaller man than I was, but I watched him carefully nonetheless.

"You're not wearing a recording device by any chance, are you?"

I shook my head. Dory was good at reading bluffs and after looking at me closely, he went back to his seat.

"It's just that I don't want to spend the last years of my life sick in jail," he said. He leaned back and pulled a handkerchief out of a side pocket and blew his nose. "Several weeks ago I found out that I'm HIV positive. No doubt, Ponzini would have found out when I started taking the AZT."

"I'm sorry to hear that, Dory," I said honestly. "But actually I'm sorrier that you decided to take things into your own hands."

"Be careful"—he winked—"conscience makes egotists of us all."

"Wilde again?"

He nodded. "You're a quick study, Costas. I'm sorry you never took my class."

"I'm willing to start now," I said. "Why don't you begin by telling me how you did it? There are lots of things I'd like to know; like why the bar you hit Ponzini with was missing before ten when Matthews and his friends arrived even though he wasn't killed until after one."

Stabler thought for a moment. "Why not? Not much you can do about it anyway." He picked up another red pencil from his pencil cup and absently wove it through his fingers. Then he started telling me exactly how he had killed Victor Ponzini.

"I had planned to do it once before, as you guessed," he said. "But the gym was being used by those guys you mentioned, whom I didn't expect to be there. Matthews?" He raised his eyes.

I nodded. "Some of Verne's friends."

"Anyway, I watched carefully for the following week and saw that Ponzini was going for his workouts Tuesday and Thursday nights, late, around nine-thirty, ten o'clock, directly from one of his evening classes. And nobody was there on Tuesday. As you recall I left the poker game early last week complaining I had to prepare a lecture on Shelley. But instead, I went right down to the weight room. I had left one of the emergency side doors of Cameron open by wedging a small piece of cardboard against the jamb. No one saw me. Ponzini was standing there doing curls so both his hands were tied up. I had left an empty heavy bar by the door and as I came over, pretending to be looking for weights, I landed a single blow in the face with all my strength. He never saw it coming." Stabler paused and watched my expression. I've heard many confessions over my years in the police department, but few have been delivered with such a lack of emotion as Stabler was showing. After a moment, he continued.

"I think he was dead before he hit the floor. He wasn't moving anyway. And curiously, there was very little blood. Maybe not so curious. Roger always claimed he was bloodless." He chuckled over that for a moment, then went on. "What there was I cleaned up with a towel I had also left. I was all set to prop him into the position I had planned, to make it look like an accident, when I heard the noise of the heavy steel staircase door open two flights upstairs. God, I panicked for an instant before I noticed the storage closet a few feet away, where I dragged everything: Ponzini's body, the bar, and the towel. I just managed to get inside, close the door, and pull one of the extra mats over both of us when the men walked into the weight room." He smiled thinly. "It was my misfortune that I had to stay next to Ponzini's dead body for the next two hours under the stifling mat in the closet. Fortunately, I had been smart enough to lay him on his back so that the lividity would collect in the right place." He smiled. "You see, reading is an obsession with me, even reading police procedurals. Not that forensic methods are entirely reliable. I read with

181

amusement afterward that the time of death had been placed around one A.M., probably because the mat and my body had insulated him from heat loss."

"So that's the reason Matthews didn't see the murder weapon. You'd already used it."

Dory nodded. "So the corpse and I waited. Can you imagine what it was like under the mats with that man's body? Horrendous, I assure you. Finally, the other men left, not once coming into the supply closet. Immediately, I lifted the body onto the press bench, and set the scene with another bar of heavy weights. With all my strength I was barely able to lift it and place it where I had already hit him to pick up a smear of blood and tissue. Why people bother to use weights I'll never know. It's such a strain. During all of this, of course, I was using gloves. Then I wiped off whatever blood was on the mats we had waited under as well as the bar I struck him with, after which I put a few additional weights on the ends just to be sure everything was hidden. Then I made a quick and careful exit. It was that simple. No one saw me go, either. Aside from the near-fatal interruption right after I killed him, everything went off as planned." He paused. "Except, of course, for your involvement." He flexed his fingers and the red pencil bent enough for a small cracking noise to fill his office. He looked at the pencil curiously, then put it back in the cup again.

"Did you tell Roger Simmons you had killed the man who had been blackmailing him?"

Stabler shook his head. "I thought it best he didn't know. He has this rather Victorian notion of me as being above reproach. I hated to disabuse him of it." Stabler grinned. "Roger is impossibly romantic . . . or was." He turned in the direction of the painting and shook his head slowly. "What a lovely summer we could have had. Instead it was all anguish over his disease and his having to leave teaching. He knew what was coming this fall after Ponzini began his rumors. He shrugged. "I think I'm more philosophical about the whole thing. Nothing positive can come out of self-remorse. I have, at best, a few years, so I simply thought I'd make the most of them."

"By murdering someone?"

"By selective refinement." Dory leaned back in his chair and put on a theatrical voice. Or maybe it was a pulpit voice given what he was saying. "I did nothing more than any good gardener would, pruning away the rotten and foul from the healthy stock. It's a job that is never ending, for behind every just person attends a pack of knaves."

"Oscar Wilde again?" I interrupted.

"No, Dory Stabler."

No one spoke for a minute as I tried to make sense of what he was saying. Stabler, the righteous and avenging gardener of morality? I had known Dory for almost a year, but never had I seen this side of him. It seemed like there was a screw loose somewhere.

"Dory, what are you telling me?"

"I'm telling you I killed Ponzini because he deserved it, and also that he's not the only one who's guilty." The flourish was now gone from his voice and he was speaking in as hard a tone as I'd ever heard from him. "Ponzini could only get away with what he did because the school had such a conservative and fearful view of everything. And that can be traced to the doorstep of only one man."

"You mean President Malloy?"

Stabler crossed his hands over his chest and looked at me stonily.

"Enough said. I'm tired of doing all the talking. I want to know now what you're going to do."

"Tell Dougherty, of course. You don't think I can forget everything you've told me? I can't turn my back on what you've done. By all accounts Ponzini was a ruthless bastard but that still didn't give you the right—"

He interrupted me. "It won't do any good, of course, Costas. There's no proof. I'll deny I told you. There's not one thing you can do."

I shrugged. "Dougherty will try his best, especially if I tell him where to look. Maybe you weren't as careful as you think. The laboratory already has the second bar with the blood smear on the end. That's enough to blow this into a full-fledged investigation. But then again, maybe you will get away with it. It's happened before. Then you'll just have to live with the knowledge of what you did. Who knows, maybe you'll even decide to confess, officially that is."

Stabler smiled. "Doubtful. I think I can handle the guilt for a couple of years."

I got up to go. "But you're wrong about something, Dory. There is one thing I can do." I took a breath. "I can tell Simmons. He'd believe me."

I saw him stiffen. "You wouldn't," he said. "The man has less than six months to live. That's a cruelty beyond even Malloy's imagination."

I put a hand on the doorknob, then turned toward him. "How long have we been playing poker together, Dory, one year? Have you ever known me to try a bluff when I didn't need to?" I opened the door, took one last look at him, and passed through. I didn't get too far before I heard the brittle sound of a cracking pencil coming from his office. Like they said, no one used more of them than he did.

THIRTY-NINE

Verne was seated behind his desk going over the plan for the following evening's game as I walked into the security office. The Wagner game was shaping up to be the hottest of the year, and even though Verne was working what he thought was his last week at St. Bartlett's, he was taking it seriously. I told him right away that Malloy had come to his senses and decided to keep Verne on as director. After he got over the shock of that, I told him to call up Gonzales and bring him back in. A smile lit up his face as brightly as if he had drunk a cup of Johnnie Walker Black.

"You're shitting me?"

I shook my head. "I just happened to bump into President Malloy and he told me to tell you."

Verne has been around me for enough years to know when I'm floating a bald-faced lie, but I didn't care. I had no intention of going into the details and this was a shorthand way of letting Verne know not to press too hard. He got the message and leaned back in his chair, still smiling.

"I don't know how you did it, but to tell you the truth, I

don't care. Magicians are never supposed to reveal their tricks."

I changed the subject. "Have you seen Dougherty around at all? I got to speak to him."

"Not today." Verne looked at me sideways. "You're not kidding me now, Costas? Malloy's really keeping me on?"

"That's what he said." I took a few steps closer and looked over the floor plan and roster Verne was preparing for the game. He usually puts on six guards, four for the doors and two inside, but this time it looked like he had put on an extra man. He followed my eyes.

"I put you inside," he said. "That way you get to see the game. One of the few good perks that goes with your job." He reached into his jacket pocket and pulled out an envelope. "Oh, and here's Hector's ticket. He's right down in front with me."

I took it and put it away. "Thanks. I'm not above bribing my kid for affection. That's all he's been talking about for the last two days."

"And everyone else at the college. Christ, let's hope we win. I don't want to have to deal with an arena full of angry St. Bartlett's students. I can just about deal with the alcohol and reefer. Stoned and angry undergraduates got to be the worst. I think I'll call in Gonzales and put him as the extra inside." He grinned. "He will be one happy dude to hear from me."

I looked down at the floor plan of the arena with its four large entrances and its five thousand seats and realized that for a small college, St. Bartlett's had a pretty impressive facility. And the alumni that had help donate it were still waiting for the team to justify the expense. Well, maybe tomorrow night.

"What does Hap think the chances are?" I asked, on my way toward the other desk in the office. The afternoon shift had me answering the phones and walkie-talkies until five-thirty. That was okay by me, I needed some peace and quiet in my life.

"I don't know what Hap thinks, but Roselyn, his secretary, has St. Bartlett's eighty-five to eighty in the pool. I figured maybe she knew something, but I boosted my bet up to eighty-six to eighty-one, St. Bartlett's. You want to play the pool?"

"I never win those things."

"Hell, this one is up close to two thousand already. "Only costs a couple of bucks."

I laughed. "Sure, what the hell. My last extravagance before the Agonomous go on their austerity plan." I reached into my pocket and pulled out two dollars and handed them over.

"What do you want?"

"St. Bartlett's," I looked down at my little tin badge number. "Eighty to seventy-nine."

Verne wrote it down, put the money in an envelope, then searched for Gonzales's number in the Rolodex. He was about to dial when he looked up and stared me squarely in the face. "Seriously, Costas, how did you do it? From what I hear Malloy doesn't change his mind so easily."

I looked back at him steadily. "Let's just say we came to a gentleman's agreement and leave it at that. You got me my job, I saved you yours, we're even."

I guess he finally accepted that because he bent down and started phoning Gonzales. While he was doing that I called up Dougherty on my line. I was hoping to find him at his desk, but he was out of the office, so I left my name and asked for a call back. Typical. I had a murderer for the guy and he was God knows where.

I waited all afternoon, but Dougherty didn't call, and by the time I left that evening I was convinced that he had decided simply not to bother with me. I picked up Helen and drove home, and along with Hector we spent a quiet evening trying not to think about the upcoming operation. Even though it was supposed to be a simple procedure, the atmosphere around the house was unnaturally strained. Hospitals were places other people went, places of strange sharp smells and rubber-soled shoes squeaking around turns, of overlit shiny corridors and sadness and pain, and the whole thing gave me the creeps. Helen was being very brave in not even mentioning it, but she had a look to her face that frightened me. Hector was unnaturally subdued, even after I gave him the basketball ticket. After dinner I asked him if he wanted to go out to the high school and shoot some hoops, practice the alley-oop, but he just shook his head. A good son, he didn't want to leave his mother for even a half hour.

The place was getting to feel like a morgue, so I decided I could surround myself with the same silence in my little office and get in some work on the baseball cards. Nineteen thirty-nine needed a little rearranging now that I had to shift Charles Ernest Keller over from 1940, where I had mistakenly placed him as a rookie. In my tight system that was like stuffing Kate Smith into a crowded elevator. Helen went to watch TV, Hector sat on the couch next to her pretending he was reading a history book, and I headed for the inner sanctum.

I was still rearranging 1939 when the phone rang. I glanced at the clock and noticed that it was close to ten o'clock. We weren't used to getting calls so late so I was kind of wondering who it might be when a voice I had only recently heard asked to speak to Mr. Costas Agonomou. It took me only a second to place it. Mr. Roger Simmons was on the line. A Mr. Roger Simmons sounding very upset and, I might add, scared.

"Yes," I said. "I'm here."

"You told me to call if anything ever came up," he began. "I mean anything important."

I closed the book on Charlie Keller and Tommy Henrich and concentrated on the nervous voice on the other end of the line.

"What's happened?"

"I had a visit this afternoon from"—he paused—"from Dory. You told him you knew about our relationship? Needless to say this was something that was best kept quiet at a place like St. Bartlett's. Especially now for his sake."

"Because of his diagnosis?"

"Yes. Dory was very upset that you had found out about

188

us." He took a deep breath and I waited for him to continue. "Very upset. He wanted to know if you had visited me and whether you had mentioned anything about him."

I guess my little threat to expose Stabler's murder to his lover was having some positive results. I was thinking to myself that things were moving in the right direction and that maybe Stabler would confess on his own when Simmons blew that idea out of the water.

"For as long as I've known him," he said over the phone, "Dory has had this side to him I can never understand. Very unpredictable, very impulsive."

"How impulsive?" I asked. I wasn't sure I liked where this was going.

There was a long pause on the phone and finally Simmons came back. "It took me awhile to decide to call you on this, you understand. Dory has been my sole emotional support for the past year. Without him I don't know where I'd be. . . ."

"How impulsive," I pressed.

"The gun," Simmons finally blurted out. "He took the gun."

I felt my tiny office get even smaller, as though all the air had been sucked out and the walls were reeling toward each other.

"Why?" I finally managed.

"He wanted to scare you," he said nervously. "To stop you from continuing your investigation and possibly exposing our relationship."

"That's what he said? Exposing your relationship?"

"Yes. I don't think he's actually capable of doing any harm, Mr. Agonomou, but I thought finally it was best to warn you. He could never hurt a fly, but sometimes he is very single-minded."

I knew for one that he certainly could hurt a fly, especially if there was a heavy steel bar nearby, but I wasn't ready to wound Simmons yet, if at all.

"The gun is loaded?"

"With six bullets. I thought I'd only need one, but Dory was with me when I bought it and he knew I had a full box of bullets. He loaded it before he left. I'm sorry, I tried to argue with him but he had this look about him. . . ." Simmons started to cry, heaving great sobs over the phone. "It's this fucking disease," he shouted, "it destroys everything. Your body, your mind . . . Now Dory's got it." The cries rolled over the line and I waited patiently. Finally, they subsided.

"Do you know what he plans to do?" I asked. "Or when?"

"You have to understand he was beside himself," Simmons said in apology. Then added, "Tomorrow. Something tomorrow. But I don't know, maybe overnight he'll forget about the whole thing."

Not likely. If anything, Stabler showed that as time went on he got more calculating. The real question was who he intended to scare, me or someone else, someone more closely associated with his anger. Simmons had said it was me, but I wasn't convinced. But I didn't want to find out the answer at the last minute staring down the barrel of a loaded revolver.

"Where the hell is he now?" I asked. There was always the chance I could still raise Dougherty and mobilize him into action.

"Not at home. He told me he wasn't going home, that he had to think and the best way was to walk the city. Mr. Agonomou, he doesn't know I've called you. He made me promise not to tell anybody."

"Thank you," I said. "I'll be careful." I couldn't think of anything else to say so I hung up the receiver softly and sat back in the chair. I spent a long time just staring at the phone, not moving, wondering what the hell Stabler had in mind. I put in another call for Dougherty, but it looked like I had already become pariah of the year at his precinct. When I gave my name again no one knew where Dougherty was or when he would be coming in. For all I knew he was making *ixnay* sign language to the guy fielding his calls. That left me alone with one hell of a problem.

I put the books I had been working on back on their

shelves, turned off the light, and went to check the locks on the doors. Helen was already asleep by the time I got back to the bedroom. I tried as quietly as I could to slip myself in between the sheets without waking her. She rolled over, settled into a new position, but didn't open her eyes. I rolled over and turned off the light. In the darkness everything seemed so peaceful, so routine. Who would have guessed that someone with a gun was out after one of us and someone with a laser was out after the other?

FORTY

I checked Helen into the hospital the next morning and left Hector keeping her company. He was supposed to leave her in the care of one of our neighbors later that afternoon. This platooning was solely to keep Helen's mind off her operation. Before I left I told her I would try to be there before she went under anesthesia the next morning, but definitely would be around when she woke up.

By the time I got to the college, the place was jumping. Classes were still being held, but everywhere there were signs with verbs like crush, maim, decimate, paralyze, massacre, and mutilate, followed by a single word, Wagner. No one could concentrate on anything except the big game. You heard it in the halls, you heard it in the cafeteria, you even heard it in the library, where you weren't supposed to hear anything. Game time was 7:30 P.M., and since I was covering it my shift had been slid back four hours.

After leaving the hospital, I had spent the morning trying to find Stabler. When I called the English department they had told me that Thursday was not a day he was scheduled to teach, so I hung out around his apartment, but he never showed. I hate stakeouts, every cop does, especially on days that are cold and moist. Then I reminded myself that I wasn't precisely a cop still, and that made me feel even worse. I waited until around noon when I finally managed to reach Dougherty on a nearby pay phone. The rain was coming in through the cracks of the little cubicle but I felt lucky just to find a phone that worked. I felt even luckier to get through to Dougherty. He listened patiently but didn't seem to buy anything until I mentioned the gun. Cops don't like loaded, unregistered guns rattling around the citizenry, so he agreed to put a man on Stabler's apartment to relieve me. I also told him I thought it would be worth his while to take in the Wagner game that evening. I had a suspicion that if Stabler was going to do anything he'd do it with a flourish, and I couldn't think of anything bigger than the game. He said he'd try to get there although the tone of his voice didn't sound encouraging. For a guy that probably got all the Knicks tickets he ever wanted, seeing St. Bartlett's play was a little like listening to Dean Martin doing Verdi. He had rung off sounding noncommittal in a voice he used for all his annoying, pesky callers, even ones claiming that a murderer had just confessed to them. But that was nothing new. When I was covering phones on the force I used to average a call a week with a murder confession from people whose TV had broken and had nothing better to do.

Around six that evening the busloads of Wagner supporters started arriving, and by seven the campus was crawling with people. St. Bartlett's games are rarely televised and only on stations in the swampy area of the cable range, but for some reason a WPIX crew had set up to do play-by-play. The press section, which usually consisted of a table with two chairs, two pads, and two pencils, had been enlarged into a section with eight chairs with enough electronic gadgets to mystify Captain Kirk. The alumni in the stands must have been swooning. All of this intensified the already swollen emotions of the players, both from St. Bartlett's and from Wagner, but from the pregame noise, its effect was most apparent on the fans. The posters had been brought inside and were being paraded back and forth in front of the two cameras to the shouts and jeers of both sides. Stabler could have been anywhere in the crowd, armed and intent on using his weapon on any one of at least five thousand targets. My job, Verne had told me, was to make sure there were no incidents in the stands or courtside. By incidents, however, I didn't think Verne meant anything more than a little unruliness. God knows what he'd do if I told him there might be a homicidal maniac in the crowd. Laugh at me? Order everyone out of the stands? I figured I had to do this one on my own.

At 7:15 P.M. Malloy came in and sat down in the third row right off the midcourt aisle. Verne was four seats to his left, and right next to Verne was Hector. Great seats. I hadn't seen him come in, but he was looking right at me and grinning. I waved and he gave me the high sign indicating, I hoped, that his mother was still doing fine, but more probably that he approved of his seat assignment. He was wearing a Mets cap to cover the bandage that was still over the cut in his scalp. I heard the noise level increase dramatically and turned to see the players come onto the court to warm up. I walked back down, stepped onto the wooden floor, and said hello to Hap.

"Ready?" I asked him.

"If you gave me Michael Jordan and Patrick Ewing, then I'd be ready." He grinned. "Right now I'd say I was prepared. The boys are as keyed up as thoroughbreds before a big race." He nodded into the stands a few rows behind me. "See those five guys, the ones in suits?"

I looked behind me in the direction he had indicated. There, about seven rows back, were five men in suits looking like they had assembled in their Sunday best to take an exam for

193

sanitation inspector. They had eyes that looked sharp enough to spot an unwashed spoon at a Lubavitcher bar mitzvah and each had a notepad on his lap.

"NBA scouts," Hap said. "Looking over the merchandise. We usually get one or two all season. Tonight it's like an opening on Broadway. Guys that never take left-handed turnaround jumpers will be rammin' and jammin' like crazy. My problem is to try to keep the lid on and get everyone to play team ball. Of course, our opponents have the same problem." I saw a ball hit off the rim hard and come bouncing in our direction. Before it got halfway there, Jason Sanders scooped it up, took a little easy step to the left, then sent it back with seeming effortlessness. The ball arced in a pure parabola ending in a graceful swish. Hap smiled and turned toward the bench. "Well, maybe you could say we are ready, as ready as we'll ever be. I'll catch you later, Costas. Got to go to work now."

I moved down the sidelines toward midcourt and all the bigwigs sitting in section A. The stands were just about full. There weren't many empty seats anywhere, and everyone was anticipating the beginning of the game. The noise level increased as the announcer welcomed everyone to the arena and the last game of the regular season. I peered into the seats trying to spot Stabler but didn't have any luck. I turned in at the center aisle and walked the three rows back. Malloy glanced up at me and held my eyes for a moment, then turned to his wife sitting next to him and said something casually. He must have felt that we had cut a deal and now he didn't have to socialize with the hired help. That was fine with me as long as he kept up his end of the bargain. Verne was pointing something out to Hector on the scoreboard, so I just kept walking up the aisle, kept looking for a familiar face with a bulge under a jacket where it shouldn't be.

I had covered the entire section when the referees called the players on the court and checked the starting time on the clock. Everyone sat down for the opening tap.

In all the excitement around St. Bartlett's, few people had stopped to consider that not only did Wagner have as good a record as we had, they also had more experience in clutch game situations. The year before they had won the Division One championship over a streaking St. Eustace and most of their players were back.

The tap went to their player, number twenty-three, a white kid with shoulders like a middleweight wrestler and a torso like a panther's, who wove his way through traffic, faked a dish-off and went in for a surprise lay-up. If there was any doubt that St. Bartlett's was in for a tough night, the kid dispelled that with this opening basket. The noise level dropped before the basketball hit the floor and a chastened St. Bartlett's player, a guard by the name of Luther Dokes, picked it up. Hap has told me that the opening moments of a game are important to set a rhythm and so I knew that St. Bartlett's had to do something right away or be playing catch-up through the first quarter. But I wouldn't see it. I moved over to section B, put my back to the court and looked up at the spectators. I was finished inspecting the first three rows of the section when I heard a roar and turned just in time to see Sanders pick himself up off of the floor. The scoreboard read two, *two*. Great, it was probably going to be the best game of the year and I had to spend it ass backwards looking for one desperate face in a throng of crazed fans. I could think of better ways to spend an evening. I turned back and continued checking the people in front of me. Stabler, for all I knew, could have been in some kind of disguise, and so I went over the section person by person and when I was finished, the score was eight all.

As I moved over to section C, I spotted Dougherty down by the north door. It looked like he had just come in because he was still wearing his raincoat and hat. I walked over and asked him if Stabler had shown yet at his apartment, knowing somewhere in my gut that it was a false hope. Dougherty shook his head and a few drops of rain spilled off the brim.

195

"I guess you haven't spotted him yet either?" he said.

"There are eight sections and I've only checked two of them. But the first quarter's not over, so there's time."

"You want to describe him? Maybe I'll get lucky."

I gave Dougherty the best description of Stabler I could, but the idea of him picking out someone he'd never seen in a place like the auditorium was crazy.

"I'll wait over there," he said, and pointed to the top perimeter walkway at midcourt, up near the roof. "I'll keep an eye on you." I watched as he walked up to the back, his head moving from side to side in case Stabler was right nearby.

For a moment I let myself look back on the court. St. Bartlett's had the ball and they were trying to get it into the center. Dokes tried a bounce pass which was batted away by one of the Wagner guards, but somehow Dokes got his hands back on the ball. With two seconds left on the shot clock he had no choice but to throw up an off-balance shot from way outside. It hit the rim, took a bad bounce, and spun off the backboard. A figure shot through the welter of bodies making an attempt to grab the rebound, cradled the ball for a second in his large hand, then slammed it in for the two points. The announcer shouted, "Saaandeerrss with the dunk!" The people around me were out of their seats, screaming. Like I said, a great game.

By halftime I had checked all the sections from A to F and had two more to go. There was no sense in continuing during the half when people were milling around, so I walked over to midcourt to talk to Hector. The score was forty-six to forty, St. Bartlett's. I hadn't been paying attention to the little details, but if there was anyone who could cite statistics, Hector was the person. I found him in the aisle, stretching.

"How'd you like the game so far?" I asked.

"Great. Did you know Sanders has eighteen of the forty-six points, and six rebounds? Four points above his average. He's just incredible with a basketball."

I didn't have the heart to tell him that Mr. Sanders was also great with a brick. Nor did I tell him what I had decided to do at the end of halftime. Sanders was in for a big surprise when the team came back on the court.

"Catch you later," I said, and started walking back casually toward the wooden court. By the time I reached the floor, the first players were just coming back from their halftime pep talk. Once again the practice basketballs were taken out of their mesh bags by the scorer's table and both teams went in to their five-minute warm-up. Being an official person I had certain privileges. I parked myself right on the sideline and waited until Jason Sanders came close on one of his practice jump shots.

"Sanders," I said, loud enough for him to hear. "I got a message." He looked around, saw who it was, and hesitated. His hands were still holding the ball for a shot, but instead he dribbled twice and turned to face me.

"Yeah, from whom?"

"Me. I found the invoice for the seven-thousand dollar ring Ponzini bought you at Cipriotti's. Tomorrow copies are going to be on three desks in town, Hap's, the sports writer for the *New York Times,* and the eastern regional commissioner of the NCAA. With it will be a statement from the salesman that the ring was delivered to you. I thought you'd like to know now since this will probably be your last few minutes on a college basketball court." I looked at him for a moment, but the only change I saw was in the line of his mouth. The hard set of the first half had turned into a curving sneer.

"Fuck off," he said, and turned back to the court. He took two steps, pumped once, and jumped three feet before releasing the ball. It took a beautiful curve through the air but came down a good foot short, a complete airball.

"You big fuck," I muttered. "Let's see you play with that in your belly." As I turned back into the stands a little smile was playing across my face. I had no intention of releasing the information because I guess, deep down, I agreed with Lisa Cunningham. Life in the ghetto is hard enough and sometimes

197

good kids get caught up in bad situations or with creeps like Ponzini. I didn't think Jason needed to spend time in prison, and I was quite willing to let him dig his own grave. I glanced over at the scouts who had resumed their seats and were talking to each other. One of them pointed to Sanders and said something and the other four nodded. Whatever happened, I figured it would be well documented and stay in Sanders's file for a long time. Top players, like horses, get reputations; and this, the biggest clutch half for St. Bartlett's basketball in over seven years, would weigh in heavily on anyone's report card. I headed over to section F as the referees were blowing their whistles to start the second half. My only regret in the whole deal was that St. Bartlett's would probably lose.

Everyone was back in their seats by the time I worked myself over to section G. Once again I started the painstaking search for Stabler in the crowd, but by now I had a suspicion that I wasn't going to find him in the last two sections. As I searched the faces, I heard several groans from the crowd nearby and an equal number of cheers from over in sections D and E, where the Wagner supporters were seated. I fought the urge to turn around after each crowd noise, but when I finished with the section I glanced up at the scoreboard and flinched: St. Bartlett's 52, Wagner 56. A run of sixteen to six against us. I let my eyes travel down to the court in time to see Sanders have a pass blocked and the Wagner guard go all the way for an easy lay-up. I suppose there is some justice in the world, but it would be hard convincing the St. Bartlett's fans that's what they were witnessing. Hap looked on in agonized dismay as the Wagner player went in with the steal. I could see him motion for a time-out. I worked my way over to section H and once again turned back to the crowd.

There was a collective dismay settling in that was quite obvious. People were whistling and shouting advice, most of it with a hard edge of anger. They were so buoyed up at the half, and now they were watching it all slip away. The whole offense was based on Sanders, and now the freshman wonder

198

was playing like a forty-seven-year-old office manager at a company picnic. Hap would have to do something soon, but I didn't think he was quite ready. I had finished with a few rows when the team came back out on the court, the same team that had just left. I watched for a few minutes, but it didn't seem that whatever Hap had to tell them in the time-out had stuck. I saw some sloppy offense leading to a Sanders hook shot from the top of the key, which never found the backboard, sloppier defense, and no coverage on the defensive boards. I turned back and continued looking at the crowd. Things were getting ugly in the stands. People were throwing paper airplanes and standing up. It made my job harder, but by the end of the quarter I had finished. No Stabler. I took one quick walk around the top walkway and stopped when I came to Dougherty.

"Nothing," I said. "If he's here he's not in the stands."

"I wouldn't come either to watch this bunch of bozos. They just coughed up sixteen points this quarter."

I looked back up to the scoreboard and saw the awful results: St. Bartlett's 60, Wagner 70. They had ten points to make up in the final quarter, but if things kept going the same way, the score would end up even more lopsided.

"They should replace that guy Sanders," Dougherty said.

"You know it and I know it, but does the coach know it? It ain't easy coming up with a new game plan in the last fifteen minutes." I glanced down in the direction of the scouts and saw that one of them had already left. This was not the kind of game that was going to produce glowing reports on anyone.

"I'm going to check the outside corridors and the four entrances," I said. "Maybe he's just loitering."

"You mean like the team?"

"Give it a break," I said, and took off in the direction of the nearest door. On the way I passed by Section A again and saw the pained look on Malloy's face. Verne didn't look all too happy either; but hell, it was only a game. Their combined looks, however, had nothing on the expression I saw on Lisa Cunningham's face. I had seen her earlier in the back of the section and she was now sitting quite still, with all the color drained out of her face. She knew, as did the players, the scouts, and the coaches, that what was happening was much more than just a game. It was an opportunity to grab onto a gold-plated brass ring for the future, and she was watching her boyfriend blow it right before her eyes. It must have been hard for her because there was not a single thing she could do. I suppose I should have felt sorry for her, for all she had gone through to get Sanders to this point, but I didn't. I feel sorry for battered little children and helpless old people, not six-foot-five athletes who go around throwing bricks. I kept walking and within a minute made it to the door. Gonzales was there and I gave him a smile. The little man was back in uniform and looking happier than a kid at his own birthday party. I'm sure he said hello personally to each and every fan that came through his door. But he was the only one standing there, so I passed through to the outer corridor.

Compared to the noise and activity inside, the corridor that ran around the building connecting the four doors was silent. The game still had a quarter to go, and as bad as it had developed, few people were ready to leave just yet. I took a walk all the way around, then checked the two men's rooms. Still no Stabler. I was beginning to feel like a real jerk. Even Roger Simmons didn't think anything would come of Stabler taking the gun and here I was acting like I was on the trail of Charles Manson or something. I decided to give it up. There was still a quarter of basketball left and I was hoping that Hap had the good sense to finally use the hook. Besides, stranger things have happened in college ball than a team coming back from a ten-point deficit. I walked back into the corridor and as I passed the main entrance, I noticed that no one was on the outside gate or turnstiles. The place was wide open, but there was nothing I could do about it. I shrugged and went back into the auditorium.

200

I decided if I was going to see the game, I'd do it right. I walked over to Section A, headed down the aisle to the court floor, and knelt down just behind the scorer's table. No one paid me any attention because there was too much going on in front of them. Hap had finally come to his senses and pulled Sanders. In his place was somebody named Callahan, a senior player who hadn't seen much court time since the beginning of the season. He was a big Irish kid with the looks of a Larry Bird but without the touch or smart moves. But everyone in the place was screaming because he had just driven around Turgeon, the all-city Wagner guard, and gone in for a reverse lay-up, getting fouled in the process. I guess the guy figured this was his last gasp as a college player and he was taking no prisoners. He converted the free throw and charged back on defense. It was the kind of play that pumps up the adrenaline and changes momentum, but I looked up at the clock and saw that there were only seven minutes left. The differential was still ten even after the three pointer. Was it enough time? I glanced over at the bench and saw Sanders looking down at the floor with a towel over his head. I had no idea what he was thinking, or for that matter, what the scouts had put down as a final comment on him. No doubt it wasn't flattering. Seven minutes, I thought, sure, plenty of time.

St. Bartlett's went into a man-to-man defense, which held up long enough to force an outside shot with only three seconds left on the shot clock. It hit the rim and bounced to the side where there was a flurry of bodies until finally Dokes came up with the ball. Build slowly, I told myself, don't throw away that little precious edge of the three pointer and turnover. Momentum in a basketball game is as delicate a thing as the shifting balance point for a tightrope walker. St. Bartlett's had the slimmest of toeholds on clawing their way back, but a single bad pass, or forced shot, could close them down for the rest of the game.

Dokes maybe got my message because he brought the ball up the court deliberately, watching with catlike eyes the spacing of his opponents. Bodies were moving, picks were being set and reset, but Dokes kept the slow dribble off to the side where the ball was protected. When the shot clock read ten seconds, he passed the ball into the center, cut around his defender and got the return pass for an easy jumper from eight feet out. I made a fist and smiled as the crowd came to life. Back to the basics, the old give-and-go. Score: St. Bartlett's 65, Wagner 73. I looked behind me. Three rows away Malloy was standing and shouting also, as was Verne. The precious little toehold of a comeback was widening into a real ledge. Five unanswered points. Wagner called a time-out and when they came back on the court, they went into a stall. Six and a half minutes left and they were working the clock. I know I'm in the minority, but I've never felt defense is the best offense. I looked on the Wagner tactics with great hope. Defensive alignments overlook easy opportunities and force more difficult late shots from the forwards. Having analyzed their strategy to be in our favor, I was crushed when Turgeon took a baseline pass and threw in a swish. Except for over in sections D and E, the crowd quieted. Roller coaster time. Six minutes left and back to ten points down. Still, with a little luck . . .

In the next five minutes, St. Bartlett's kept chipping away at the ten points. They still hadn't lost that fragile edge and Callahan was playing like a man possessed. He hit a fadeaway jumper from twenty feet, and then a minute later stuffed in an offensive rebound. A point here, two points there . . . it all added up to an exciting last quarter. With a minute left Wagner called a time-out with the score seventy-seven to seventy-four. When they inbounded they stretched out the guards and tried to isolate Turgeon on a one-on-one. He made a swing around the outside toward the basket, but Callahan stepped over and blocked his way. Rather than taking a bad shot, he threw the ball back. It was tipped by Dokes, spun in the air and landed back in one of the Wagner player's hands. With two seconds left, he threw up a quick shot that hit the rim and rolled in. There was a groan in the auditorium from behind me. Thirty-six seconds left and down by five. Even Jimmy the Greek wouldn't have touched the action for St. Bartlett's. Hap called a time-out. He looked like a man about to go in front of a firing squad, but he huddled with the players and went over a play. I hadn't been keeping count, but I heard one of the scorers near me say there was one more time-out left for both teams. Then the St. Bartlett's players came out at mid-court and the crowd quieted. Thirty-six seconds is a long time in basketball. In the NBA they're even breaking it down to tenths of seconds, but St. Bartlett's didn't have the luxury to use more than ten of them. That would guarantee them a final two- or three-second possession, but they'd have to score on this possession and then keep Wagner from scoring. Ten seconds is also a long time, but Dokes used only six of them. He got the inbound pass, dribbled ahead five feet, faked over to his left, then lofted a shot that was off by at least a foot. I got this sinking feeling as I saw the Wagner players tense for the rebound, but they were already too late. Callahan soared up a second earlier, timing it just perfectly to catch the ball before it hit the backboard, way above the rim, then jammed it home. I perfectly executed alley-oop. What a goddamn beautiful call. Hap had made it. I looked back up at Hector and he was on his feet screaming. Then he looked down at me and saw me watching him. He flashed me a big smile and also our little two finger hand signal for the oop. St. Bartlett's was still alive, but just barely. Down three, thirty seconds left, Wagner ball. Wagner time-out. The sweat was running down my back. And this was supposed to be fun.

I could hear the announcer for WPIX telling his viewers what kind of ball game they were watching, as if they needed any help. Four St. Bartlett's cheerleaders came out and went through a number with a few somersaults and a couple of leg raises, but clearly the fans' interest was not on gymnastics. Then the time-out was over and the ten players came back out on the court. Wagner needed something to put the game on ice, either a field goal or a foul. The seconds started ticking away as soon as the ball was inbounded, and it was obvious that Wagner was milking the clock. Their center worked himself into the low post position and was calling for the pass, but Turgeon held back, brought the ball out, dribbled back in, then finally managed to get it to him. The center pulled a head fake to the left, swiveled right, pumped once, then jumped. Callahan had two opportunities to be faked right out of his jock, but he stayed right with him. When the center went up, he went too, with his big beefy Irish hand outstretched in front of the ball. The shot never made it more than a foot away. It hit Callahan's palm and dropped straight down to the floor. Turgeon made a lunge for it, and so did seven other players not including the two who were floating back to earth. Turgeon got a hand on it, but Dokes pulled it away, turned his back on everything and everybody, and called time-out. The referee signaled St. Bartlett's ball. The crowd was going wild but I wasn't turning around for anyone. Eight seconds left to score three points. Two points wouldn't do anymore, and this was the last possession.

Once again Hap bent down with a play, working furiously with a small board and crayons. This time the cheerleaders didn't come out to fire up the crowd, they didn't need to. And once again, at the end of the time-out, the crowd quieted. I could see across the way everyone was standing and watching the court. That precious little crack had widened to a road leading straight to the heart of victory in overtime. The momentum of the game had swung as forcefully as the pendulum on Big Ben and there wasn't a person in the auditorium who couldn't feel it. The teams broke again, Dokes inbounded to the other St. Bartlett's guard, worked his way up to the three-point line, and got the pass right back. Six seconds left. I was counting in my head, afraid to take my eyes off the action. Dokes had the option to take the three-point long shot, or go for the drive and hope for a shooting foul. I think there were better odds on the long shot, because the moment he stepped over the line the Wagner players should have backed off from him like he was poison. Give him the easy two points and they win the game. But with six seconds left and the game on the line, players don't calculate odds or numbers, they go on instinct. Dokes faked the three-pointer, then drove in under the defender and streaked to the basket. Four of the defenders backed off, willing to concede the two points, but Turgeon stayed right with him. Instinct this time was working against the all-city guard who had never conceded anything on defense. He went up with Dokes while he was shooting and touched his wrist. The ball banged hard against the rim, ricocheted against the backboard, spun around the rim once, then finally dropped through. The referee signaled the basket and the foul, and then all hell broke loose. I looked up at the clock and saw that time had run out.

Turgeon was fuming. I had read that he was the best player on the Wagner team, but that he had a temper second only to Billy Martin's. There was no dust on the court to kick onto the referees shoes, but Turgeon was doing the best he could with his voice. He was claiming complete innocence of the foul, which was making him look like such a goat. The foul was the first real stupid mistake he had made all year, arguing the call was his second. I could see all his teammates trying to pull him away, but he wasn't about to suffer humiliation in silence. They had almost managed to get him away when his elbow accidently brushed the referee's chin. That was an automatic technical foul and the man with stripes raised his hand to show everyone. The St. Bartlett's fans went wild: seventy-nine to seventy-eight with two free throws coming.

First came the technical and Dokes stepped up to the line all alone. The sweat was beading up on his shoulders, but he looked cool and composed. He studied the basket for a moment, bounced the ball twice, then bent at the knees and let the shot go. I watched as it floated up as softly as an early morning cloud of mist off a summer pond and then dropped over the rim for a swish. I could almost feel the auditorium expand with the one collective shout that followed—seventy-nine all with one shot to go. Maybe this was going to be a night of realized dreams, realized for everyone, that is, but the Wagner fans and Jason Sanders. Dokes stepped back from the foul line, wiped his brow with a bit of his tank top, then he asked for the ball. Since the other players had cleared off for the technical, and there was no time left on the clock, there was no one else on the court with him but the referee. He took two steps forward to take the final shot. Everyone in the auditorium was standing, hardly breathing. A silence descended like the silence before a verdict is read. Again Dokes bounced the ball twice and looked up at the rim. He took a deep breath, squared his shoulders and bent at the knees.

And then, in the deathly stillness, two shots rang out. To me it sounded like someone had set off two cherry bombs in the row behind me, but when I turned, I realized I was off by a couple of rows. What I saw made me feel like I had just come to a halt in a plummeting elevator. Stabler had his hand on Malloy's throat from behind, and in his other hand he was leveling the gun right at the president's head. The two shots must have gone in the direction of the roof because Malloy was still very much alive, his eyes looking like they'd been inflated with helium. He was standing rock-still and staring straight down at the court and at Luther Dokes who had, at the sound of the shots, stepped back from the line. Five thousand pairs of eyes shifted to the action in the third row center. Stabler looked around at the stunned audience and a nervous little smile played across his face. In the continuing stillness his shots had punctuated, his voice boomed out.

"This man has caused, by his intolerance and prejudice, the humiliation and suffering of some of this institution's finest teachers. He deserves to be shot." There was a gasp from those nearby who could hear him, but those who could not certainly got the message. So did Malloy, who stiffened like a day-old corpse. But, from my vantage point it didn't look like Stabler was quite ready yet to pull the trigger. He had the spotlight, had somehow worked himself up to this bizarre confrontation, and was not about to let the moment slip away. He looked around him and decided he was too close to the row behind, so he pulled Malloy out into the aisle, then backed off half a step and pointed the gun at his back.

"It is onerous that this man should be allowed to direct this institution's policy on AIDS hiring," he now shouted. "His insensitivity to the problem is staggering." The muscles in Stabler's neck were starting to stand out with his effort, and his face had turned a shade redder. He had the entire auditorium riveted with the sleek-looking revolver he had pointed at the president. Even Dokes, down on the court, and the referee had turned up toward him.

Well, not quite everyone was rooted in place. As I glanced around, out of the corner of my eye I spotted Dougherty slowly slipping around the upper aisle into the section A aisle. He was still about twenty rows back, but slowly edging down closer toward Stabler from behind. Then I noticed Verne was slipping carefully by the person next to him in the direction of Stabler eight feet away. I didn't like what I saw. A crazy man with a loaded gun in a full auditorium is enough to give anyone an uncomfortable feeling. With two determined men making a move on him and your own son standing five seats away, that feeling turns into white fear. I glanced over at Hector and saw him concentrating on the gun. He was two feet behind Verne, close enough to be hit by a pulled shot or a bad ricochet. Not to mention that I was standing in a direct line below Malloy, presenting as easy a target as a cigar store Indian.

But Dougherty kept coming, a row at a time, very carefully.

"I want," Stabler continued, "President Malloy to renounce his policy on AIDS in front of this entire assemblage. I want him to show some compassion and apologize for the removal from this campus of Roger Simmons." He looked down at the sports announcer, then motioned with his free hand. "Over the PA system." He motioned again, and the announcer came up with the microphone trailing fifteen feet of wire behind him. He handed it slowly to the president.

"Go ahead," Stabler hissed, "so everyone can hear you."

Malloy took the microphone and held it in front of his face like it was contaminated. He drew back a few inches and looked behind him. Stabler nudged him with the gun. Then, almost in the same motion, he swung the gun over to his left and pointed it straight at Verne's head. My boss had worked himself to within two seats of the aisle, with only one person between him and the president, but Stabler must have seen him coming.

"Don't try it," he said in a low growl to Verne. "Take another step and I'll put a bullet in your neck."

Verne stopped moving and took a deep breath.

"You're making a big mistake," he said. "Drop the gun and no one will get hurt."

"I'm hurt already," Stabler said. "This is the only way I know to make me feel better." He pressed the gun into Malloy's back again. "Go ahead, Mr. President. We're all waiting to hear you apologize."

Malloy cleared his throat and started speaking slowly. What came out sounded more like a croak than a human voice.

"What's that?" Stabler prompted. "We can't hear you Malloy."

"Perhaps I have been too narrow in my policy on AIDS here at the college," he said more clearly. His words reverberated around the silent auditorium. "While I had the interests of the student body in mind, I expect some people have gotten hurt and I apologize for the problems I have caused them."

"What a euphemism, Mr. President. Problems? Try suffering," Stabler hissed, loud enough to be picked up on the loudspeaker system.

Malloy looked around the large auditorium slowly and brought the microphone up close to his mouth. I could see this was difficult for him. He was having a hard time getting the words out. Finally, he took a deep breath and said, "Yes, you are right, some have suffered."

"Thank you for telling us all the truth for once in your life," the English teacher said.

But I changed my focus from the two men to Dougherty, who had now worked himself down to within five rows of them. I could see him slowly reaching underneath his coat for what must have been a gun. Terrific, I thought, now we're going to have a shootout in the middle of the St. Bartlett's Alumni Auditorium. But Stabler saved me the trouble of having to duck a bunch of bullets. For a guy who couldn't see his way to a winning hand at poker, he had a knack for protecting his back. He let Malloy feel sorry for himself for a moment and took a quick look behind him. His memory must have registered the new body five rows away, or maybe he recognized the police captain as the person who had conducted the interrogations on campus, but he immediately saw the threat as the man's hand went reaching under his coat. With one hand he grabbed onto Malloy's collar, and with the other he pointed the gun at Dougherty's feet and pulled the trigger. The explosion once again filled the gymnasium, even louder this time since the microphone was so near. The bullet must have caught the cement and splintered because the police Captain cursed but didn't seem to be wounded.

"Let's have the gun," Stabler said. "I don't want anyone getting hurt that doesn't deserve it." He held his own gun on Dougherty while the policeman walked slowly down the incline. "The gun," Stabler repeated. "Put it on the ground."

Dougherty took it out slowly and placed it on the cement incline just in front of him. Stabler swung Malloy around and told him to pick it up and bring it behind his back, slowly. He released the grip on his collar just long enough to get the policeman's gun and drop it into his pocket. Then he swung Malloy around again and motioned for Dougherty to sit in Malloy's vacant seat. He was still on top of the situation, with his gun behind the president's head and a grip on his collar, facing down onto the court. He allowed himself a small, self-satisfied grin.

"I don't have much more time," he said, almost to himself. "And it would be a shame to come this far and not see St. Bartlett's make it into the NITs." He paused for a moment and looked down at the court and at Luther Dokes, who was still holding the basketball. He seemed to be making a decision about something. "I'll make a deal with you, Dokes," he shouted at last. "You make the basket, and I'll give myself up. You miss, and I'll do what I have to do. Go ahead." He brought the gun back behind the president's head. "Take the final shot."

Dokes's eyes got as large as half-dollars and he shook his head.

"Yo, you're crazy, man," Dokes shouted back. "Lay down the piece."

"I will after your shot." He looked around for a moment. "We're all waiting anyway. You got it coming."

Dokes looked behind him at the referee, then up at the basket. He bounced the ball once, then walked over to the sideline. Hap stood up to meet him. As he did, I took a step to my right, and then another. Stabler was concentrating on the little meeting at the sidelines and at Dougherty and Verne sitting just to his left. He didn't spot me bend down to the mesh bag next to the scorer's table.

Dokes was trying to find out from Hap what to do, and I heard Hap give him good advice. "You make the basket," he said, "and the game is ours, you miss and we appeal because the shot was taken under duress. You can't lose."

"Yo, what if I miss man. He gonna shoot dat guy."

"No, he won't. He doesn't have the guts to do it." He pushed him back gently onto the court. Dokes turned and walked slowly back to the foul line shaking his head. All the players were up off their benches and facing the basket as the St. Bartlett's player got set to make the shot. All the audience

210

turned in the same direction. I fished around and got one of the practice balls. I didn't trust Stabler. The little weasel had gotten out of anteing up too many times at our poker games to take his word for anything.

Once again Dokes bounced the ball, squared his shoulders, and bent at the knees. But instead of letting the shot go, he eased himself up like he was on a set of shock absorbers, bounced the ball again, and stepped back from the line. You could tell the pressure was more than he could deal with. The perspiration was now rolling down his neck and his arms making little drops of moisture on the court. The referee walked over and said a few words to him. Dokes shook his head, took a deep breath, and stepped back to the line. Another bounce, another bend, and this time he let the ball soar upward. I could see that he kept his fingers on the leather as long as possible, trying to give it whatever last-minute spin he could to get it to go into the hoop. At least four thousand St. Bartlett's fans helped it on its flight by willing it into the basket. The gymnasium was absolutely silent as the ball arced upward, hit the front rim, rested there for a heartbeat collecting its momentum, then rolled over and through the basket. St. Bartlett's had won the game, eighty to seventy-nine, but inside the airless gym there were only a few shouts. Everyone now turned back to Stabler and Malloy.

"It's your move, man," Dokes called with relief. "Lay it down like you promised."

Stabler's face went from his little smug grin to one of fear. The games were over and the next ten seconds would be the most important in his life, or what was left of it. He took a glance over at Dougherty and at Verne, both still sitting watching him carefully, and then down at the gun in his hand. Malloy was still standing in front of him fully aware that his life was on hold for the next ten seconds. I looked over and desperately tried to catch Hector's eye. He was standing two seats farther away from Verne, about ten feet from Stabler. I had our little two finger sign up in front of me, but my son was not looking my way. He was looking, like the other people in the gym, at the crazy man with the gun.

"Get down on your knees," Stabler said to Malloy softly. His eyes had taken on a new resolve. I knew I was right not to trust the son of a bitch.

"People with AIDS are dying like flies. What's one more death? I guess what we just saw wasn't the final shot."

"No," Malloy croaked. "You can't."

"I can't? I already have. The second time will be easier. My life's over anyway. I'll be dead before anything gets to a jury." His facial muscles were twitching like a horse's flank and he had a faraway look to his eyes. "Get down now," he said again. "You got five seconds to pray to your sanctimonious, upright, homophobic God." He pressed the gun into Malloy's back and the president sank down in front of him on his knees. He bent down, put his hands together, and started muttering something. Stabler took a step back, cocked the hammer on the gun, then pointed it down at the base of Malloy's skull in front of him. "Five seconds," he repeated. Malloy moaned, then started weeping.

I was frantic. A man was about to be executed in front of five thousand people and no one was going to do anything. I tried again to get Hector's attention, but still nothing. And then, just briefly, with maybe three seconds to go, Hector turned away from what he knew would be a gruesome sight and spotted me. I waited only for a split second for his eyes to focus on my signal, then threw the basketball. It sailed back up into the stands in a high arc, much too far from Stabler for him to be concerned. He watched out of the corner of his eye as it floated lazily five feet above everyone's head several seats to his left, and then concentrated on the business before him. But what he didn't see was Hector who had sprung up as high as he could and just managed to grab the ball at the height of its arc. Stabler must have finally seen the blur of Hector moving because he turned his head to the left at the same instant

212

that the boy, suspended in the air above him, slammed the ball down in one fluid motion. The heavy ball sailed down straight toward Stabler's gun hand, swinging now toward Hector, and connected with a resounding thud. The shot went off and in that instant, both Dougherty and Verne moved. Hector sank down on top of a woman sitting in the row in front of him. I screamed and ran up the aisle trying to get to Hector to see where he had been hit. I noticed as I ran that Dougherty had Stabler in a choke hold, and Verne had his gun hand, now pointed at the ceiling. Another shot went off, and then I heard a thud as Verne crashed a fist into Stabler's face. As I turned into the row where Hector had landed, Stabler sank to the ground, unconscious. The screams coming from all around were deafening. People were hiding under the seats and running up the aisles, but nothing really registered. I was concentrating on getting to Hector. I told myself over and over it had to be done, it was the only way, but I didn't feel I could really convince myself. I had acted instinctively, a cop saving a life. I reached his aisle and leaned in, but by that time he was already on his feet with the biggest, most self-satisfied grin I'd ever seen.

"Goddamn," he shouted. "That was beautiful! I did it, the best alley-oop ever." He held up his hand to slap me five. "Perfect pass, perfect timing, perfect shot."

"Good Christ," I said with relief. I held up my hand weakly and shook my head. "Sorry, I couldn't think of anything else. If I had thrown it at him from so far away he just would have ducked."

"I hope they have it on tape," my son said. "For mom."

I smiled and hugged him. After a good many seconds I let go and started to lead Hector out to the aisle. Then the two of us headed out of the row and into the glare of the television lights now focusing on the scene in Aisle A. Malloy was still on his knees sobbing with relief, Stabler was unconscious with blood coming out of his nose where Verne had hit him, and Dougherty was speaking urgently over a Walkie-Talkie. As for the rest of the people in the gym, I couldn't even guess what they were thinking. But hell, St. Bartlett's had won, the rest was just window dressing. Well, not quite that meaningless. I looked up at the scoreboard once again, at the eighty to seventy-nine, and realized I had just won the goddamn pot. Like I said, luck sure has a funny way of working.

· FORTY-ONE

Hector and I made it home that night, exhausted after all the lights had gone out and after all the interviews had ended. We locked the door, set the alarm clock, and slept, no doubt each reliving the moment in our special way. The next morning we made it out early, before any reporters got the idea to do more interviews, and drove over to the hospital. Helen was just being prepped for the operation and neither of us mentioned what happened the night before. Helen worries over the least little thing, and telling her that Hector had been a split second from being shot would have set her insides churning. They finally took her away and the two of us were left to sweat it out in the waiting room. Scattered around were the morning's editions of the three papers.

I have to admit, the front-page picture in the *Daily News* was a classic. Patrick Ewing would have been jealous. There was Hector, hanging in the air with his arms extended after throwing the ball down at Stabler. The ball had just hit the gun, but it could still be seen pointing off at an angle. The headline read oops!! I love the *Daily News* headlines. If Stabler had murdered Malloy it probably would have read TEAM WINS, PRES LOSES AT THE GUN. Anyway, Hector was pleased. The caption on the photo read simply, "The Final Shot."

I had been told when we were still there that Stabler's bullet had wounded somebody in the shoulder a few aisles away, but we were too busy to find out who it was. By the time the commotion had died down they had taken the unfortunate man to the hospital. The *Daily News* reporter had followed up and gotten a name. I didn't like the idea that anyone had gotten hurt in those frantic last seconds, but I suppose there is some kind of weird justice in the world. Of all the people in the auditorium, I would have felt the least sympathy for Howell Tandy, and sure enough, that's just who got wounded.

Stabler, of course, recovered from Verne's left hook and was now in custody. The reporter didn't have the full story yet but that would surface in the next day or two. I guessed that even now there were people camped out on our doorstep at home. I put the paper down and looked over at Hector.

"How do you think she's doing?" I asked.

He looked at his watch. "We'll know in a couple of hours. You want to go out for a coffee?"

"No, I'll wait."

I read the article over again, then handed it to my son. Then I sat back to wait. I hate hospitals, and waiting inside one with nothing to do was torturous. I lasted an hour before I decided to go for a little walk. In one of the corridors I found a pay phone.

For some reason I wanted to call Verne and see what was happening around the school. As much as I had tried to distance myself from caring about St. Bartlett's, the morning after the big victory I couldn't help being curious.

Verne told me I should be glad I wasn't there, the place was such a madhouse. The kids were going wild, the reporters were camped out on Malloy's doorstep, and the police were all over the security office. Everyone wanted explanations and few people had anything to give.

215

"Dougherty's pieced a lot of it together, but not all of it. They're looking for you, pal." Verne said. "But I didn't tell them where you were. I didn't think you'd want to be disturbed at the hospital."

"Thanks, Verne."

"Which reminds me, strictly out of the blue I got a call a half hour ago from one Everett Barnet. You know who he is?"

I felt my heart drop down to the level of my kneecaps.

"Yeah, I know."

"He wants to talk to you. It's not often the chief of police makes his own appointments. The way I figure it, Costas, he wants to cash in on one of his policemen stopping the murder. You get my drift. Son of a bitch didn't even thank me for putting Stabler down. Hey, but that's all right, you deserve it. Way I figure it, I'll have to hire a new guard soon."

When I came back to the waiting room a few minutes later the surgeon was already there, smiling. He was a big guy with hands like a meat packer's, but somehow I guess he had trained them to manipulate delicate little lasers. I don't know what I was expecting, maybe Jascha Heifetz or something. He came over and told me Helen was resting comfortably, the operation had been a piece of cake, and we could go into the recovery room. Hector and I crept in and waited by her bedside until she opened her eyes. She smiled, held out a hand for each of us, then raised an eyebrow.

"You're done," I said. "With a fifty-thousand-mile warranty. The doctor said you would be able to leave tomorrow evening." I saw her body ease back into the bed and she closed her eyes for a moment. The anesthetic still hadn't fully worn off. In a minute she was back with us.

"Thank you for being here," she said. "I was kind of nervous. I never got to ask you how the game was last night?" She struggled to keep her eyes open.

I looked over at Hector and he returned my smile.

"You know Helen, nothing's ever exciting without you

around." I leaned over and kissed her. "We won. Now go back to sleep. When you wake up we can watch the news together."

"The news?" she barely managed.

"Yeah, they might have some clips from the game."

"I think," she answered weakly, "this is one day I can miss it." In a few seconds she was back asleep.

"You going to tell her at least about the money?" Hector asked. "That's the first time you won anything in your life, isn't it?"

"I thought I'd show her." I said. "I found this little jewelry store over in Brooklyn . . ."